THE US OR THEM WAR

Also by
WILLIAM GARNER

★

OVERKILL
THE DEEP, DEEP FREEZE

THE
US OR THEM
WAR

*

WILLIAM GARNER

THE
COMPANION BOOK CLUB
LONDON

This edition is published by
The Hamlyn Publishing Group Ltd.
and is issued by arrangement with
William Collins, Sons & Co. Ltd.

Made and printed in Great Britain
for the Companion Book Club
by Odhams (Watford) Ltd.
600771210
600721215

The gulf between how one should live and how one does live is so wide that a man who neglects what is actually done for what should be done learns the way to self-destruction rather than self-preservation. The fact is that a man who wants to act virtuously in every way necessarily comes to grief among so many who are not virtuous. Therefore if a prince wishes to maintain his rule he must learn how not to be virtuous, and to make use of this or not according to need.

MACHIAVELLI: *The Prince*

. . . a tough struggle going on in the back alleys all over the world, and there's no quarter asked and none given.

U.S. Secretary of State DEAN RUSK

GIGO—*In the beginning* . . .

LIGHT CASCADED from triple-tiered chandeliers. The Marine Corps band played a selection from 'East Side Story'. Flunkeys with trays of drinks threaded through the multi-coloured throng like shuttles on a loom. A thickening of the crowd towards the far end of the room marked the progress of the President and his wife.

In an alcove some distance away, the President's adviser on national security nursed an empty glass and two ambassadors from under-developed countries. The deceptively acid look on his lined, non-committal face was betrayed by the laughter lines radiating from the corners of his eyes.

At the moment he was peering, head bent, over the tops of his rimless lenses, his eyebrows raised exaggeratedly. He said, 'A computer? A myth, your Excellency, I assure you! A space age myth!'

The ambassador from Central America displayed mock regret. 'Such a pity! It would be so perfectly in keeping with your great technological society that one would like to believe it.'

The ambassador from South East Asia, bright as a jungle flower in his national dress, said, 'Is that not a definition of a myth? A fiction everyone would like to believe, because in myths good always triumphs over evil?'

The White House aide said, 'Isn't that a definition of fiction too, your Excellency?'

The Central American ambassador took his long cigarette holder from his mouth, shook his head in mock sadness and said, 'Such cynicism is uncharacteristic of an American. It is a pity the story of the computer is not true.'

The White House aide signalled a passing waiter and disposed of his empty glass. He wondered just what stories were floating around Washington at the present time. He took off his spectacles to polish them and said, 'A pity? Does your Excellency have more faith in computers than men?'

The Central American ambassador said innocently, 'But of course! A computer is dispassionate, incorruptible, errorless. What better qualifications could be found? And no one will dispute that what is good for the United States is good for the whole of the free world.'

The White House security aide replaced his glasses, studying the other's olive-skinned, patrician face for any trace of irony. There was none, but the man was a diplomat, of course.

The South East Asian ambassador moved smoothly into the conversational gap. 'In my country,' he said, 'the tribes who live in the mountain foothills believe that the world is borne on the back of a great elephant. In their rites they propitiate the elephant, for if it should forget its burden and move by so much as one inch, the world would fall off and be shattered into a million fragments. Of course, these people are very primitive.'

The Central American ambassador smiled. 'But the elephant, like the computer, never forgets.'

The Asian briefly permitted himself to look scrutable, curving his full lips upward. He said, 'Another myth, alas.'

The White House aide had taken the analogy in another way. He said, 'I guess you don't have to be primitive to have your elephant myths.'

They were joined by two more guests. One was very tall and gangling, with a vague air and eyes that were far from vague. The White House aide looked up at him and said, 'Hello, Henry. His Excellency here tells me there's a rumour going around that the U.S. has replaced the President with a computer. The guy down the other end of the room is just a front man.'

Henry half drew a pipe from a pocket, remembered regretfully and put it back. He said, 'Why don't you tell them the truth?' He stooped towards the Central American ambassador and told him solemnly, 'The character you see making his way up the room isn't even a front man, Mr Ambassador. He's a robot, controlled by the computer.'

He put an arm around the shoulders of his companion who was even smaller than the South East Asian ambassador, and said, 'I'd like you to meet a friend of mine, your Excellencies. Mr Robinson, over from England on a little business of mutual interest.'

The small man shook hands, bowing gracefully as the two ambassadors repeated his *nom de guerre*. He seemed a little reserved and preoccupied, as Englishmen often do. Behind him, the White House aide flashed his compatriot a glance that was a compound of amusement, warning and question.

The tall, lanky American said seriously, 'I hope the revelation hasn't come as a shock to you, your Excellency?'

The Central American ambassador said, 'On the contrary! I had only just remarked that infallibility and incorruptibility are very desirable virtues in a head of state.'

The small Englishman emerged from an almost frosty withdrawal to say, 'Or the appearance of infallibility and incorruptibility. No doubt you recall Machiavelli on desirable virtues. A prince who has them all may be ruined by them, but if he only appears to have them they will give him good service. He should seem—he may even be—a paragon of all the virtues, but he should also be capable of the opposite. In essence, as Machiavelli said, he should do good in all things if possible, but he should know how to do evil if necessary.'

He smiled at the two ambassadors but his eyes, when he flicked them briefly at the Americans, were cold, guarded, hostile.

The man called Henry thought: Cold as an icicle, ever since he stepped off that plane. It must be the Bohm affair, but he can't possibly know . . .

9

1. BOHM—*One of us*

No ONE but the police photographer was taking any notice of the man contorted on the concrete. For the two of them it was a private, professional business, like a modelling session with a corpse standing in for a half-dressed girl.

Every noiseless explosion of light from the electronic flash bound them together in a transient intimacy. Each time the brilliance split the night at its seams the dead man's wide-open, permanently fascinated eyes glinted, as if his brain, like the camera, were recording events for future reference.

The big Jaguar arrived from London. It swept between the parked police cars, their blue flashers still winking at the stars, and drew up at the foot of the steps leading to the main entrance. Three men got out. Doors slammed; a ragged three-gun salute fired with damp powder. They went past the photographer, up the steps towards the bright lights of the entrance hall.

The photographer took his final shot. The dead man lay unobtrusively in the dim glow of reflected light, his short spell of publicity over. The photographer lit a cigarette and began to pack his equipment.

The three men pushed through the big double doors. The plain-clothes chief superintendent came forward to meet them. One of the newcomers, tall, well-built, with a kind of tough, self-mocking elegance, took a plastic-sheathed card from his wallet. The plain-clothes man looked at it carefully and handed it back. He said, 'This way, sir, please.'

He led them into a large office. Hooded typewriters sat silent on empty desks, like cage-birds covered for the night. A uniformed chief inspector was waiting with a P.C. They all glanced at each other like men unacquainted but not entirely strangers. There was also a middle-aged civilian with a nose that twitched like a rabbit's and an acute case of nervous anxiety.

The man who had produced the identity card looked around. He said, 'Where is he?'

The chief superintendent said, 'I thought we'd better have a word first, Mr Morton. This is Chief Inspector Norcott of the uniformed branch. His people were here first. And this is Mr Parsons, of Pargeter Electromation.'

The civilian said, 'Research and development director. They sent for me. You're——'

Interrupting ambiguously, Morton said, 'Yes, that's right.' He looked at the chief superintendent. 'Has Mr Parsons made a statement?'

'Not officially, sir. We thought we should wait for you.'

Morton said, 'I think it would be a good idea if he did it now. After that we needn't keep him. It's getting late.'

Parsons said, 'Oh, but it's no trouble.'

The chief superintendent was an old hand. He said, 'We don't want to keep you hanging about, sir. The chief inspector'll be glad to look after you.'

The chief inspector took the hint. Nodding at his constable, he shepherded Parsons towards the door.

Reluctant to leave, Parsons said, 'You do appreciate the importance of absolute security and discretion? I told Sir Ben——'

Morton said, 'Sir Ben spoke to the Minister, Mr Parsons. We've been fully briefed. Incidentally, that was a piece of very quick thinking. We're most grateful.'

The chief inspector took the opportunity of pushing Parsons through the door without actually appearing to do so. Morton and the plain-clothes officer exchanged smiles. Morton swung himself on to a desk and crossed his legs.

He said, 'All right. Before we see Bohm—that's his name, yes?—let's just run through things again. The dead man's name is Lusty. He was an employee of this company, a research scientist. Pargeter's night watchman, who's based on the gate-house, gave Lusty the key to the administration block around seven-thirty. Lusty said he was going to work in the library. He's done it on other occasions. Right so far?'

The chief superintendent said, 'Quite correct, sir.'

Morton nodded. 'Right! After that, nothing happened for the best part of an hour, except that the lights of the library were on. Then the watchman heard some kind of a shout. He ran across here. He found Lusty lying on the concrete. He'd apparently fallen quite a way although the library's on the ground floor. Lusty was dead. Broken neck and spine. The watchman left him to find a telephone.'

'Here sir,' the chief superintendent said, pointing. 'This is the nearest phone that's put through to an outside line when the switchboard operators go off duty.'

'From here, then. He phoned for the police. Also for Parsons, who lives quite near, I gather.'

'Mickleham. About two miles away.'

Morton nodded again. One of his companions lit a cigarette. The other was sitting wrong way round on a seat, resting his arms and chin on its back.

'While the watchman was waiting,' Morton said, 'he thought he heard a noise. He went out into the lobby we've just come through. He saw a man leaving the building by the main doors. The watchman shouted. The man ran for it.'

'That's right. The watchman didn't see the intruder's face, but enough of him to give a useful description. Height, colour of clothes, hair and so on. You'll see it fits when——'

'Thank you,' Morton said politely. 'Can we come back to that later? The watchman started after the intruder, realized he'd never catch him and decided to stay where he was until someone else arrived. Sensible chap.'

'Ex-police, sir,' the chief superintendent said with quiet satisfaction.

'Is he? Then he'll know how to hold his tongue. I'm still getting things right?'

The plain-clothes man said, 'Spot on, Mr Morton. You'd make a good policeman if you weren't——' He stopped in a certain amount of confusion.

12

Morton smiled. 'Very complimentary! Now, where were we? The intruder's done a bunk. The watchman's waiting for assistance. Meanwhile, back at the ranch, so to speak, a police car is on its way and our twitchy friend, Parsons, has also set out. I think you said he'd only two miles to come?

'Parsons was almost here when he was nearly forced off the road by a car going like a bomb. He managed to note the other car's registration number. He arrived here, heard the watchman's story, put two and two together and guessed that the driver of the other car was the intruder.

'Up comes the first police car. Parsons gives them the story and the registration number. They radio through to control and car and driver are picked up inside twenty minutes. Very smart work.'

'Norcott's pleased,' the chief superintendent said, grinning. 'He admits his blokes had a bit of luck, but there isn't a law against that.'

'Your chaps,' Morton said, 'brought car and driver back here. The driver, who spoke with an American accent, gave his name as Bohm. By that time you'd found something of interest on the top floor of this building. Someone had dropped a camera but there was no film in it. You made Bohm turn out his pockets. Among other items there was a roll of unexposed film.'

The chief superintendent went across to a table. On it was a miscellany that included a camera and a roll of film. Morton picked up the camera. He examined it briefly before passing it to his companions. He said, 'Exacta. Made in Dresden. East Germany. A favourite with Redland agents.'

The chief superintendent said, 'Bohm apparently stayed behind after Lusty fell, to get the film. We decided it must be important.'

Morton was looking at other, more personal items, taken from a wallet. One was a Kodacolor photograph of a woman in early middle age, not pretty but attractive. She stood next to a boy in the uniform of a West Point cadet. Either side of them were two bonny girls in their 'teens.

13

'Bohm's family, presumably,' Morton said. He picked up something else, a transparent plastic envelope. Sealed in it was a pass embodying the head-and-shoulders colour portrait of a man. The card had been die-stamped across the corner of the photograph with the eagle seal of the United States of America. Underneath was an angular signature: Charles David Bohm.

Morton turned it over. There was more printing on the reverse. He read it in silence and passed it to the other two. Nobody said anything.

The chief superintendent said, 'Bohm refused to make a statement of any kind. He asked Chief Inspector Norcott to contact the American embassy. When Norcott suggested it could be done from the police station, Bohm showed signs of alarm. Finally, he produced this identity card and asked Norcott to ring a certain number. In view of the nature of that number, Norcott contacted me and I got in touch with you. Standing orders and so on.'

'All very proper,' Morton said. 'A complete clamp-down. Who knows, apart from the police?'

The chief superintendent considered. 'Well, the watchman, of course, but I told you—he's ex-police. Very convenient. Now, let's see. Mr Parsons. Oh, and Sir Ben Pargeter, naturally. Mr Parsons insisted.'

'Well,' Morton said, 'after all, this place belongs to Sir Ben's company. In any case, Sir Ben immediately passed the word along, through the appropriate channels as they say.'

The chief superintendent said, 'I'm not prying, but I take it that what we're dealing with comes under the Official Secrets Act, sir?'

Morton said shortly, 'Yes.'

He thought for a moment. He said, 'We'll take over. Deal with press inquiries, give you a cover story. Everything. In the meantime, there's just been an accident. I'm not even sure of the existence of anybody called Bohm. Officially, that is. But I think we could see him now.'

They followed the chief superintendent out into the corridor

14

and through another door. A police sergeant stiffened to attention. The other man in the room didn't get up.

He wasn't unlike his picture, Morton thought, but a little older, a lot more tired-looking. He was somewhere in his forties, rather overweight, with thinning hair. He looked unwell. He was also anxious and trying to hide it.

Morton said, 'Mr Bohm?'

Bohm said, 'That's right. Would you mind telling me who you are?'

Morton held out his official card. 'Will that do?'

Bohm looked at it for a long time. He said. 'I guess so. I guess it'll have to.' He was trying to be ingratiating. Morton remembered reading somewhere that it was a common response in small animals trapped by something larger and fiercer. He was sizing Bohm up. Normally, he thought, Bohm's complexion would tend to the florid, as his photograph had suggested. At the moment the man's skin was underlaid with a blueness that gave it an unhealthy whiter-than-white appearance. His breathing scratched the silence like a stylus stuck at the beginning of a record.

Bohm smiled again, returning Morton's card. 'I'm out of condition, I guess. I'm not too used to running.'

Morton said, 'Nobody made you.'

Bohm made an odd movement of his head, half reluctant, half rueful. He said, 'You can say that again. Want me to tell you about it?'

Morton said evenly, 'Could we dispense with the coyness?'

Bohm said, 'I had them call that number when they refused me the embassy. Give you any ideas?'

Morton said, 'I'm full of ideas. We had another call about you. From quite a different source. We'd have come anyway.'

Bohm pulled a face. 'I seem to have kicked over the pot!' He sat thinking, his breath still sawing the stillness. Morton thought: He's worried. Worried as hell!

Bohm looked up. 'If you're the top man I'll talk to you. Alone.'

Morton considered. In the silence the sergeant sneezed. He went a little red, mumbling an apology. The chief superintendent stared stolidly at the nearest wall. Morton's colleagues stared at Bohm. The sergeant fished out a crumpled handkerchief and blew his nose loudly.

Morton turned to the chief superintendent. 'I'm sorry. I hope you understand?'

The man said, 'Of course, sir.' His voice betrayed his expressionless face. He said, 'Sergeant!'

The sergeant said, 'Sir!' very loudly. Both policemen left.

Morton said, 'Andy, you stay. Mac, we'd better give the little boss-man an interim report on the radiophone. Scrambled. After that you could stay in touch and wait for us.'

McIntyre followed the policemen.

Morton said to Bohm, 'Andrews is my right-hand man. He'll sit in a corner and go to sleep, but he stays.'

Andrews found himself a seat behind Bohm. Morton pulled up another to face the American. He said, 'You could begin by telling us how you knew the phone number.'

Bohm said, 'It's a long story. The best way to begin would be with another phone call. To the American embassy.'

Morton said, 'We're wasting time. Later, perhaps.'

Bohm tried a small grin for size. It didn't begin to fit. He said, 'Look, the explanation I'll have to give you is nothing to the one my own people'll want. The sooner you make that embassy call, the faster things'll move. Diplomatic incidents and that stuff!'

Morton's face was particularly blank. He said, 'If we're worried about diplomatic incidents, I'd say your own problem's king-sized. Unauthorized operations in the sovereign territory of a friendly power. Something like that.'

'Unauthorized, yes!' Bohm said. 'That's the whole point, but there's no need to make it sound like a military invasion. What do you think I am? We're talking about industrial espionage, not the real thing. The guy Lusty was spying. I came across it by accident. I reported it. After that I should have washed my hands but I guess I was carried away. I didn't

16

even mean to come inside this place. I was going to brace the guy when he left but the security here is so lousy . . .'

Interrupting, Morton said, 'Are you trying to tell me you're out on your own?'

Bohm sighed. 'Boy, *am* I out on my own!' He waited a while and said, 'How far out you'll find out after you make that phone call.'

Morton said, 'Whom do we call? The London liaison office of the Central Intelligence Agency? Or do you have someone who pretends to be a second secretary at the embassy?' He took Bohm's identity card from his pocket, looked at its back and said, 'Accredited for special employment. That could mean a lot of things.'

Bohm's stare was half-way to convincing. He even managed to laugh. He said, 'Oh, now look! Let's keep this thing in proportion. Listen, if I can't phone the embassy straight off, I want to do a deal.'

Morton stood up. He said, 'No deals. How are you feeling?'

'I could feel better, but I'll live.'

'In that case we'll continue the conversation in London.'

Bohm bit his lip. He looked like a man with a crisis and a shortage of solutions. He said, 'Look, I didn't kill him, you know. After all, he was spying. I stumbled across the whole thing by accident. Everything I've done has been against orders. When I got up there I was just watching him but I made a noise. It scared him. He tried to take off down the fire escape. He slipped. I'm telling you, it scared the living daylights out of me. Except it was dark,' he finished, but nobody played up to the laugh line.

Morton said, 'You weren't so scared you forgot to wind on that camera and pocket the film. Or can you explain that, too?'

Bohm said, 'I could explain everything if you'd agree to a deal.' He looked at Morton's stony face. He stood up. He said unhappily, 'Well, if you want to do it this way.'

Morton said, 'We do.'

The chief superintendent was in the hall, trying to look as if he hadn't been hovering. Morton said, 'Bohm hasn't exactly committed any offence. He's what you might call a friendly alien. We're taking him back to London.'

The other man stared. He said, 'You mean he's—well, one of us?'

Morton said, 'You could put it that way. It's all going to turn out to have been an unfortunate accident that only involved Lusty. Nobody'll know anything about a man called Bohm.'

The chief superintendent said, 'You'd better stick to that promise about taking over. It's going to be hard to make so many people forgetful.'

In the Jaguar McIntyre was just replacing the radiophone. He said, 'Reinforcements on the way.'

Morton said, 'Thanks, Mac. Stay behind and cheer the police up, will you? At the moment they're not very happy, and all because there's no such man as Bohm.'

McIntyre said laconically, 'It's hard for a copper to keep a sense of humour, let alone a suspect.' He trudged off.

Bohm said, 'Now you're showing some sense. You'll be glad of it later.'

Bohm and Andrews got in the back. Morton took the wheel. As they drove off, Bohm said, 'Incidentally, I thought you people had no powers of arrest.'

Morton said, 'Who's arresting anybody?'

Bohm laughed. He said, 'Oh, fine!' He firmed up his voice. 'I know I'm not in much of a position to insist on rights, but this is a civilized country. How about if I tell them you wouldn't let me call the embassy?'

Morton swung the car through the main gates. He said, 'Let's discuss it later. In the meantime, take it easy. You had a bit of a shock. It's probably taken more out of you than you realize.'

To himself he thought: But not one half so much, you poor little bastard, as is going to be taken out of you quite soon.

2. BOHM—*One of them*

THE DEAD LIGHT of a half-awake dawn glimmered bluely outside, making the artificial brightness of the room look unreal and tawdry. All four men showed dark, unshaven jowls. Two of them looked fatigued. The third, not much over five feet tall even when standing, which he wasn't at the moment, seemed as brisk and inquisitive as a magpie. His pink skin glowed with well-being. His green eyes, bright and penetrating behind contact lenses, gave his bland, espiscopal features a worldly look that was somehow disconcerting.

He sat with his small, neat hands on his lap, one folded inside the other. Above them swelled the discreet curve of the small paunch his tailor had not quite succeeded in concealing. He leaned forward, watching. The fourth man lay on the bed, his white face glistening like Carrara marble, his wide eyes staring glassily at the ceiling.

Morton, too, watched as Andrews repeated the question. The man on the bed, his jacket and tie removed, his shirt front unbuttoned, the shirt sleeve of his right arm rolled up past the elbow, showed no interest. He stared vacantly at the low ceiling.

Andrews fed a little more of the colourless liquid from the hypodermic into the bared forearm. He said again, 'Why? Come on, Bohm, tell us why. Tell us why.' Instead of answering, the man on the bed suddenly stiffened. His eyes opened wide, agonized in shock and terror. The blueness lurking beneath his skin had concentrated in his lips, nose and cheeks and he fought for breath as if he were strangling. He struggled to sit up, made a brief gurgling noise like a plumbing system being drained, and relaxed with an air of permanence.

Andrews bent forward, as if straining for a reply. His eyelids fluttered several times. Otherwise his face was expressionless. He withdrew the needle of the hypodermic. He said, 'End of conversation.'

The small man exhaled sharply, his brows arching and then straightening into a frown. He said, 'No, he can't. He mustn't. Not yet.'

Andrews shrugged. Moving slowly, heavily, as if he himself had been part-anaesthetized, he rattled the ampoule into a waste bin along with the disposable hypodermic and its ripped-open plastic container. He said stiffly, 'He obviously didn't know the rules. Perhaps we should have explained that dying wasn't allowed.'

The small man said, almost querulously, 'Damn! Damn! This really is too much. One had hoped for—'

'—more consideration?' Morton asked ironically.

Andrews said, 'The doc did warn us. You can't put a man through that kind of questioning for that long without a hell of a strain. And he'd already had a rough night.'

He stared at Bohm for a moment. He reached out and brought the dead lids down over the staring eyes. He went to the bottom of the bed and began to draw up a blanket. Inch by inch, Bohm changed into an impersonal, morgue shape, a series of hidden curves terminated by the awkward, undignified upthrust of the feet. Watching the sweat-varnished face disappear, Morton thought: You don't look much like your colour picture now.

Andrews sat down again, heavily. It wasn't just his tiredness.

Morton said, 'Well, have we learned anything?'

'Learned anything?' the small man said. 'Perhaps. Though more in what he attempted to avoid saying than in what he said.'

He lifted his hands from his lap. From one of them, incongruously, something spilled out on a slender chain. It was a neat golden whistle, cylindrical, almost elegant. They all watched as it described small, hypnotic arcs under the yellow light.

The small man said, ' "O whistle, and I'll come to you, my lad." But who?'

Automatically Morton said, 'Robert Burns.' He added, 'I know that isn't what you mean.'

The small man said, 'No. Not in the least.' He was still studying the pendulum action of the golden whistle. Watching it, he said, 'We can guess why he wore it, but the knowledge is

20

useless. A keyhole without a door. Or a key without a keyhole.'

'It might not even be London,' Andrews said.

Morton said, 'It could be anywhere in the world.'

The small man said, 'And we had scarcely begun.' Almost to himself he added, 'Though we are relieved of a difficult and unpleasant decision. I mention it as fact, not mitigation.'

Morton said bleakly, 'You mean that whether he died under questioning or was killed later, we would have had him murdered.' He touched the closed lids of his eyes gently, wearily with the tips of his fingers and added, 'I mention it as fact, not mitigation.'

The small man abruptly halted the swinging of the whistle, trapping it in his neat, pink paw with a swift, dexterous movement. Distastefully, he said, 'Nothing so crudely put. But it would have been impossible to allow him to walk out alive. He may perhaps have thought of that in attempting to strike his bargain with us.' Bouncing the whistle and chain on the palm of his hand with a tiny chinking sound, he said ' "Thou wretched, rash intruding fool, farewell!" How easy it is to dismiss stark reality with a quotation!'

Now the light outside almost balanced that in the room. The window looked across a shadowy, serrated panorama of rooftops still flat and unreal in the fading umbra of the night. The small man stood up and walked to a table beneath the window. On it, Bohm's personal possessions were spread out in the kind of arrangement that rates about thirty seconds in a memory test.

The photograph of Bohm's family lay between a mono-grammed Zippo lighter and his Diners' Club card. The small man toyed with the picture briefly, disinterestedly. He said, 'You realize that he used our telephone number because he thought he might strike a better bargain with us than with Five or Six.* He thought that with us there might be room for bargains, for manœuvre.'

*M.I.5 and M.I.6, the two chief branches of British intelligence. M.I.5, counter-intelligence, is confined to the United Kingdom and the Common-wealth. M.I.6 is responsible for espionage in the world at large.

Morton said, 'Knowing you, he was probably right.'

Abstractedly, the small man said, 'Perhaps. Perhaps. His information we might have used. *Will* use, such as it is. But he had to——' He left the sentence not so much unfinished as guillotined. He was still looking at the table. To one side were the spool of film and the Exacta camera. The film had been developed now. Beneath it was a series of enlarged prints.

He picked up one of the prints. He said, 'Clumsy, the use of the Exacta. Everyone knows the Russians and their allies favour it for this kind of work. But it hardly matched up, once Bohm was caught. Of course, he hadn't expected it. If he had escaped, the evidence would have suggested Russian handiwork, but it's clumsy. So very clumsy. Just think! The intelligence expenditure of our American friends is enormous, perhaps a hundred and fifty times bigger than our national total, but they are still capable of this kind of *bêtise*.'

Morton said cautiously, 'We can't be sure. He went too fast when we got down to the real business.'

The small man was looking at the photographic enlargements. Either Lusty had been uncertain of his skill or he had been making trebly, quadruply sure. The grainy prints were all of the same subject, a few lines of mathematical notation, written in a large, almost childish hand. There was also a rough sketch. It could have been anything—some arcane geometrical problem—or nothing more than the kind of thing technocrats who have wined and dined too well are apt to doodle on tablecloths.

The small man dropped the print. It drifted over the edge of the table to the floor.

Outside, a starling floated down to the soot-sprinkled window-sill, whistled shrilly at the strengthening light and began to preen itself. It saw the men in the room and plunged away with a startled flurry of wings.

The little man turned round. Picking up Morton's last remark, he said, 'Sure? Of course not! When can one ever be sure in this business? However, I am prepared to assert

22

that Bohm's story was substantially false but nevertheless a clue to the truth.

'That is to say that Bohm was *not* working on his own, let alone against the instructions of his employers. He endeavoured to avoid an exceedingly delicate diplomatic situation by trading us Lusty as a Russian agent in return for a quiet coming to terms. Of course, he was safe in the knowledge that Lusty was dead.'

Morton said, 'He tried hard enough to sell us the industrial espionage idea on the way back to London.'

The small man said, 'Naturally. It was admirable as a thing to be disbelieved so that a story equally untrue might subsequently be accepted. As something concocted after the death of Lusty and the equally shattering capture of Bohm himself, it was nothing less than brilliant. If he had once succeeded in establishing contact with the American embassy, we would have been compelled to accept it as the truth, for the sake of the alliance. But things began to go wrong faster than Bohm, or anyone else, could possibly hope to deal with them.'

Morton shook his head. 'Nobody could beat that kind of luck,' he said. 'It could happen to any of us.'

'One devoutly hopes not,' the small man said primly. 'However, one is not interested in speculation. Only facts. Such as we have. They may be summed up quite concisely. No Russians! Just Americans! Allies! The Central Intelligence Agency knows what's going on at the Pargeter research centre, made a determined if clumsy attempt to take a closer look and very nearly brought it off.'

'Where does that leave us?' Morton asked. 'What next?' He stood up, stretching, and rubbing his chin. It made a grating sound.

The small man glanced quickly at Andrews from the corners of his eyes and stroked his own chin. He said, 'A shave. Coffee. A thick rasher of ham. I shall go to the club. Andrews!'

'Yes, sir,' Andrews said. He was still looking a little pale.

'He died. You understand? He died.'

Andrews looked very unhappy. He said, 'Maybe. It's hard to be sure. I don't like the idea of living with the thought that I killed him.'

The small man's face was suddenly much less benevolent. He snapped, 'I will tolerate no woolly, emotional thinking. What killed him was something impersonal, the business in which we are all engaged. And in which Bohm himself was engaged. He knew the risks he was taking. He took them for the good of his country. Well, he died for the good of ours. If we don't believe that that's preferable, we believe in nothing. Now, be a good chap. Go and see what arrangements "D" group have made for the disposal of the body. They'll have all the relevant information by now. Thank God the man's family's already gone back to the States! He's less of a problem, living alone.'

Andrews stared. He said, ' "D" group? Then you'd already arranged that he was going to die?' The small man made an impatient gesture. Andrews left the room.

The small man looked at Morton. Almost defiantly, he said, 'Our kind of work comes complete with a kind of built-in absolution. All-purpose remission for every imaginable kind of sin on the grounds of higher national interest.'

As if to himself he added, 'A worm that devours its own tail.'

Morton said, 'They won't be fooled, naturally.'

The small man turned to look at him. 'The little accident to be arranged for Bohm? Of course not. But what can they do? An official complaint? We're sorry we were spying on you, dear ally, but you really shouldn't have killed our spy? Hoist with their own petard, my dear chap, for the sake of unity. They're unlikely to have another Lusty to step into the breach, so we may feel reasonably safe. At least until after the Geneva conference.'

'With the appropriate precautions,' Morton said. 'All the Pargeter people will have to be vetted now. We were caught out over Lusty.'

'Of course. A discreet watch on that idiot-savant at Leather-head. A general tightening up of security procedures. And perhaps——' He stopped, nibbling the tips of his fingers thoughtfully. Morton waited.

Eventually the small man shook his head. 'No,' he said. 'At the moment I don't see how it's to be done. I would like,' he explained, 'to place a scarecrow in a rather conspicuous position. Not so much to scare the crows, which are intelligent and mistrustful creatures, but as a sign to those skilled in reading signs. I shall think better when I am washed and fed.'

Morton turned off the light. A thin torch-beam of sunlight shafted across the room at a sharp angle. It laid a bright escutcheon on Bohm's mummy-form. Morton said, 'It could hardly be one of us. We couldn't afford another direct confrontation. One dead man's enough.'

The small man made a noise of impatience, following Morton to the door. 'One is aware of all the consequences. Bacon quotes a Duke of Florence as saying that though we are commanded to forgive our enemies, there is nothing about forgiving our friends. For my own part, I don't ask that they should forgive me in this instance, nor do I forgive them. My only concern, and I hope theirs too, is that we shall remain friends in spite of everything.'

As he closed the door on Bohm he said softly, 'However, there is another area of interest. If Lusty was suborned by our friends, we have a further suspect. Because we know now who recommended him to Pargeter. Does that not stir your curiosity?'

Morton began to see, He said, 'Oh, yes!' He pressed the button for the lift, He said, 'Schramme!'

The small man nodded. 'Exactly!'

The lift arrived almost at once. They stood aside while the men with the big basket wrestled it out. Andrews was with them. The basket had the name of a non-existent laundry stencilled on it. It was big enough to hold a man.

As he passed, Andrews said, 'For the dirty linen we don't want to wash in public.'

Morton smiled perfunctorily. He held open the lift door and said, 'After you, Master.' The small man stepped in, still thinking about Schramme.

3. SCHRAMME—*Someone else*

MYRA OPENED HER EYES and found herself staring into Schramme's stubbly jowl at close quarters. He was breathing heavily into the pillow, close to her left ear. His breath was male, sour with the smell of whisky and those damned cigarettes he imported from some place in the fundament of Europe.

She turned away, shoving impatiently. He moved, his belly peeling away from hers like adhesive plaster. For a moment his breathing almost stopped. Without opening his eyes he turned towards her, fumbling his lips at her cheek although she knew he was immediately wide awake. His right hand slid down her flank. Dutifully, she thought. Dutifully! She had guessed some time ago that he was weary of her.

She moved as far away from him as his weight permitted. She pressed one of the buttons on the panel in the bed-head. The heavy drapes rolled back from the windows with the long, prim shushing sound of an audience settling down. Pale morning light fanned across the room like the opening of the first act.

Schramme opened his eyes. As always, it was as if someone else looked out, someone alert and aware, guarded and cynical. The eyes looked into hers, trying to read her thoughts while the mouth below adjusted its automatic smile.

Her own mouth reflected the smile precisely. 'Schramme,' she said softly, half mockingly, half impatient. 'Shhh-ram!' She found the slender, gold-plated whistle that lay among the coarse, dark hair of his chest. She tugged and twisted. The thin chain that secured the whistle cut deeply into the muscled

26

flesh of his neck. He put up a hand to disengage hers. He did it gently, but the curbed strength was implicit.

She pouted, malice tugging at the corners of her lips. 'Diddums want ums ickle whistle, den?' she said. She snatched at it viciously. His hand was there first. For a moment they struggled. She fell back, closing her eyes and opening her lips on a sharp intake of breath. Inwardly she damned the uncontrollable urge of her body.

He was staring at her with those scalpel eyes that hardly ever matched the look on his face. He pressed his mouth down on hers, grinding his stubble against her soft skin. He could see the fine crow's-feet at the corners of her eyes, the bruised shadows beneath them and the pores in the skin of her pinched, aristocratic nose. He thought, as if he were conducting one of his interviews: Age is beginning to imprison her in a cage of lines and wrinkles. She will pursue her youth like a necrophilist, long after it is finally dead.

But she was still attractive. Experience was worth more than mere beauty. She had been a pleasant fringe benefit of his hidden occupation. He concentrated on arousing her.

She slid her mouth away, sighing. 'You allow me no more freedom than a puppet. Why can't I stop you, Schramme?'

He propped himself over her on his forearms. 'Perhaps you would find it easier if you tried pronouncing my name more accurately. Scramm-er! But no, you are English. When I first arrived in this country, after the war, I abandoned any hope that the English would pronounce my name properly.'

She began to laugh, a laugh with a tincture of venom. 'Scram, Schramme! When I think! It's really too bloody silly!'

He nodded, smiling faintly. 'Of course! Ralph Schramme, one-time refugee and nobody. In your bed. Wife of a knight, daughter of a baronet. And yet, believe me, this woman, this aristocrat feels like, behaves like, makes love like any peasant girl.'

She declined to be annoyed. She said, ' "For the Colonel's Lady and Judy O'Grady are sisters under the skin." '

He frowned.

27

She said, 'Kipling. A poem.'

He shrugged. 'Kipling is like earls and knights, a relic of a dream world. Why does your extraordinary country not free itself from the cerements of its dead past?'

She said, 'Why do you speak its language like a prissy, pedantic old maid? You've done well enough out of our extraordinary country. But of course, you haven't any past. You've turned your back on it. You represent the present. Or perhaps the future? The aristocracy of merit. The peerage of progress. You still have serfs, but they're not people, just patterns of holes in computer cards.'

He could feel her quivering beneath him. She was laughing again.

He said, momentarily disinterring his past and as quickly reburying it, 'Yes. I was forgetting. I owe much to this country.'

She said, 'Balls, ducky! What you have you took. With both hands. And you're so grateful you can't wait to leave us for America. Except they won't have you.'

'Not today,' he said mildly. 'But tomorrow, perhaps. These things take time. And it's nothing to do with ingratitude.'

'Of course not. New York's your Mecca, your Holy City. The high temple of the people processers. Doesn't that strike you as funny? The great champions of democracy and they make the Russians and the Chinese look like children when it comes to turning people into ciphers! What are all those tall buildings full of? Not people. Credit ratings, Nielsen ratings, social security numbers, blood groups. No men! And no women! Just that mindless, unholy trinity of bust, belly and buttocks that they call our vital statistics!'

She took a long breath and said, 'Or something,' but the lightness was lacking.

Schramme looked down at her, the gold whistle about his neck swinging gently across her breasts. He thought: And the more highly developed the system of personal statistics, the greater the need for a carefully established background. Such as mine will be when the time finally arrives.

28

He shook his head at her, making the whistle dance a little. He said, 'There should be a rule. Never go to bed with an intelligent woman. Only with assemblies of vital statistics.'

He rolled away from her, reaching out for his cigarettes and his gold lighter. He lit a cigarette and switched on the bedside radio. It was news time. There was another welter of hopeful speculation about the forthcoming Geneva conference. Well, perhaps something would come of it. He would believe it when it happened. He snapped the radio off. It reminded him of things he chose, at this moment, to forget.

He lay on his back, smoking and staring out at the gilded tops of the trees. A pigeon was doing an imitation of a man doing a clever imitation of a pigeon. A big jet rumbled over, high and remote, like summer thunder.

He said, 'You are reluctant to destroy your past, you British, but it is already dying.'

She said, 'We British, ducky. *We* British, *ja?*'

He ignored the gibe. 'This is no longer the country I found when I came here. The greyness, the outward respectability and decency, still there. But something else, hard to describe and not at all pleasant. A discovered taste for brutality and eccentric vice in middle age? Hectic, heartless, a little nasty. The old kindness, the old tolerance, going, going. I am not sure what eventually will replace them. A kind of honesty, perhaps, but I think I shall not like it very much.'

He meant it. You came to like a country.

He pointed. 'He will. It will be his kind of world.'

He meant the large, silver-framed photograph that peered at them from its tactful, meaningless position on the escritoire. It showed a superficially handsome, middle-aged face, the firm jaw tamed by well-fed flesh, the eyes hard even in two-dimensions. The general effect was one of calculating opportunism behind a façade of worldly tolerance. Immaculately groomed hair, thick and fine, swept down to silver wings at the temples, added to a slightly theatrical air. The face was still well known to newspaper readers, television viewers.

29

She fell back on her pillow. She said, bored, 'Oh, him! He'll make sure it's his kind of world. It's being made by his kind of people.'

He said, 'Were you not his kind of people, once?'

She said, 'Oh yes, ducky. Once! Our courtship was as romantic as a company merger.'

'But he will end up as a lord. Or so they say. A lord for merit. A little better than being born a lord?'

'Rags to riches? Crap, ducky! Middle class to meritocracy. And who says he'll make it? He's waited a long time. His lordly ambitions are becoming a bit of an Establishment joke.'

She took the cigarette from his fingers, drew on it. She made a face, coughed and handed it back. 'God! When are you going to give those things up? Hand-rolled in the sweaty armpits of Bessarabian peasants!'

'You must give your husband some credit. He believed in me, all those years back. He used me. He still does. So do others, because of him. I owe him a great deal.'

'Which is why you're shacked up with his wife. Look, ducky, he used you because you were new. He couldn't have cared less whether you were actually so marvellously good, so long as you weren't too obviously *not* any good. You sounded good. I've told you before. You fitted in with his image—progress, enlightenment, efficiency. Think of the publicity he got from you.'

'And I from him.'

'All right.' She was becoming irritated. 'So you benefited too. It didn't cost him anything. All that lovely stuff about deep probing, inner conflicts, shock interrogation. Whatever his failings, he knows a headline-maker when he sees one, and you were it, ducky. You were it!'

'Why do you use the past tense?'

'All right! Are! But not for him. That's why you don't see so much of him. But come up with something new, something sensational, today, and he'll be in your office with the morning mail.'

'Hardly tomorrow. He's in Düsseldorf.'

'From Düsseldorf! But until you've something that's news you're *vieux jeu*, yesterday's tune. So far as Ben's concerned, anyone who isn't news, just isn't.'

That amused him, privately. In certain circumstances he could have given Sir Ben Pargeter enough headlines to satisfy even him! He suppressed the joke. He had his rôle to play, though it was becoming increasingly irksome. He slid his arm under Myra's bare shoulders, cupped her breast. For no particular reason other than force of habit, he said, 'And what is news with Sir Ben at present?'

She shrugged, snuggling against him and letting her hand wander. 'Don't ask me. As a matter of fact, he *is* up to something. I can always tell. I don't know what it is, except that it pleases him. Excites him, even. I know the signs. He's so damned conspiratorial, like a little boy with a secret. I can't imagine—My God!'

She had stiffened suddenly. 'My God!' she said again, wonderingly. 'Do you suppose——?' She turned towards him, her eyes bright with malicious curiosity.

'Ralph ducky,' she said. 'You know everything. Or nearly everything. Or everything worth knowing. Do you know a good 'tec?'

He stared. 'A what?'

'A detective. A private eye.'

His alarm bells clangoured. He didn't know what she meant, but she had his full attention. 'Why do you ask?'

'Because I want to know, you fool. I mean, I want to know what he's up to.'

'Sir Ben?'

'Look, ducky, you're not usually stupid, but at the moment you're being the teeniest bit thick. Yes, Ben, of course.'

'What do you think he might be up to?' He was taking part in two conversations, one with her, the other within himself.

She sighed. 'If this is the way you question all those top brains who come to see you, I wonder you manage to recruit so much as an office boy. What do I think he might be up to!

31

If I knew, I wouldn't want a private detective, would I? But he might—he just *might*—be up to getting himself a mistress. And if he were, I'd have him in the divorce court before he could say "Pargeter Electromation Limited". Then perhaps you and I could cloak our naked lust in the grey fustian of respectability. Should you like that? No, don't answer!'

For a moment her eyes were bitter. Then, with one of her lightning changes, she began to laugh. 'My great-aunt Lucy,' she said with a gaiety as brittle and synthetic as cheap plastic, 'who could hardly hear herself speak as a young girl for the sound of lecherous Royals slurping champagne from her slippers, and is now deceased, once told me when she was tipsy that you hadn't lived until you'd made love under a cloak.'

He drew her round to face him. She misunderstood. She began to nibble his ear.

He shook her, controlling the strength of his fingers. 'Wait,' he said, pushing her hand away. 'Let us attend to one thing at a time. You think Ben has a woman?'

'How do I know? He has something. Perhaps it's a woman. He would be terribly discreet. Scandal terrifies him. He's afraid it might keep him from the ermine.'

She laughed at his expression. 'We British!' she said. 'You're only British on the surface, like those pathetic coloureds who say "Goodness gracious me!" A British peer in full drag, ducky, wears ermine on his robes.'

Her eyes darkened and the lines strengthened sulkily on her face. 'I don't know whether he's got a bloody woman or not. But I know he's got a secret.'

She began to mouth the lobe of his ear once more, her interest fading. Schramme closed his eyes. It gave him a little time to think. What she had said confirmed a feeling he had had for some time. His basic, long-term purpose required a comparative inactivity. The request to handle Lusty had been a brief break in planned inertness, like a man turning over in his sleep. But for some considerable time he had sensed that he was on the edge, was being deliberately kept on the edge of something that might be very big.

The Lusty business had come to a bad end. Whether it had also been an unsuccessful end was something he had no present means of finding out, not in any of his capacities. It was all very well to be earmarked for a long-term rôle but it placed a great strain on someone in his position. He came to the provisional conclusion that no harm would be done in advising that Sir Ben Pargeter had a secret.

Myra was rubbing her nose in the hollow of his neck. 'Perhaps he isn't in Düsseldorf at all,' she said. 'Perhaps he's teaching some young bitch new tricks.' She didn't sound serious.

He said, 'So no private detective, eh?' But the time might come when the idea would have its use, so he added, 'In any case, a private detective is not a genius, you know, or he would earn his living in another way. He can watch, he can follow, he can report, but only someone with all the facts can interpret correctly. And it is best not to give outsiders all the facts.'

She wrinkled her forehead. Watching, he saw that she was making up her mind to be bored with her own idea. Before she could say so he took the matter to a neutral but potentially useful conclusion.

He said, 'Think about it. If you really wish it, tell me how Ben's secret appears to be developing. I will advise you whether it would be worthwhile to proceed to the construction of a detailed picture.' It would be only too easy to provide her with someone to act as a private detective.

Her mood had changed again. 'Not a picture,' she said, pulling him round to her. 'A portrait. Like the one of Dorian Gray. Or was it Oliver Cromwell? Warts and all.'

He put his mouth to hers, noting a growing reluctance in himself. What had begun as a convenient piece of amusement was becoming a mechanical bore. He found himself half-pretending that Myra was her daughter. It made things just a little more interesting, though in this, as in his other occupation, there was no substitute for reality.

4. THE PRESIDENT—*I*

THE PRESIDENT was angry. Not with his frequent, off-the-top anger that boiled up, died quickly and did no more than ruffle feelings. He was angry from deep down inside. The main symptoms were a cold slowness of response, an apparent lack of attention that could bring swift disaster to anyone taking them at their face value.

His special assistant came in to announce the arrival of the Director of Central Intelligence. The President went on reading the dispatch just in from Moscow, as if no one had spoken. His desk was covered with black-headlined press clippings. The assistant tightened his lips resignedly. He turned away, glad of the view through the windows across the south lawn towards the Washington Monument. He let his eyes wander along the hedge-lined walks of the rose garden and the beds studded with the showy vividness of late-summer flowers. In this big, oval room, with its sound-deadening carpet and its off-white, picture-hung walls, a minute could sometimes feel like eternity.

Eventually, without looking up, the President said, 'Have him come in.'

'Here, Mr President?'

The President was already unwinding his big frame. He went to the door. 'No. Next door.'

He loped the few steps down the hall to his private study, the dispatch still in his hand. When the Director, duly warned, opened the door and said, 'Good morning, Mr President,' he was once more deep in the dispatch, reading it for the third time to confirm his view that it said nothing at all.

He said, 'Take a seat, Mart,' in a voice that was abstracted, neutral and yet dangerous. The Director knew it well. He quirked his lips and said to himself: Fasten your safety belts!

He relaxed. He looked at the frontier scene paintings. When he tired of them he stared at the wooden eagle with *E pluribus unum* lettered on a ribbon the carver had streamered from its uncompromising beak.

The President came to the end of the dispatch, flipped slowly through the sheets once more and placed it carefully on the desk. He adjusted its edges with a precision normally foreign to his temperament. Beyond him the heavy green curtains were partly drawn against the sunlight. The room was quiet enough to pick up the muted thump of an electric typewriter somewhere in the distance. He looked at the Director over the tops of his rimless half-lenses and said, 'Well, Mart?'

The Director uncrossed his legs. He made a wide gesture with his square, tanned hands. 'Mr President,' he said, 'I just don't know.'

'You don't know?'

'I don't know. We don't know. Nobody knows, not yet.'

The President leaned far forward. The desk light was merciless on his thinning hair. With equal ruthlessness it emphasized the deep ravines of flesh that ran from his ears to the corners of his mouth, delimiting the lower part of his face like the edges of a mask. His lenses glittered.

The Director waited but the President said nothing. He just stared. It was an intimidating gambit. The Director, wise in the ways of presidents, still had to fight for his balance.

He said, 'Hell, Mr President, we only just had the news ourselves. You know the way they work, like a conspiracy of Byzantine eunuchs. It was completely unexpected. You probably know more than I do.'

The President stroked the end of his long nose, his hard, granite-grey eyes looking through the Director. He said, 'You get more than five hundred million bucks a year for finding out, and I probably know more than you do! What are you doing with all that money? Infiltrating the American Legion?'

The Director flushed. The President, a master of personal relations, saw that the time had come to ease the pressure. He slipped into folksiness. He said, 'Don't get sore, Mart. I was just joshing. Okay, so I'm mad. Who wouldn't be? Those bastards didn't even signal the play. Just that goddamed so-called Tass man arranging to meet Frank at the Statler-Hilton, the way they've done a dozen times before, and calmly saying that the deal is off. Then, nothing until the reports come through on the speech in Moscow. And this.' He slapped the dispatch on the desk. 'All it tells me is that those guys in the Moscow embassy don't know worth beans what's going on out there. Did you get anything from your Moscow station chief?'

The Director said, 'Not yet, Mr President. We've signalled world-wide watch-and-listen. You'll be getting summaries every twenty-four hours.'

The President frowned. 'Twenty-four hours? It's going to take that long?' His toughness was showing again. He said, 'Listen, Mart. You're a civil servant and I'm a politician. Do you really understand what this means?'

The Director said stiffly. 'I believe so, Mr. President.'

The President dragged the sides of his glasses over his big ears. He pointed with them. 'Okay! Maybe you do at that, but let me tell you how I see it. Your understanding might be a little different from mine. We have a nuclear non-proliferation treaty virtually in operation with the Soviets, right? It's a start, but only a start. So we open secret discussions on the possibility of some kind of agreement on arms limitation. Something that would achieve a meaningful slow-down in the arms race. Something we both want.

'It hasn't been easy, Mart, not on either side. You know it. I have the generals and the admirals, the big corporations and the America First blood-and-gutsers hammering at my door twenty-four hours a day, demanding more and better hardware. And it isn't too different with the Soviets. They have their Old Guard and their hard-line fire-eaters and enough suspicion to freeze the Atlantic clean over.

'But we were getting somewhere. It's taken a lot of talk, a lot of patience, but we were getting somewhere in all those secret talks. We wouldn't have agreed to the public announcement of a date for the Geneva meeting unless we'd been given cast-iron assurances by the Kremlin. As you know, they finally guaranteed us that if we held a full-scale arms limitation conference, they'd match us cut for cut, missile for missile, warhead for warhead.'

He jabbed with his glasses, lowering his voice. 'You know the price we've paid for those guarantees.'

The Director nodded. 'Near nuclear equality.'

'Something pretty close. You can't expect the other guy to agree that you'll each throw away your gun when his is the only one he has and he knows you have two or three more in back. But if you both have four and the agreement is to scrap three apiece, he's a mite more enthusiastic. So we've turned a blind eye while the Soviets caught up a little.'

The Director said, 'I may not be a politician, but you don' have to spell it out. The U.S. public doesn't realize how close the Russians are to equality. But they're beginning to suspect. When it sinks in, there'll be a lot of bottles thrown from the bleachers.'

'Who says they'll stay in the bleachers? They'll come out on the field.' The President put on his sincere look. 'Mart,' he said, 'there's not too much difference between home and foreign affairs in one respect. They're both games of chance. You make your play. The other guy makes his. The one with the lucky streak wins. So far in my political life, I've had the luck. It's a thing you get used to, so you graduate from taking little chances to taking big ones. This one was the daddy of 'em all. If we came back from Geneva with an arms agreement—and we would have, Mart, we would have!—no one would care peanuts about equality except the cranks. We'd be scrapping missiles, not building 'em. And anti-missile and multi-warhead programmes that will cost five billion dollars just for a down payment would be dead before they got off the drawing-board.'

'Except,' the Director said, 'that since this morning that Geneva conference is going to be a mockery. It won't produce any kind of agreement. We'll be all set for an arms race that'll make the present one look like a swords into ploughshares contest.'

37

'And,' the President said, anger thickening his voice, 'the Russian prime minister, in a public speech, accuses me of calculated deception and bad faith. Damn it, Mart, what happened?'

He pushed himself up, his hands clenched, blood suffusing his jowly face. He smacked his right fist into the palm of his left hand with a violence that made the Director's palm tingle in sympathy and walked across to trade glares with the wooden eagle.

He said, 'Bad faith! Can you beat it!' as if, the Director thought wryly, he'd never heard the words before. Over his shoulder the President said, 'My good friend the senior senator from the Poison Ivy state telephoned me just before you arrived? Can you guess why?'

He didn't wait for an answer. 'He was speaking as a friend, of course. I should need such friends! And as chairman of that goddamed Senate sub-committee. Even before that committee began its hearings I had him in for a private briefing. I pointed out that if he dug too deeply into the question of parity he'd create a public outcry that would wreck any chance of reaching an understanding with the Soviets.'

He swung round.

'Mart, I as good as guaranteed him that if he'd go easy, I'd be announcing some kind of disarmament agreement with Moscow inside three months.'

Now it was the Director's turn to keep his silence. He knew, but not officially. He simply nodded, looking down at his feet.

Chin jutting, eyes hard, the President said, 'This morning that sonofabitch would read the speech from Moscow practically the same time I did. He knows damn well something's gone wrong. He thinks I won't be announcing any agreement, then or ever. And with that possibility out of the way, he knows what's going to grab the headlines, once that committee resumes its hearings. Parity! Can't you just hear it? The U.S. hasn't just lost its commanding lead over the communists,

38

no sir! Ladies and gentlemen, this administration has made the Kremlin a *present* of parity! That's going to be his line, Mart, and he'll work it for blood.'

The Director said quietly, 'My job is the security of the United States, Mr President, not the maintenance in office of your party.'

The President drew in a breath so deep that the fine lawn of his shirt rucked across his big chest. His neck swelled and his eyes bulged. Then his gaze flickered. He sat down again at his desk. He looked at his glasses, nodded almost imperceptibly and slipped them on. He dropped his elbow on the desk and pointed a long, spatulate finger at his Director of Central Intelligence.

He said in a soft rumble, 'All right! I'm a politician. I was born shaking hands with the doctor. But I still put country before party and an arms race isn't going to help either. Mart, here's your brief. I want to know what made the Kremlin change its mind and I don't care how you find out. After that, we can decide what we have to do to make them change it back. The world needs that disarmament agreement. I'm human enough to want to go down in history as the President who gave it to 'em. I don't intend to let anyone or anything stand in the way of it. So let me say this. If I don't manage it, so many heads will roll in Washington it'll sound like family night at the bowling alley.'

He stood up to show that the interview was over. He squeezed the Director's elbow on the way to the door and said, 'My old daddy used to say, "If you're dyin' of a snake bite, knowing the name of the snake won't save you but you'll be able to concentrate your cussin' a mite." Mart, find out what kind of snake bit us.'

The joke was perfunctory. Anger threaded it through like barbed wire.

5. SCHRAMME—*Who?*

JANICE came into his office with her coat on, her bag in one hand, the tear-off from the teleprinter in the other.

She said, 'Geneva, Mr Schramme. It's a long time since we heard from them. Not that they ever seem to pick one of our recommendations, anyway.'

He looked up casually, though he'd been expecting the telex ever since he'd received the letter from Manchester at his home address the previous day. The envelope had only contained a circular but under the stamp had been a microdot, a minute photograph reproduction of a page of five-figure groups.

He said, 'We have to keep on trying, Janice. The Bureau pays a good retainer. Sooner or later we shall do better from them.'

She was only half-listening. It was one of her virtues that she did her own job very well without taking more than a polite interest in what didn't directly concern her. That was one of the reasons he'd chosen her over other, more imaginatively intelligent candidates. She said, 'Someone over there must be working late, too. I heard it coming through as I passed the door of the telex room.'

He said, 'Yes, I've kept you much longer than I should. Don't bother to wait any longer, Janice.'

She picked up the two sandwich plates and the empty coffee cups. 'You're sure there's nothing else?'

'Quite sure. The telex will keep until tomorrow. It was good of you to stay so late. I'll see it doesn't happen again for a while. Good night and thank you.'

She said, 'Good night, Mr Schramme. Don't be too long yourself.' She went back into the outer office. She'd re-done her hair and make-up and refreshed her scent. She would be off to the man she was sleeping with. Schramme had considered her himself at one point, but it would have been too dangerous.

The man who'd won her favours was a solicitor's clerk,

married, with two children. His wife had taken the kids and walked out on him. He was perfectly clean, according to Ida. He'd been checked for weeks. The report had revealed a life of stupefying respectability, apart from his somewhat frenetic sexual activities. Of course, Schramme had had Janice herself checked right at the beginning, before he'd given her the job. It was highly convenient to be able to call upon two vetting services so utterly independent as well as highly efficient! It was safe enough, too, so long as he didn't overdo it.

He waited until he heard Janice close the outer door, humming under her breath as she left. Then he picked up the telex again. It said: BURRECAD GENEVE. SCHRAMME EXRES LONDON REF. 203 FOLLOWING REQUIREMENT WORK GENEVA SOONEST. INTERVIEW GENEVA 7 DAYS NOTICE. GRADUATE CHEMIST SENIOR RESEARCH POSITION ORGANO-SILICON LUBES HIGH ALT HIGH TEMP KNOWLEDGE MILTEST PROCEDURES ADVANTAGE AGE 30/40 SALARY BRACKET 5 FRENCH AND/OR GERMAN SPEAKING. CONFIRM EARLIEST. BOURQUET.

He pulled a face at the thought of another series of spurious interviews, another spurious recommendation. It was time-consuming, but it was fool-proof and that was all that mattered. One of these days he'd have to insist that dear M. Bourquet of the *Bureau de Recherche et Recruitement des Cadres Supérieurs* actually accepted one of Schramme's recommendations and found him a job. It would set them all by the ears but it could certainly be arranged and it would deepen the cover. However, it could wait. Direct communication from Geneva was rare enough. He wondered what was so important.

He ignored the text of the telex, simply extracting the ciphers. He went through the mirror, took out the current gamma pad and thumbed through until he found a red page with 20375 as the first five-group. He had already transcribed the groups from the microdot. He fed figures into the Swedish electric calculator, pressing the operating button each time to produce the fresh groupings. He made the final transpositions, humming the tune Janice had hummed as she left.

41

The message, when he completed the deciphering, read:
CONFIRMED PARGETER DISCONNECTION DUE TO VIOLENT COM-
BINED ACTION SAM AND JOHN. LUSTY APPOINTMENT IF QUERIED
MUST BE STRAIGHTFORWARD FAILURE YOUR PART. NO PERSONAL
THREAT CURRENTLY PREDICTABLE BUT MAXIMUM CAUTION
REQUIRED. ADVISE IMMEDIATELY ANY APPROACH DIRECT OR
THROUGH LONDON LADY EMPLOYER.

He read the message several times. Lusty had been killed,
then. He'd suspected as much, piecing together guarded comment, gossip and rumour, though Sir Ben had been
uncharacteristically uncommunicative beyond putting it down
to a crude attempt at industrial espionage. He hadn't dared
press.

But joint Anglo-American action! That was surprising.
Fortunately he'd already covered himself in the way they were
suggesting. It had been the only thing to do. According to
what little Sir Ben had revealed, they'd already found out
about Lusty's wife, though she'd left him back in the Wiltshire
days. Schramme, according to the claims he made for his
techniques, should also have found out. So he'd had no
choice but to confess that he'd missed it, that his system wasn't
infallible. It might weaken his standing with Pargeter in the
long run, but it had been the safest thing, as the decoded
telex now confirmed.

As for inquiries from Ida, so far there'd been none, but
again he'd already anticipated the possibility. He could only
wait. Once again he had the feeling that he stood on the edge
of something big, something vital. It was maddening to sense
so much and know so little, but his own rôle was clearly
defined. He had been chosen, among other things, for his
patience. The long-term objective was overriding.

He'd felt all along that he shouldn't have been involved at
all with Lusty. His unique position, he supposed, had made
his direct participation inevitable, but the involvement had
been brief and he very much hoped that he'd heard the last
of it. Only something of paramount importance should be
allowed to jeopardize the work and planning of years.

42

Especially when the time to take the final, decisive step was so close at hand.

He put the used red gamma sheet in an ashtray and touched it with the tip of a freshly lighted cigarette. It flared and vanished immediately. Back on the other side of the mirror, he flushed down the lavatory the semi-soluble sheets he had used for deciphering.

When he left the office he walked along Charles Street towards Berkeley Square, looking for a taxi. He decided to go straight home. Sir Ben was still in Düsseldorf but Schramme was increasingly tired of Myra. It would be quite a pleasant change to spend a night on his own. And it would give him time to think.

6. JAGGER—*No one*

THE MAN with the thin, taut face and the disbelieving eyes sat alone at his pavement table, watching the summer and the evening die together. They were overdoing it, he thought, like Romeo and Juliet in a school production.

Plane trees, tasselled with prickly fruits, paraded their mottled bark in diminishing perspective towards the shadow-camouflaged outline of the Chelsea Royal Hospital. Two scarlet-jacketed and tricorned pensioners, medals gleaming, ambled homewards, filled with a nostalgia that had more to do with beer than past glory.

The man at the table felt in his pocket for a cheroot, remembered he was giving up smoking and groaned inwardly. Part at least of his spiritual unease was due to withdrawal symptoms. He began to swirl the Scotch in his glass, frowning unconsciously at its play of amber light. The gaudy parade of the King's Road turned imperceptibly into a funeral procession, as if his inner ear had subtly retuned itself to the endless, inaudible death rattle of the universe.

Drinking a little more whisky, he thought incredulously of

the days, so far behind that there seemed to be no real proof that they had ever existed, when his major preoccupation had been with the exciting question of what he was going to be. Now, with his fortieth year climbing the temporal horizon like a rain cloud, it was time to reconcile himself with what he had become.

Thirty-nine years stretched behind him like an empty, dwindling road. It came from nowhere and was heading for the same destination. He could think of nothing he had ever done that mattered.

The last brilliance of the setting sun struck across rooftops, igniting the crowns of the plane trees like torches. Starlings chattered and whistled. A passing aircraft flashed sudden brilliance in the high, salmon-pink haze. From the King's Road a busker's trumpet made 'These Foolish Things' sound as heart-breaking as Mahler's *Abschied*.

The man at the outside table tried to think of something, anything that might serve him as a *raison d'être*. Not, he thought contemptuously, that he felt any need to justify himself, at this or any other time.

He had risked his life, time and time again. In the service of others, he supposed—of humanity, but what of it? Hazarding the meaningless was like gambling with matches. He had killed. Killed in anger and killed in cold blood. Did that give him any significance? Or did it perhaps give meaning to the victim but not the executioner? When he had killed he'd seldom been concerned with value judgements. Some of his victims, he supposed, might have been corrupt, unfit to live. Others, without doubt, had been as good as he. Probably better; it wouldn't be difficult. But they'd all had one thing in common. They were unique, irreplaceable. And consequently significant?

If so, the same must apply to him. Did his significance lie in his uniqueness, in the fact that, good or bad, never before had there been, never again would there be another exactly to match him. He thought ironically: Give thanks for small mercies!

44

But was uniqueness a positive quality? You were what you were, *ab initio*, not what you made yourself. In my beginning is my end. He fingered his glass. A few more double Scotches, if he chose, and it wouldn't matter one way or the other for a while. But he never chose.

A red Lotus Elan turned the corner of the street and boomed towards him in low gear. It dropped through another gear with an arrogant flourish of horsepower, stopped on the tips of its tyre-toes and reversed with nicely calculated panache into a gap just across the road. The driver was a boy with a pink vapid face. He had a golden-haired girl with him. They were arguing.

The girl ended the argument abruptly. She opened the door, slid out and slammed it violently. She leaned across it to make some last pungent comment, her face hidden by long wings of yellow hair, and turned away. The boy watched her for a moment, shrugged petulantly and started the car on full throttle. Spinning the wheel furiously, he shot out of the parking place and jetted away, exhaust blaring, tyres squealing tormentedly.

The girl walked across the road with studied indifference. She wore a snakeskin jacket, a green silk crepe shirt and tailored black cord jeans as far removed from Levis as the Champs-Elysées are from San Francisco. She had a butterfly-bright face, a generous mouth and eyes that advertised her feelings more than she would have liked if she'd known. No more than nineteen or twenty, she made the man at the table feel very old and as alien as a Martian.

Until the car had gone, she walked as purposefully as if she had an appointment with destiny, but she slowed down as she reached the pavement, her fingers playing small arpeggios of indecision on her bag. She glanced behind her, caught the openly interested stare of the man at the table and accidentally dropped her bag.

She bent to pick it up at the same time as he stretched out a hand to help. She straightened up immediately, her eyebrows coming together in a V of potential annoyance. He saw it and withdrew his hand. The impasse disconcerted her. She hesitated.

He smiled.

'Shall I, or will you? My hands are quite clean.'

She said 'Thank you,' a little uncertainly. Her sophistication, he thought, had been acquired without a full matching set of experience. She wasn't quite sure how to handle him, or even whether she should try.

He bent and picked up the bag. She took it, thanked him again and half turned away.

He said, 'The secret now is just to go.'

She glanced at him, decided he was harmless and said, 'I'm sorry. I expect I seemed very rude.'

He said, 'Not in the least.'

'And you're very polite.'

'A disease of middle age, as a substitute for communication.' Christ, he thought, how phoney can you get!

The red Lotus suddenly reappeared, bellowing like a bull with a sore throat. She sat down hastily, smiling brightly and giving him her full attention for the first time. She blinked rapidly and said, 'That remark—very cynical. Is it supposed to be true?'

'True? I shouldn't think so. Very few would-be epigrams are, even when they're cynical. And that's real cynicism! It's all right. He's gone now.'

She raised her eyebrows. 'Who cares?'

'What I mean is that you don't have to stay.'

'What if I choose?'

'I shall be flattered and you'll be bored.'

'That's up to me, isn't it? What's your name?'

'Jagger.'

'Your first name, stupid.'

'Michael.'

'Not Mike, or Mick? Just Michael. Like the archangel.'

'Michael, but not in the least like the archangel.'

She laughed, her brown face, white teeth and young, honest eyes giving his bruised feelings a twinge. She said,

'When I first saw you, you were glooming. Why? It's too gorgeous an evening.'

'I'm an incipient manic depressive, with thirty-nine inescapable reasons for glooming.'

She looked puzzled. Then her face cleared. 'Oh! Years? You shouldn't let it matter. It's not how old you are. It's how old you think.'

He laughed as if laughing was a matter for consenting adults in the privacy of their own homes, but she found herself thinking there was something oddly attractive about him in a dark, prickly sort of way. He said, 'I think very ancient thoughts. Don't let it bother you.'

'I won't. Neither should you. If you don't like things as they are, do something to change them.'

'Agreed. I have, haven't I? And now's the time for you to take your own advice.'

'Me?'

'You've stood him up. What next?'

She flushed slightly. 'Him? A baby with a new toy! I didn't stand him up. I'm not sufficiently interested. He's the kind who waits for things to happen to him and gets bored and sulky if they don't.'

'And you're the kind that makes things happen.'

'I am. Aren't you? You look as if you were. My name's Patricia, but everyone calls me Patti. Would you like to come to a party?'

She took him by surprise, swooping down on the last question like a bird from a thicket of inconsequence. Watching him, her mood changed. She pushed her hair back from her face with a hasty, nervous dab, her surface assurance cracking a little. 'I'm sorry. It was stupid. Sometimes I am. Goodbye, and thanks for—well, talking.' She started to get up.

He caught her wrist, holding it gently but firmly. She stared at her captive hand as though it might come off if she pulled. He said, 'I'm not very good at parties, but I didn't say I wouldn't go. What sort of party is it? And will my car help? It's not far away.'

She said, 'What kind? Oh, there'll be all sorts there, most of them pretty pukey and not really my thing, but you have to do something or nothing ever happens. No, it won't help. We're not going far. You can call me Patti. If you want to, I mean. I won't call you Michael, though. I'll call you Jagger. It suits you, somehow. All sharp and spiky.'

He winched. He said, 'Do you tell fortunes, too?'

The sun had gone. Even across the Atlantic, in Washington, it was several hours past the zenith, its fierce, Indian Summer heat dropping fast towards the cool of evening. Cars were arriving for the meeting.

7. THE COMPUTERS—*Neither*

THE MEETING was in an eight-storey building in a secluded, heavily wooded section of the town of Langley, Virginia. Built in white concrete, it sits among tightly packed parking lots and looping service roads, like an out-of-town shopping centre or part of a college campus.

It could probably staff several colleges. Its ten thousand employees include chemists and physicists, psychiatrists and anthropologists, mathematicians, agronomists, cartographers, oceanographers, linguists and economists, as well as specialists in more esoteric subjects.

It has greater fame than any university. Visitors call from all over the world. Once, all the roads in the area were sign-posted to help them. Today, the one sign to be found points to the Fairbanks Highway Research Station, but the white building in the woods takes more interest in back alleys than highways. It is the headquarters of the Central Intelligence Agency of the United States.

In the seventh-floor operations room a battery of high-speed teleprinters and picture transmitters receives information from every corner of the earth, every minute of every hour of every day of the year. It comes from places widely different and far apart—a waterside bar in Matanzas, a barracks in Szombathely, a male brothel in Ayuttha, spy satellites orbiting the earth at 17,000 miles an hour.

It comes as reports, figures, data, drawings, maps, photographs and tape recordings, as gossip and just plain rumour. Expertly studied, painstakingly interpreted and assessed, the cream finds its way into an average four or five pages of single-spaced typing. Bound in white, with the C.I.A.'s emblem stamped in blue on its cover, it goes to the White House between six and seven every evening in a black C.I.A. car. It is known as the President's brief.

One of the few additional copies is held by the Director o Central Intelligence himself. He was holding the current edition as he came into the meeting. In a sense it was worth nearly two million dollars, the amount the Agency spent on a single day's operations. The expression on his face suggested that he thought it poor value for money.

He sat down next to his Head of Plans, tapped the summary with the tip of his third finger and said, quietly, 'I won't shock you by telling you what he said.'

Head of Plans, the Agency's operations department chief, said, 'I shock as easy as a cat-house madam and I know as many dirty words as the President. More. I'm polylingual.' He stuck an empty pipe in his mouth and felt for tobacco.

The Director nodded at the President's security adviser, whom he respected, the Deputy Secretary for Defence, whom he liked, and the Undersecretary of State, whom he didn't. He nodded particularly to the admiral who had only recently taken over as director of the National Security Agency and was still feeling his way around. He raised his voice and said, 'Gentlemen, I don't need to waste your time on preliminaries. We all know why we're here. It's three days since the Soviets reneged on their secret promises concerning the proposed Geneva conference. Since then, we've checked every source that time has permitted. Net result so far: zero. Normally, it wouldn't signify. Three days is no time at all. There're thousands of corners we haven't even begun to explore. One of them may hold the answer. But the President doesn't have time for the waiting game.'

State Department interrupted. In his gravelly voice he said, 'You have to admit the President has a point, Mart. He knows the Russians wanted some kind of agreement as badly as we do. So it must take something pretty big to make them go back on their word before talks have even begun. Something too big to hide in a corner.'

Defence came to the rescue. He said, 'The State Department hasn't been able to come up with anything either, Jim. And it's State's business if it's anybody's.'

The White House security adviser said, 'It's everybody's business, especially if the President says so. And he does say so. Let's make progress.'

The Director exchanged fleeting glances with his Head of Plans, who was stuffing his pipe bowl with tobacco. They were used to reading each other's thoughts. Head of Plans was thinking: Bastard! He meant the Undersecretary of State.

White House said, 'Mart, let me say one more thing. The President isn't gunning for the C.I.A. He isn't gunning for anybody. He wants that arms agreement and right this minute he doesn't see his way clear. That's why he's mad.'

Head of Plans lit his pipe carefully. He thought: That and the fact that the chairman of a certain Senate sub-committee is going to make things very, very awkward for the President if he's given away parity without getting some kind of disarmament.

Defence said to the Director, 'Mart, does this meeting mean you're on to something?'

The Director hesitated, then said, 'I think we have a good idea how to get something.'

White House said, 'Great! Why don't we hear about it?'

The Director said, 'Well, let's start off with some automated speculation. We've been using STARCOM.'

Although protocol made his presence this afternoon essential, the admiral was looking worried. His professional deputy, glancing apologetically at the Director, began to whisper.

The Director used his tact. He said, 'Admiral, forgive me if I tell you things you already know. STARCOM stands for Strategic and Tactical Assessment and Review Computer. It has one great advantage over the rest of us. It only knows what we tell it but it knows as much as all of us put together —the entire U.S. security, defence and information services. Also, it never forgets anything, and we do.

'It can answer a pretty comprehensive range of questions on security and defence matters. Or, more exactly, given a choice of answers, it rates them in order of probability, which is the way most human beings think. Only STARCOM does it a hell of a lot faster than human beings and without missing any tricks.'

Defence chipped in. He said, 'The Russian Chiefs of Staff would vouch for that.'

The admiral was looking puzzled again. The Director saw it. He said, 'What the Deputy Secretary for Defence means is this. At the time of the Arab-Israeli war in 1967 the international situation could have turned pretty nasty. The Russians were officially backing the Arabs and the U.S. could hardly have stood by and let the Israelis be overrun. On the surface of it, there were all the makings of another Cuba.'

Defence said, 'Eyeball to eyeball.'

White House said, 'Only glass eyes. The Russkis, anyway.' Everybody laughed.

The Director said, 'Needless to say, we knew damn well the Israelis weren't in any danger. We had all the facts. The Joint Chiefs of Staff prepared a forecast for the President. They gave the Israelis two weeks to wrap the whole thing up.'

White House said, 'STARCOM said six days, only the Joint Chiefs didn't believe it. Six days is what the Israelis actually took.'

The Director, talking to the admiral, said, 'The question was, had the Russians come to the same conclusion? It was important they should and we could hardly send the Joint Chiefs of Staff to Moscow.'

'So we sent STARCOM,' Defence said. 'Not in person, but in the form of a complete tactical and strategic review. Fact studded, as the reference book ads always say.'

'On the hot line,' the Director explained. The admiral's face began to clear a little. Head of Plans leaned back in his chair, staring at the diffused lighting panels in the ceiling. He puffed gently at his pipe, well content with the general trend of the conversation.

The admiral laughed doubtfully. 'You mean that story was true? I heard it at half a dozen cocktail parties, computer talking to computer. I thought it was a joke. So did everyone else, so far as I could see.'

'That's one of the things Washington cocktail parties are for,' White House said. 'Talking the truth to death before anybody gets around to believing it. Baseless rumour's always so much more interesting.'

'Why would the Russians believe a computer any more than they'd believe anything else?' the admiral asked. 'Or am I being stupid?'

The Director said, 'You're not. They have a STARCOM of their own. We didn't just send the assessment. We sent the data, in computer language, and let their computer make its own assessment.'

'In their computer's language,' Head of Plans said. 'We thought they'd be interested to see we knew what language their computer speaks.' It was his first contribution to the meeting. He took his pipe from his mouth to make it.

State Department said impatiently, 'This is history. History's dead the moment it's made. We didn't have to fight the Russians over the Middle East. What does STARCOM say now?'

The Director said, 'We couldn't give it many additional facts, because we don't have them. So we asked it to consider possibilities.'

'We don't have too many of those either,' State said.

'Call them speculations,' White House snapped, 'and we have an inexhaustible supply.'

'Exactly,' the Director agreed. 'The thing was to have them assessed in order of probability. I could show you the whole thing but it would be wasting your time. All that matters is which came top.'

'Let me guess,' Defence said. 'The Russians have developed something new, something they figure will give them enough edge to do away with the need for arms limitation. Something that makes missiles old-fashioned.'

The Director said, 'Stu, you're warm but not hot. If you had the ultimate weapon system you'd be happy to cut down on things like missiles.'

White House thought. He said, 'Okay, Mister Director! Surprise us!'

The Director said, 'It's the other way round. It also explains those accusations of bad faith. They think *we've* developed something new.'

White House stared. 'They think *we* have? Oh, come on! We haven't and you know it.'

The Director said, 'Of course I know, but this isn't me. This is STARCOM. And STARCOM isn't considering facts, it's considering probabilities.'

Defence was interested, even a little excited. 'How high a probability rating does STARCOM give this, Mart?'

'Eighty-three plus.'

Defence whistled.

The admiral said, 'That's high?'

'If they go much higher,' the Director said, 'they aren't probabilities. They're facts.'

The admiral said, 'But if the Russians thought we'd developed something that good, what would it be?'

Suddenly enlightened, Defence said, 'Shortchange!'

There was a long silence. Head of Plans puffed enigmatic smoke signals. White House looked sceptical, State Department shocked and Defence calmly expectant.

The admiral said, 'Shortchange? Is that——'

The Director said, 'Yes. It is. And you're right, Stu. That's what STARCOM says. The Russians think we're seeking a

53

general reduction in nuclear and conventional arms because Shortchange makes them all obsolete.'

Defence said, 'Shortchange would make everything obsolete. Including people.'

White House was smiling, his glasses flashing, but the smile was tight and sour. He said, 'Fine! Fine and dandy! Only one flaw, so far as I can see. We don't have Shortchange. Mart, we aren't any nearer breaking through now than we were two years ago, and you know it. The meeting knows it. The President knows it. The only one that doesn't know it, apparently, is your cute machine.'

The Director was smiling sympathetically. He said, 'Wait. I didn't say we had Shortchange. And STARCOM didn't say we had it. All STARCOM says is that the Russians think we have it. And STARCOM, gentlemen, backs its judgement with an eighty-seven point four-three probability rating.'

That silenced everybody except the admiral.

The admiral said doggedly, 'But weren't the Russians working on a version of Shortchange themselves? Code name Witch Baby, because in Russian mythology the Witch Baby eats its own parents. This is the thing we're talking about?'

Defence said, 'Right on the button, Admiral. The British did some work, too, but they abandoned it a while back. We and the Russians stuck with it. We're bogged down to our ears and so are they. The old problem of the universal solvent or the irresistible force. What do you keep the universal solvent in? How do you handle the irresistible force?'

White House shook his head, reluctantly impressed. He said, 'Eighty-seven per cent is one hell of a lot of probability. It has to be right, I guess. It just has to be.'

The Director said, 'Well, we think so. But we need a little more evidence, even with that kind of probability.'

'So will the President,' White House said, his glasses flashing as he nodded. 'What do you have up your sleeves, you two?'

The Director gathered in their glances like a conductor mustering his orchestra for the downbeat. Head of Plans chuckled. The Director said, 'An ace! What else?'

Head of Plans took his pipe from his mouth, laid it in an ashtray and said quietly, 'An extra one.'

White House drew in an audible breath, flung himself back in his chair and said, 'Fifth Ace?'

The Director nodded once. 'Fifth Ace. So called because you can't play it often without being found out.'

White House took off his glasses, flicked the neatly folded handkerchief from his breast pocket and began to polish them. 'It would be one hell of a risk, Mart.'

The Director said, 'The President said he didn't care what means we used so long as we found out. And we're in the risk business.'

State, apologetic for once, said, 'Gentlemen——?'

The Director turned to his Head of Plans. 'Henry.'

Head of Plans said, 'Fifth Ace is the code name for something very special. You heard how we let STARCOM talk to the Russian computer in its own language. Well, that's because we know that Red computer like we built it. We also know its servicing routine.'

He picked up his pipe, rubbing its hot bowl against the palm of his hand as he talked. 'Like ours, their computer has to be on duty pretty well full-time. They don't take it out of line for servicing. There's a complete duplicate set of sub-units. Each sub-unit in turn is replaced, serviced and put back next time round. Well, it just so happens we have a—friend in the outfit that does the servicing. And it just so happens that our very good friends in the National Security Agency figured us out a very special replacement for one of those sub-units. Which is why the admiral's here today.'

The admiral, hastily briefed by his deputy before the meeting, found himself trying to look modest. He cleared his throat angrily.

State said, 'And this unit can read a computer's—mind, for want of a better word?'

Head of Plans said, 'There's a few extra micro-circuits in the N.S.A. unit. On receipt of an outside signal they stimulate the computer to run through any selected part of its storage system and transmit the results on low power. We place a booster fairly close, somewhere outside the computer building. It collects and stores that low-power transmission, scrambles it and gives it to us on demand. It works. Let's leave it at that.'

The Director cut into the silence, summarizing. 'We know we don't have Shortchange. Until we find out why the Russians think we have, the President won't be able to get his waggon rolling again. We should be able to find out why by playing Fifth Ace.'

Head of Plans, quietly knocking out his pipe, said, 'We have one new item of information. The Presidium met secretly in the Kremlin the day before they ratted. The man in charge of their computer was there. If we tickle that computer's memory over the week before that meeting I think we'll have all we need to know.'

The Director said, 'Gentlemen, as you know, we need the approval of this committee for all "black" operations. I'm asking your formal permission to play Fifth Ace.'

There would be quite a bit of argument. It was almost obligatory before any covert operation was approved. But, looking round the table, the Director knew already that he was going to get his approval.

Afterwards he found himself walking down the corridor with the Undersecretary of State, who was unusually subdued. He had something on his mind, something he'd only just thought of.

State said, 'Mart, what if the Russians turned the table on us one of these bright days and sent us a computer assessment that showed they could lick us one-handed in a war. And what if our computer agreed with their data? What would we do? Surrender?'

'Jim,' the Director said, 'that's a question I hope I never have to answer for real.'

8. JAGGER—*Himself*

JAGGER was dancing, in a space the size of his feet, with a plump, ungirdled girl in sandals and a Happi coat. She rolled her pelvis over him like an erotic massage machine and murmured wetly in his ear, 'You're dishy! No, I mean it!'

Patti reappeared from somewhere and waved before she was engulfed by a beard with ears and huge, steel-rimmed glasses. The Jefferson Airplane gave way to the Mind Zap, the Mind Zap to something called Gullible's Travels. The twitter of electric flutes and sitars merged into a confusing double beat with a loud pounding from the street door.

Somebody was shouting, 'Police! It's a raid!'

Jagger told himself he must be slipping. The musky-sweet smell of marijuana had been there all the time, interlaced with the rough-edged odour of the incense. He thought, dismally, that a bleary-eyed early morning appearance at the nearest police station was all he needed to square life's circle.

He broke free from the scared, bedroom clasp of the plump geisha. On the far side of the spectacled beard he caught a glimpse of Patti. He pushed over to her, sweeping her towards the stairs. Somehow, with a minimum of gentleness, he forced an upward path as blue and silver shouldered into the room.

Gullible's Travels came to an abrupt, screeching end. An authoritative voice said, 'Stay where you are, ladies and gentlemen, and you'll come to no harm. We've men at both exits.'

He could hear Patti's breath, fast and excited. Her eyes shone. She smiled at him. Someone tried to stop them on the basis that troubles shared are troubles halved. Jagger gave him some fresh trouble with a short expert jab to the arch of the ribs. They reached a second-floor landing. The smell of pot was unmistakable. Nothing but a blank wall lay ahead.

He looked up. A skylight. He bent, cupping his hands. He said, 'Quick! Up you go!' and felt her foot against his palms and laced fingers. A hard thrust and she was on his shoulders, leaning against the wall while she pushed at the skylight.

It moved aside. Her trousered legs slid out of sight in the darkness above her. He took three steps back, threw himself up and grabbed the edge of the opening, hoisting himself until he could get his forearms over the rim of the skylight. He wormed his body out, Patti's fingers plucking at the suede of his jacket and then pulling at his legs.

Below, someone shouted, 'Look! We could get out this way.' Jagger smiled with the first genuine pleasure for some time. He waited until a face appeared against the light, put the butt of his palm under its chin and shoved. The face went backwards with an obscenity cut short by a crash. Jagger slid the skylight back in its frame.

He looked for Patti. She stood waiting. Even in the dark he could tell she was enjoying herself. The flat roofs ran away into the night-glow, chimneys, railings and changes of level making a kind of half-seen maze.

He said, 'Come on. It isn't over yet.'

They crossed a low parapet on to the next roof and then over five more, her hands warm in his, her face pallid in the fungoid phosphorescence of the night.

They reached the end of the block. He found another skylight, fumbled and sighed with relief as it came up. The landing below had one dim light and a steel ladder that served as a fire escape. A radio played something from 'The Desert Song.'

He said, *'De l'audace, et encore de l'audace, et toujours de l'audace!'* and walked downstairs without any attempt at concealment. She followed. On the ground floor a door flew open. A woman with curlers in bright ginger hair and gin on her breath stared at them furiously. She said, 'I've told him. I've told him a 'undred times but does he bloody care? Not him, little shit!' She popped back like a puppet, her eyes bright with rage. The door slammed behind her. Jagger opened the front door and they went out. Far down the street blue flashers winked dazzlingly and a crowd grew as they watched.

He said, 'All over. Were you very frightened?'

She said, 'Frightened? I haven't had so much fun in years! You thought so fast. As if you did that kind of thing all the time.'

He said, 'I'll take you home. My car's not far away. Where do you live?' The address made him raise mental eyebrows. Her daddy certainly wasn't a standard bearer in the ranks of the underprivileged. The exclusive little square, barely five minutes away, was near enough to the river for him to be able to smell the rank tidal water. On the far side of the Thames, above intervening treetops, Battersea power station scribbled steamy plumes on a blackboard sky. She said, 'Come in for a drink. Yes, you must! Please!'

He stepped into a rich-smelling darkness that came alive like a high-class store window when she switched on lights. Everything was conspicuous, overpowering, mummified good taste sold as a package deal and looking as lived in as the Victoria and Albert Museum.

She flung herself down on a chair. She said, 'I admit I was scared about one thing. All the time. If the police had caught me, Daddy would have blown his stack.'

Behind them a woman's voice, cool, faintly amused, said, 'Would he, darling? Why?'

Jagger turned, then got up. The woman, as assured as a film star at her fifth marriage, wore a frothy peignoir over night clothes. The relationship to Patti was obvious, but Patti was spring and daisies, her mother *fin de saison*, like a Riviera flowerbed in autumn. Looking at Jagger she said, 'Introduce me, pet,' her voice softer, throatier.

Jagger thought: If you were a real cat, your fluffy tail would be straight, straight up. Her appearance had driven Patti behind a barrier of brittle unease. She introduced Jagger off-handedly, her attitude a blend of impatience and amused contempt.

The elder woman said, 'Gin and something for me, pet. I expect Mr Jagger would prefer Scotch.' Patti sighed exasperatedly and went to pour drinks. Her mother whispered silkily over to sit next to Jagger on his sofa. 'Perhaps you could tell me why Patti was scared and what the police had to do with it?'

Patti said, 'I wasn't scared. It was nothing. Really, Just a kinky party.'

Looking at Jagger, her mother said, 'Do the police raid all the parties nowadays? How Chelsea must have changed.'

Jagger said, 'Patti wasn't involved. She's right. It was nothing.'

'But you helped her. How kind of you. Have you known her long?'

Patti said, 'Bloody hell! Does it matter? No! We only met tonight.' She gave Jagger his Scotch and pushed a glass at her mother. She said, 'It was a pot party, if you must know. If it hadn't been for him I'd be appearing in court tomorrow.'

Her mother raised her eyebrows mockingly, a faint smile twitching her mouth. 'Pot? That's marijuana, isn't it? Weren't you taking rather foolish risks, Patti dear?' Her indulgence was as artificial as her maternal concern.

Patti stared coldly. She turned to Jagger, thrust out her hand and said, 'I'm going to bed. I hope I didn't bore you too much. Good night and thank you again.'

Jagger stood up. He said, 'On the contrary, I hope I didn't bore you. Time I went too. Thank you for a most entertaining evening.' Unseen by her mother, he winked.

Patti smiled suddenly, ravishingly. She switched it off like a lamp. In quite a different voice she said to her mother, 'Say good night to Ralph for me. Or is it his night off?' She marched out, her quick steps almost inaudible on the thick carpeting.

The elder woman blinked, her fingers tightening about her glass. It was all over so rapidly that Jagger almost missed it. She recovered, smiled and said, 'So much for a Swiss finishing school! Must you go? It's barely one. Have a nightcap.'

He shook his head. 'I really must. Don't worry about Patti. She wasn't involved.'

She stood up in a graceful swirl of silk and expensively sultry scent. 'Sometimes it's more fun to be involved. You must leave your telephone number. My husband will want to thank you. He's in Germany at the moment.'

He said, 'There's no need.'

She said, 'Oh, but I insist,' as if she were surprised that it should be necessary to insist. She found a small pad and a gold pencil.

He hesitated, then gave her his number. She said, 'I don't seem to recognize the exchange numbers.' He told her where he lived. Once again there was a fleeting reaction, this time to the wildly unfashionable South London address, but she continued to write.

She said, 'I'll show you out.' She opened the door on to the square, standing so close that he was forced to brush against her as he left. She held out her hand. He felt a slight pressure from her fingers.

She said, 'Perhaps I should get to know Patti's friends better. Some of them, anyway. They're not all quite so mature. She seems to attract the retarded type. I can't think why. There was one boy whose name was Tinn—well, *boy!* Man, I suppose, though you'd never guess.' She began to laugh and changed it into an exaggerated sigh. 'One's *so* out of touch! I hope we shall see you again. I know my husband will want to thank you personally.'

He said, 'It's rather stupid, but I don't know Patti's—your surname.'

She laughed again, a rich, intimate gurgle. 'How ridiculous! Really! These young! I'm Myra Pargeter. My husband's Sir Ben Pargeter. I expect you've heard of him.'

Driving across the Albert Bridge, with the embankment lights wriggling on the Thames like electric eels, he thought: Pargeter! Brummagem Ben Pargeter! Well, well, well!

9. THE MASTER—*Us*

IN SPITE of every attempt to improve it, thought the neat little man who occupied it, the office had a prefabricated and built-in ugliness that not even the pick of the National Gallery and the Wallace Collection could have hidden. Though the modernists at the Tate, he reflected with conscious malice, would doubtless have found something to match its inhumanity.

His rosewood desk, transposed from other and happier surroundings, glowed in its sterile, clinical environment like— like a gem of purest ray serene in the dark unfathomed cave of Ocean. For a moment, smug to have avoided the hackneyed companion image of the flowers wasting their sweetness on the desert air, his gloom lightened. Then he looked at his flower prints, as unhappy on the barren buff-coloured walls as vegetarians in an abattoir. He sighed deeply, looking like a sad, pink-pawed mole in his dark Huntsman suit.

He saw himself as a victim of modernity, where modernity meant the sacrifice of the old virtues to the new Philistinism: to the convenience not of $\delta\eta\mu o\varsigma$ but of architects, property speculators and bureaucrats.

Modernity, in this particular case, stretched from Abbey Orchard Street to Old Pye Street, Westminster, and was known as New Strutton House. It accommodated some twelve hundred civil servants, all of them dispassionately devoted to the new god of social security.

All of them, that was, except a small group of men and women unobtrusively tucked away at the river end of the building, sealed off like a secret compartment in a smuggler's suitcase. Yet they too, technically speaking, were civil servants, equally concerned with security. On their choice—the small man took off on a Shakespearian flight—depended the safety and health of the whole state.

Once a don, always a don, he told himself. In any event he was reminded continually and poignantly of his academic past by the grey Gothic pinnacles of Westminster Abbey, looming hugely through his window above the far side of Great Smith Street.

Morton came in, laid the daily summaries on the desk and said, 'Good morning, Master.' He had an air of suppressed anticipation.

The other shook his head reproachfully, his contact lenses

adding glinting depths to his eyes. 'Ah, Morton, Morton!' he said. 'You little know what tender nerve you touch. When I was Master of that small but delightful Oxford college I thought the world my oyster. Now my business is to pry open the oysters of the naughty world with never the smallest hope of a pearl.'

Morton said, 'Sorry. I know it's a long time ago, but after all, you were Master when I was a member of the college. Old habits die hard.'

The Master blinked. 'Morton,' he said, 'your aim this morning is unerring. Since we moved into this dismal affront to architecture and humanity, my old habits have struggled through an unending convulsion of death throes.' He smiled slyly and added, 'However, *levius fit patientia quidquid corrigere est nefas*. Yes?'

Morton nodded impassively. 'Patience helps us endure a great many things. *Durate, et vosmet rebus servate secundis, Magister*.'

The Master chuckled appreciatively. 'A Roland for an Oliver, a Virgil for a Horace!' From the street below his windows the road drills began their ear-shattering clatter. He winced and said grimly, 'I shall indeed endure and hope for better times.'

He pulled the pile of summaries towards him. 'Anything fresh on the Geneva situation?'

Morton said, 'Not really, but there doesn't seem much doubt that Washington and Moscow had some kind of secret understanding, or that it's gone sour.'

The Master said, 'I'd like to know why. I hope we're still doing everything we can to find out.'

'Everything within reason,' Morton said, 'but the field reports all mention furious C.I.A. activity. I suspect the Yanks don't know much more than we do.'

'They certainly seem to have been much too busy to follow up on the Bohm affair,' the Master said, 'even if they'd wanted to. Well, if that conference still takes place it can produce nothing but propaganda and deadlock. So much the better for us. We shall carry all the more weight once we have a *fait accompli*.'

'If,' Morton said.

'We can but hope,' the Master said. He picked up the top file. It was the previous day's Pargeter surveillance report. He looked at it without opening it. 'One can't help thinking that one might be wasting one's time,' he said. 'Our manpower's stretched thinly enough, in all conscience, and it begins to look as if we'll get nothing from Schramme without long-term surveillance.'

Morton said, 'You're changing your mind?' He looked surprised.

The Master said, 'No, but after the Bohm business, he's certainly been told to lie very low. Not that I wouldn't like to see the Minister's reactions if he knew that we suspected Schramme, or that Schramme and Ben Pargeter's wife were *inamorati*. He'd come apart like a jellyfish doing the splits.'

Morton said, 'Because of his friendship with Sir Ben?'

The Master said, 'Friendship! The man wouldn't know how to spell it.' He slipped a finger inside the cover of the Pargeter file. 'I wager I can tell you exactly what happened yesterday, without looking. Our young Dr Tinn went home at six-thirty on the dot, had his bachelor dinner at seven, listened to Schoenberg on his high-fidelity contraption and played with his stamp collection until nine-thirty. Then— let me see! Was it cloudy last night? No!—then he peered through his telescope until around eleven, at which time he went to bed. As regular as a timetable and twice as dull. As for Schramme, even easier with Sir Ben away. He visited Lady Pargeter at about nine p.m. and left this morning. Correct?'

Morton said, 'No.'

The Master shrugged tolerantly. 'All right! Tinn had a rush of blood to the head, assuming he has blood. He rashly abandoned Schoenberg for Webern. Or Lady Pargeter visited Schramme.'

Morton said, 'Perhaps. Why don't you look.'

The Master opened the file, took out the surveillance reports and ran one neatly manicured finger down the blue, typed sheet. The finger stopped. His brows came together. The muscles of his face locked. The eyes he turned towards Morton were intimidating.

He said curtly, 'Was this certain?'

'Absolutely. We've been watching the house to establish movement patterns. Carter took the late turn last night. He knew Jagger well.'

The Master contemplated the immaculate whiteness of his desk blotter, pursing his lips. His voice brusque, almost menacing, he said, 'I want Jagger, Morton. Fetch him in. The fancy way. He won't come willingly.'

Morton said, 'You don't think it's coincidence?'

'No. Neither would you if you'd known Jagger as well as I.'

'I never met him but I've heard. I gather he was a security risk.'

The Master leaned back in his chair, scowling. He slipped a hand in a pocket and began to chink coins, his gaze bleak, unfocused. 'Security risk? Balderdash! At least, not in the sense of consorting with enemies of the state, if that's what you mean. It was just——' He pulled a face, reliving events. 'It wasn't so much what he did as what he was. The original Wolf Who Walks All Alone. He still is.'

Folding both hands in his lap, he looked at them as if they held a crystal ball. 'He was a first-class agent,' he said slowly. 'One of the best. But only when he could do things his own way, cutting corners, taking risks. He had a death wish. Now one didn't really care whether Jagger might kill himself, but there was always the possibility that he might jeopardize others. And in the end, as you doubtless heard, that's exactly what happened.'

Morton nodded. 'I heard.'

'Two good men,' the Master said. 'Jagger brought off that job, you know. Brilliantly. But two good men died when there was absolutely no need. He had to go.' He glanced up. 'I didn't dismiss him. Did you know that?'

Morton looked puzzled. 'I thought——'

The Master shaped his lips into something that was too regretful to be a smile. 'So did everyone else. It isn't true. I transferred him. A desk job, as a disciplinary measure. So far as I was concerned, that was the end of the matter, but it wasn't. Not for him. Because he's Jagger he did what he did. But because he's Jagger he'll spend the rest of his life punishing himself for doing it. That's why he went. He has a conscience, though he pretends otherwise.'

It was the first time Morton had heard the full story. He prodded. 'I've heard that he still—well, gets mixed up in things.'

The Master said, 'True, though on the side of the angels, broadly speaking. Depending upon where you see your angels. He even helped me out on one occasion.' This time his smile was real enough as he added, 'Not exactly voluntarily. One has to use a certain amount of guile with a man like Jagger.'

Morton said, 'Yes, but do you think——?'

'That he's up to something. Possibly. The man's addicted to risk-taking, excitement, danger, with little else to do but look for it. He's modestly independent, financially. From his father, whom he detested. That's one of the chips on his shoulder. Worshipped his mother, who died when he was a youngster, and that's another. It's all of a classical piece. Little charity, less faith and no hope at all. Nor any ties or loyalties. A dangerous combination. There was a girl, once, but she became tired of waiting.'

Morton said shrewdly, 'I suspect you're fond of him, for all that.'

The Master considered. He shook his head. 'No, not fond. I—respect him. It would be hard to be fond of him. To be fond of someone requires some kind of reciprocity. He gives nothing. Nothing at all. He's completely self-contained. He thinks life's some kind of cruel joke and he's determined to get his own back. That's an over-simplification, of course, but you see what I mean.'

He thought, and added, 'It's an over-simplification because

he pretends to care about nothing, and yet some things concern him passionately. That's why I respect him.'

Morton thought: *Like* him, just as I said, even though you're grudging about it.

As if reading his thoughts, the Master said, 'Well, perhaps the fellow's faintly likeable. And wholly fascinating. As Bacon said, "There is nothing makes a man suspect much, more than to know little." I want to know more, Morton. Fetch him in.'

Morton went out, grinning. Behind him the Master continued to think about Jagger. His association with any girl, let alone an empty-headed chit like Patricia Pargeter, was the best possible hint that something odd was happening. And there had already been too many odd happenings in the highly sensitive Pargeter area. Jagger was a harbinger of trouble. A man who could no longer find suitable employment with his own country might just conceivably find it with another.

Big Ben struck ten o'clock above the traffic rumble. Somewhere down the corridor a squeaky trolley approached inexorably, bearing its cargo of undrinkable coffee and inedible biscuits. The pneumatic drills down Great Smith Street started up again, a savage burst of decibels, like the end of a temporary truce.

The Master groaned, rubbing his forehead wearily. 'Stone walls do not a prison make,' he thought, 'nor iron bars a cage.' It was true. The civil service, always economy-conscious, confined its time-serving inmates very nicely without either.

10. JAGGER—*Himself?*

AT FIRST GLANCE Mr Morton was just another, somewhat elegant higher-grade civil servant. Then Jagger noticed the sharp eyes, the firm mouth, the general air of polite but tough competence. It reminded him of policemen, customs officials— all those, in fact, whose employment stems from human weakness and who are therefore the target of human resentment.

He blunted Jagger's planned assault by saying, 'It's very good of you to come at such short notice.'

As they walked across the lobby, Jagger said, 'I was going to make the same remark. In any case, I always thought the Special Commissioners of Income Tax had their nest somewhere out of London.'

'Their headquarters, yes, but you'll appreciate the necessity for a London office. No, not those lifts, Mr Jagger. Just over here.'

He took Jagger past the bank of elevators and steered him into a much smaller one round the corner. It surged smoothly skywards, flexing their knees. There was no floor indicator and only two buttons. One said UP, the other DOWN.

They stepped out into what seemed to be a small waiting room, a buff-coloured box with a white lid. Morton crossed to a door as glossy and unrevealing as a public relations brochure. He knocked lightly, stood aside and said, 'Would you go straight in, Mr Jagger?'

Jagger started forward, then stopped. On the facing wall was a row of six eighteenth-century flower prints, displayed with mathematical precision. He had seen them before, in another place at another time. A voice he knew very well said, 'Kind of you to spare the time, my dear chap. Come in and sit down.' Behind him, the polite Mr Morton closed the door gently.

Jagger turned. The Master said mildly, '*Please* take a chair. There's so much about this office that I already find distressing. Don't add to it, there's a good fellow.'

Jagger sat. He felt for a cheroot and remembered for the hundredth time that he no longer smoked. He continued to stare. The other lowered his eyes almost demurely, a smile waiting hopefully on his small, prim mouth.

The Master said, 'No doubt you would appreciate an explanation?'

Jagger said, 'Oh yes, but I suppose I'll have to put up with what you've already planned to tell me.'

The Master tried to look hurt. He said, 'Unkind! Let me

come to the point at once, in that case. Two days ago, at approximately one o'clock in the morning, you were in the vicinity of Cheyne Square, Chelsea. Why?'

Jagger stiffened, his eyes narrowing, his lips compressed.

'I was passing through.'

'Why?'

'To look at the view.'

'The view?'

'From the bridge.'

'At one in the morning?'

'My watch was slow.'

They went back to watching each other. The Master said, 'You haven't changed.'

'Nor you. You still don't know how to mind your own business.'

The Master sighed, holding out his hands in a gesture half placatory, half pleading. 'You misunderstand me. You always did. As Machiavelli says, everyone sees one for what one seems to be, but few get to know one for what one really is.'

Jagger said, 'I'm one of the few. You could give Machiavelli lessons.'

'Flatterer! How long have you known the Pargeters?'

'How long have you had the extraordinary idea that I'd be prepared to discuss my private affairs with you?'

'Then the Pargeters are your private affair?'

'Did you go through this buffoonery just to ask me that?'

'Would you have come if I'd asked you openly?'

'Probably not. Now I'm here, I see no need to stay.'

'How tiresome you are. Would you prefer us to trouble Patricia Pargeter?'

'I'd prefer you to trouble no one.'

The Master bent his head, briefly communing with himself. When he looked up he said, 'I am charged with certain responsibilities, as you are well aware. And I am answerable to politicians. If one bears down on others it is because one is borne down on.'

Jagger said indifferently, 'You poor old man.'

The Master breathed deeply. He had the small vanities of a fit man of sixty. References to his age, as Jagger knew very well, touched him in a tender place. He said, 'Very well. You ask for explanations. Why am I here? The old building was condemned as being inadequate, which is another way of saying full of character, charm, whatever makes a building pleasant for human beings to occupy. It is about to be demolished. That is why we are now condemned to inhabit this—this people file. As for the Special Commissioners, they do indeed have a small suite of offices here. They provide us with a convenient cover. Finally, as a department we have current responsibilities which concern the Pargeter organization.'

Jagger stared in mock disbelief. 'Don't tell me Brummagem Ben's a security risk! Why, for a smile from H.M., let alone a peerage, he'd clean every window in the Palace with his tongue.'

The Master smiled coldly. 'No one has questioned the loyalty of Sir Ben or his family. As you are well aware, there are many reasons for surveillance. For example, there is protective surveillance.'

Jagger shifted impatiently. 'Oh, come on, for Christ's sake! Either you want to tell me or you don't. Do you mean protecting girls like Patti Pargeter from men like me?"

'Perhaps,' the Master said, peering sideways at him like a bird. It was hard to tell if he was serious.

'Supposing, you dirty old man, I told you I was simply taking the Pargeter girl home?'

'She's half your age. And you don't even know her. At least, you didn't before that night. How did you meet her, and why?'

Jagger stood up. He said, 'Go to hell, Master. And if you want my opinion, I think this place was designed specifically for people like you. Faceless, soulless, heartless, miniature Machiavellis.'

He went out into the anteroom. The Master's voice came after him. 'Patricia Pargeter's almost young enough to be your daughter. Why not be reasonable? We shall find out.'

Jagger was looking for a button to bring up the lift. There was none. The persistent voice from the other room said, 'Only I can bring up the lift. I could keep you here indefinitely.'

Jagger sat down in an armchair that might have been designed to soften up visitors for questioning. He said, 'I'd bust up your office but it would be doing you a favour.'

'My dear fellow, I don't *want* to keep you. I have troubles enough.'

The lift whispered softly upwards and opened its doors. Jagger stepped inside. Nothing happened. The voice from the other room said with the merest hint of a threat, 'You've never been against us, my dear chap. It would be a pity to start now.'

Jagger said, 'Too late. I've sold myself to Automated Contraceptives as a double agent. There'll be some startlingly sinister things happening to the birthrate.'

The doors rolled shut with a muted rumble. The polite Mr Morton was waiting to show him out.

The Master placed his palms together as if his view of the grey, ribbed roof of the Abbey nave had prompted him to prayer. Instead he began to nibble gently at the tips of his fingers.

The whole thing, he thought, had been highly unsatisfactory. Interviews with Jagger had always tended to be highly unsatisfactory. On reflection, Jagger's evasiveness had been more than normally stubborn. He came to a decision. The Minister had a great many sources of information. Any one of them might report to him that a trained agent who had left the British security service in doubtful circumstances, had suddenly and inexplicably turned up in the general area of Pargeter Electromation.

The Master had no liking for the Minister. He would have been reluctant to turn him loose in the corridors of power with a vacuum cleaner. There was no point in taking chances. He picked up one of his telephones.

When Morton answered the Master said, 'I want his

telephone tapped. No, nothing else for the time being. You know where he lives? In a sort of semi-slum somewhere south of the river. All in keeping, one supposes, with his eremitic misanthropy. What? I said eremitic misanthropy.'

The slight pause before Morton's, 'Yes, Master,' cheered him briefly. Then the twin millstones of uncertainty and political oppression dragged him headlong back to his ocean floor of gloom.

11. SCHRAMME—*Himself and another*

COMING BACK across Berkeley Square after lunch, Schramme was in one of his lighter moods. The grass, faded and tired, was sprinkled with dead leaves, crisp as spilled cornflakes in the yellowing sun. The summer was over but he felt good and it wasn't simply the wine. He passed a pair of tourists, middle-aged husband and wife. They were arguing loudly in Serbo-Croat. It reminded him of how far he had come and, more important, how comfortably, compared to some. Beyond one briefly appalling setback that had since turned out so advantageously, the upward path had been smooth, even pleasant.

Of course, he could fail, even now. He could, he supposed, even be killed. After all, Lusty had apparently been killed and Lusty was native-bred, English. In the meantime Schramme felt good and because he felt good he preferred to forget possibilities.

It was ironical that his kind of ability should have such monetary value. Look at his reputation! Only one or two Americans stood higher. He even found himself, from time to time, regretting that he couldn't continue to be what he was supposed to be for the rest of his life, living on one simple level instead of two. Or three! But that would be traitorous.

He emerged through the gates at the south side of the gardens, played tag with the Berkeley Street traffic and turned along the white-painted crimson-bricked dignity of Charles Street. He would be sorry—it could hardly be traitorous to admit that—when the time came to exchange the comfortable, decent solidity of London for some glass-walled eyrie in Manhattan. He preferred London, in spite of its newfound, classless brutalism, to the desperate, competitive violence of New York. Wasn't it Henry James, an American, who had described London as the most possible form of life?

The polished plate that said *Management Search Limited* in elegantly engraved script caught his reflected figure briefly as he mounted the steps. He opened the navy blue door with its restrained gilt decoration. He smiled pleasantly at his receptionist and went into the lift. In its confined surroundings the rich odour of the cigar he smoked as an occasional counterpoint to his Balkan cigarettes added to his euphoria.

He met Janice in the corridor on the top floor. Her make-up didn't quite hide the dark rings under her eyes. They'd been coming out steadily since the morning, like a slowly developing negative. It was time her solicitor's clerk gave her a little more sleep, or was it the other way round? Either way, it wasn't something a boss could discuss with his secretary.

She said, 'Oh, there you are, Mr Schramme. I was beginning to wonder if you'd forgotten about Mr Miller. He's due quite soon. I was just bringing the file.'

He took it from her and went into his large, light office. The smell of rich leather, the sight of fine wood, of furnishings that were works of art, all added to his feeling of well-being. He liked good things. Why be ashamed to admit it? It was another reason for being grateful. Whatever he might be according to others, here at this moment he was boss class; Ralph Schramme, founder and kingpin of *Management Search*, self-made and successful. His two assistants and his secretarial staff of five were modest out of all proportion to his tremendous profitability, even discounting his hidden income. He was a model of efficiency, not merely by British but by American standards.

And the most important thing of all was that America itself

73

was beginning to take him seriously. *Fortune* had done a profile, *Business Week* an interview. *Time* had carried a story in its 'World Business' section that had been half compliment, half sneer but either way good for business. Sooner or later they'd *have* to let him in.

He looked at his watch. There was just time to make his call to Ida before Miller arrived. He asked Janice for a direct line and waited the fraction of time necessary after dialling the last digit. Then, with the certainty of long practice, he blew the single note on the whistle. It was supposed to be a gold-plated souvenir of his stay in the wartime D.P. camp at Ratingen.

There was the usual pause, the usual double click and Ida's dispassionate voice, pre-recorded, was saying:'. . . Oboe Two, no change. Papa Seven, recalled. Repeat, recalled. Charlie One, 492493 at 2315. Foxtrot, no change. Delta Tango, proceed. Repeat, proceed. Yolk . . .'

He cut off. No change. So no news for Geneva. They wouldn't be sorry and neither was he. No news was good news. Or so he hoped. He'd been instructed to lie low and 'No change' from Ida meant that Ida had the same idea, which was hardly surprising in the circumstances. He found himself shaking his head at the incredibility of it all. It was like some bizarre and complicated game, except that even the most harmless of games could sometimes turn rough if the stakes were high enough. At that stage even onlookers could get hurt. Rosencrantz and Guildenstern, he reminded himself, had been little more than kibbitzers at Elsinore, but they had eventually died more bloodily than Hamlet.

His intercom buzzed. Janice said, 'Mr Miller's downstairs. Shall I take him straight in?'

He said, 'Give me five minutes. I'll buzz you from the interview room.'

He switched off and picked up the Miller file, flicking perfunctorily through its growing bulk. Miller had reached the final stage. Today was the beginning of stress. He was deputy research manager with a leading pharmaceutical

74

company, with some very smart work on tailored antibiotics to his credit. Judging by the evidence so far, he was also an up-and-comer. Just the type Schramme kept for himself. He was pretty sure by now that he would put Miller forward for the job he'd applied for, so it was time to begin extracting some real information.

He looked at the photographs, full face and right and left profiles. They'd come out well, though Miller didn't know they'd been taken. Neither did Janice. He didn't keep things like that in the open files. The pictures had even brought out the man's barely concealed intellectual arrogance. Well, he'd know by now what he was faced with. At least, he'd think he knew. He was hooked, like most who got this far under the Schramme system. He'd consider himself capable of meeting any kind of verbal assault and he'd be eager enough to try. The salary, perquisites and status that went with the new job would put him among the top two per cent in the country. And among those that Ida liked to encourage in technical indiscretion.

Schramme left the file on his desk. He knew Miller's background by heart. He could have given Miller's answers at the last interview almost word for word. That was another advantage of his dual training. He walked across to a mirror to make sure, as always, that he was intimidatingly immaculate and went to the interview room at the foot of the corridor.

It was windowless, with blank, pale green walls, a completely bare, unostentatious desk, a chair either side and a soft hush of air-conditioning to underscore the almost oppressive silence. The chair Schramme would sit in was comfortable, the other less so, the ambience not at all.

He checked to make sure that the room temperature was set at eighty. He always stepped it up for stress interviews. That made it uncomfortable for anyone who was anxious and over-dressed. Schramme wore a featherweight suit.

He took his own chair, found a note-pad in the desk and slid his gold Mont Blanc pen from an inside pocket. The tiny but sharply audible click made by its spring clip emphasized the stillness. He switched on the remote-controlled recorder, its microphone built into the desk. The cameras concealed behind the air grilles had already done their work. He pressed the button to tell Janice he was ready.

Miller came in almost eagerly, hand thrust out. He said, 'How are you, Mr Schramme?' His North Country accent, more pronounced than usual, betrayed his underlying tension.

Schramme ignored the hand, waving Miller to his seat. Giving him no time to settle, Schramme said, 'You look pleased with yourself.'

Miller grinned. Schramme thought: Over-confident. We'll make it rough from the start.

Miller said, 'Well, it's supposed to be something, to have got this far, isn't it? Nothing to be ashamed of, anyway.'

Schramme said, 'You have other things you are ashamed of?'

Miller said, 'Oh, no, I didn't mean that.'

Schramme said, 'You didn't mean what?'

Miller said, 'The kind of thing you meant, I suppose.'

Schramme said, 'You're not making yourself very clear. How do you know what kind of thing I meant?'

Miller said, 'Well, whatever you meant, what I mean is that I'm pretty normal. No more and no less to be ashamed about than anyone else.'

'Is that for you to decide?'

'Why not?'

'You don't care what others think of you?'

'I didn't say that.'

'I thought you did. Your wife, does she think you're pretty normal?'

Miller tried a joke. 'Why don't you ask her?'

'Perhaps I should. You wouldn't mind?'

'Why should I?'

'Some men might. You don't mind your wife discussing you with other men?'

Miller said, 'Well, I don't think——'

Schramme interrupted. 'Does your wife talk a great deal

76

about you to other men? You've never suspected her motives?'

'Whatever for?'

'Talking to other men. You've never, for example, suspected her of being unfaithful?'

Miller said, 'Oh, now look!' He was beginning to blink faster.

Schramme cut across him again. 'Or is that you've been unfaithful to her? Is that what you meant when you said that you'd no more and no less to be ashamed of than anyone else? Which do you consider more reprehensible, unfaithfulness in a husband or in a wife?'

Miller said, 'I know this is only a sort of game but I'm damned if I see why I should answer that.' He was sweating in the heat.

Schramme said, 'Because you have something to hide? Why are you perspiring, Mr Miller? It's quite cool in here. Do you consider me impertinent? Perhaps you don't like foreigners? Jews, for example? But we were talking about your wife.'

The interview had scarcely begun but already it was nicely under way.

12. D.C.I.—*Them, not us*

IN THE THICK WOODS the fall blazed like stained-glass windows, yellows, oranges and crimsons licking at the blue sky as if the world burned. The sun glittered on parked cars and bled molten light from massed windshields. On the seventh floor of the C.I.A. building the Director and the White House security aide walked into the conference room together.

'Mart,' White House was saying, 'I hope you have something this time. It suits me personally to get out of Washington for an hour or two, but it makes the President ask questions. What's so special that we couldn't meet where the action is?'

The Director held the door open to let White House through. He said, 'It depends on your definition of action.'

The State Department Undersecretary was already there, ostentatiously studying a fat stack of letters and reports. He nodded without looking up. He rasped, 'Since when was the capital of the U.S. in Langley, Virginia?'

White House said, 'Trust State to be out of date with its geography,' and started to polish his glasses. He looked at the empty seats and then at the Director. He said, 'Government by triumvirate?'

The door opened again to admit the Deputy Secretary for Defence and the C.I.A.'s Head of Plans. The Director said, 'What's the fancy word for government by five?'

Defence said, 'Hi, Mart. What's the good word? Or isn't there one?' He nodded to White House and State. Head of Plans had five folders under his arm. He distributed four thin pink ones quickly, keeping a fat red one for himself. He began to stuff his pipe with tobacco.

State started to open his folder. The Director said, 'Do you mind holding off? I'd like to say something.'

Head of Plans lit his pipe and puffed luxuriously.

The Director said, 'Gentlemen, the last time we met you authorized this agency to carry out a certain operation. Well, we carried it out. Tell 'em, Henry.'

Head of Plans took his pipe from his mouth, blew out a good deal of fragrant smoke in a lazy way and said simply, 'We were nearly caught.'

Everyone sat up.

White House said, 'How near is nearly?'

Head of Plans said, 'As close as not quite. There are some things you can't plan for.'

State said, 'You mean you forgot they had an intelligence service too? Or what?'

Defence said, 'Let's hear their story, Jim.'

Head of Plans said, 'As you know, we play Fifth Ace as part of a servicing procedure.' He sucked at his pipe, found it was out and laid it in an ashtray. 'What happened,' he said, 'was that we had a circuit failure of some kind in our spy unit. As a result it had to be pulled out of the Russian

78

computer unexpectedly. Before we'd finished brain picking.'

White House said slowly, 'Do I understand that they discovered your fancy hardware in the course of an emergency servicing?'

Head of Plans shook his head, looking more imperturbable than ever. 'Nearly, but not quite,' he repeated. 'But it was a near thing. And it means that we didn't finish the job. Didn't and can't.'

State said, 'Then the operation was a failure?' There was an edge of malice to his voice.

The Director said, 'Oh, I wouldn't say that, Jim.'

Defence said, 'Come on, Mart. You're holding out.'

Head of Plans said, 'The operation wasn't a hundred per cent success. But it certainly wasn't a failure. We stopped short, that's all.' He began to ream out his pipe, his hands making quick, economical movements.

The Director said, 'We didn't get as far as discovering what the Kremlin got out of that computer. But we did find out what they put into it. The important part's here.' He tapped his pink folder. Three pairs of eyes automatically dropped to look at its replicas. State started to open his again, thought better of it and sat with one finger between the covers.

Head of Plans said, 'This is what we got out in total.' From his lap he raised the red folder he had kept. It was much fatter than the pink ones. 'It'd take you a week to digest all this stuff. We saved you the trouble.'

'Now you can open the folders,' the Director said. State had his open at once. He looked at the first page, frowned, flipped through the others, returned to the first and frowned again.

The Director said, 'I think you're going to need some explanation.'

White House looked over the tops of his glasses. 'What is it? Extracts from *Fortune*'s five hundred biggest companies' listings?'

Head of Plans said, 'Well now, let's take it a piece at a time. In the first table you have a list of foreign companies holding

79

U.S. government contracts. It's quite a list. Everything from thumb tacks to mine-sweepers and hydro-electric generators.

'Table 2 lists every company outside the U.S. that's controlled or part-owned by a U.S. company.

'The third list reduces the first to companies in the electronics field that have contracts for defence equipment.'

Defence said, 'Let me get that straight, Henry. Three's a list of foreign electronics companies that hold U.S. defence contracts?'

Head of Plans nodded. 'Right! The next table is of companies *inside* the U.S. holding defence contracts in the electronics field. And the one after that shows which companies in list number four also appear on list two.'

State was beginning to look baffled but Defence was smiling. He said, 'Mart, I don't understand it any better than the next man, but I'm relying on you to do my homework.' The Director grinned.

Head of Plans went on. 'List number six. A short one. All those companies on list five that are also on list four.'

White House was scribbling away with a ball-point. He held up a hand and went on writing while they all waited. He looked at what he'd written and said, 'That would be U.S. electronics companies holding U.S. defence contracts that have holdings in foreign electronics companies with U.S. defence contracts? Okay, go on.'

The next list brought a stronger reaction. 'All companies in the U.S.,' Head of Plans said carefully, 'that have ever worked on, or are still working on the Shortchange project.'

Defence and State looked up simultaneously. White House peered over the tops of his glasses. He said, 'This is from the Russian computer?'

'From Moscow,' the Director said.

'And it's accurate?'

Head of Plans said, 'They missed out one company. One unimportant company. Otherwise, it's accurate.'

They all thought about it for a while. Finally White House said, 'Go on. Is that all the lists? It seems to be.'

Head of Plans said, 'It's all we've given you in that file. There's one more. I'd like to save it for the time being.'

White House said dryly, 'The trick bit, where you wave your magic wand and it isn't a white rabbit, it's a bunch of roses.'

Defence said, 'There's a common factor. Yes?'

White House said, 'Ee-lucidate, Massa Bones,' but the way he said it, it didn't sound funny.

The Director said, 'Do you mind, Henry?' Head of Plans shook his head, feeling for his tobacco pouch. The Director said, 'Only one company appears on all the lists referring to foreign companies. And only one company, a different one, of course, on all the lists of U.S. companies. Lastly, one of the lists gives a direct connection between the first company and the second.'

White House said, 'I just love guessing games. The U.S. company owns a piece of the foreign company and both companies have U.S. defence contracts. The U.S. company is also one of those that's working, or that's been working, on Shortchange.' He took off his glasses and polished them carefully, hiding every sign of accomplishment.

Head of Plans said, 'I couldn't have put it better myself, but I have to try. That Russian computer was all set to tell its masters that a certain very important electronics company in the U.S. that's been working on Shortchange has a share of a foreign company with important U.S. defence contracts.'

State said, 'So what? Unless——' He stopped, thumbing through pages of closely typed data. After a while he stopped thumbing. He said, 'I don't see that it takes a goddamed computer to work that out but it does need a little more time than I have now to discover which companies are the ones we're talking about. And anyway, you're going to tell us. You're going to tell us which foreign company also has a tie-up with Shortchange, yes?'

Defence frowned. He said flatly, 'No foreign company's done any work for the U.S. on Shortchange. Hell, is it likely?'

The Director said promptly, 'No.' He hesitated and added, 'Well—no!'

White House said, 'Come on, Mart. Is it or isn't it?'

Head of Plans got his pipe going. He puffed comfortably through a short but awkward silence, beamed and said, 'Maybe I'd better produce the last list.' He took three sheets of paper from his own fat folder and pushed them across the table.

White House ran the tip of his ball-point down the list of names. He said, 'This is people. Never heard of any of them.'

Defence was checking his own list, a slight frown on his forehead. He said, 'I have. One or two, at least.' He squeezed up his mouth with one hand, thinking. 'They're scientists. Or the ones I know are.'

The Director nodded. 'All of them. All the same kind of scientist, too. Specialists in the theory of radiation physics.'

State was lost. 'So?'

Head of Plans manœuvred his pipe to the corner of his mouth. He said, 'If you're going to get anywhere with Shortchange, radiation physicists are something you need plenty of.'

White House was staring at his list, tapping his ball-point in a slow, intermittent tattoo. He said, 'I don't mind making a stab. Somewhere on this list of names is a man who works for one of our two companies. No, damn it. Who works for *the* company. The foreign one.'

Head of Plans looked at him admiringly. 'Who *needs* a computer? What's your rental charge?'

The Director said, 'All right. Now let's be serious.'

White House said, 'I was. I'm never anything else.'

The Director said, 'A bunch of lists with a couple of linking factors. You ask who needs a computer. But don't forget, we did your homework for you. And that Russian computer did ours for us. What you've seen is the distillation of God knows how much data.'

'Which is another way of saying I'm not really smart at all,' White House said.

The Director said, 'The only thing you don't know is which foreign company. The U.S. one is West Coast Radionics, of Long Beach, California. The top outfit on the Shortchange project in the industrial sector. But which foreign company, partly owned by Westcorad, has U.S. defence contracts and the kind of expert you need to have any hope of breaking through on Shortchange?'

State said, 'You mean this foreign company *is* working on Shortchange, on a U.S. government contract? But you just said——'

The Director interrupted. 'No, Jim, I didn't. But that's what Moscow thought, even though we didn't get any further with our electro brain-picking. I'll lay you a billion to one in micro-circuits the Russian computer made an eighty-per-cent-plus prediction that Uncle Sam is actively developing the Shortchange weapon system through the collaboration of Westcorad and its foreign partner. Anyway, that was COMSTAR's prediction from the same data.'

'Subsidiary,' State said eventually. 'You said partner but I imagine this foreign company is a Westcorad subsidiary?'

The Director shook his head. 'No,' he said. 'It isn't. But it's a point the Russians might have difficulty in appreciating. They may be long on secret defence information but they're short on company financial data. Foreign companies don't have to publish as much information about themselves as they do over here.'

He leaned back in his chair. 'Somebody asked me why only three people had been invited to this meeting, apart from me and Henry. If I tell you the name and nationality of the foreign company, you'll see why.'

He told them. State looked shocked, Defence puzzled. White House whistled.

'Get it?' Head of Plans asked White House.

White House shook his head reluctantly. He said, 'I thought I did. Now I'm not so sure. The U.S. isn't collaborating with anybody on Shortchange, either directly or through an American electronics company, neither under contract nor without it. So how——?'

Suddenly he threw his ball-point across the room to hit the far wall. For the first time since the beginning of the meeting, his face showed signs of excitement. It even went slightly pink. Words began to tumble out of him, so that he stammered a little.

'But if that other company,' he said, 'was—I mean the foreign company you just named—if that company was not only working on Shortchange but had made a breakthrough. Or if the Reds thought it had. Then things would begin to add up.'

Defence saw it too. 'The Russians find out that a leading company in the country of a major ally of the U.S. has made a breakthrough on Shortchange. They know that this company is a subsidiary of Westcorad—no, wait a minute!'

State had caught up. 'They know the foreign company has U.S. defence contracts. They *think* this company is a subsidiary of Westcorad and they *know* Westcorad is working on Shortchange for the U.S. government.'

White House collared the ball again. 'And somewhere around the same time, the President of the U.S. starts a big push for an agreement on arms limitation.'

State elbowed his way back in. 'Only you have to look at it all back to front. We're pretty close to an agreement on arms limitation. Near enough for the Russians to make promises in secret, for a date to be announced for the Geneva meeting. Then the Russians discover—how, by the way?—that the U.S. is double-crossing them by developing Shortchange in secret collaboration with an ally that wouldn't be subject to arms limitation. An agreement at Geneva would result in a measure of general disarmament. When both sides are supposedly equal, and not before, the U.S. pulls Shortchange out of the hat and says, "Look what we've got!" '

They were all excited now, their eyes bright, their faces flushed, as if they were playing some kind of game. White House sobered up first. He'd just seen the fly in the nice smooth ointment.

He said, 'Mart! None of this stands up unless one thing is true. Or unless the Soviets have good reason to think it's true.'

The Director was nodding. 'I was wondering,' he said, 'how

long it would take for someone to see that. It only stands up if our old and trusted ally *has* made the breakthrough on Shortchange. Or if the Russians have a very damned good reason to think they have, which amounts to the same thing. Now can you see why we didn't invite anybody else to this meeting?'

Defence broke the silence first. 'Well,' he said, 'do they? Do they have Shortchange? Or don't we know?'

'We don't know,' the Director said.

'In that case,' White House snapped, 'you'd better find out. Don't you see what it would mean? Two super-powers, to use the newspaper jargon, hold the peace of the world in balance. Slowly, suspiciously, grudgingly, they come to realize they have to learn to trust each other even if they don't like each other. They edge along, bit by tiny bit, towards some kind of understanding. It survives Cuba, the Arab-Israeli war, it even survives the recent events in Czechoslovakia. And then, out of the blue, comes a super-super-power. A former world power in new drag, raring to slip back into the old rôle. A super-super-power with longstanding delusions of grandeur and a weapon system that could relegate the U.S. and the U.S.S.R. to the bow and arrow class. Do you realize where that could lead us?'

White House was leaning across the table. His voice harsh, he said, 'If I were the Russian Chiefs of Staff I'd be seriously considering a pre-emptive strike. At the U.S.! No wonder they accused us of bad faith!'

He added, 'The President's waiting to hear what came of this meeting. I don't think he's going to like what I tell him. He's going to think the problem he had was better than the one you just gave him.'

The Director opened his own folder and slid out the list of experts in radiation physics. He underlined a name and passed over the sheet.

'If the British have solved the Shortchange problem, that's the man who did it.'

White House scowled at the paper. 'I told you. I never heard of any of 'em.'

The Director said, 'Even if you were an expert, you'd probably never have heard of this one.'

Head of Plans said, 'No more than thirty years old. A bit of a reputation as a theoretician, a bit of a screwball. But before he joined Pargeter Electromation he worked on the British version of Shortchange. He's the only man at Pargeter who did. That's why it has to be him.'

'Are you telling me,' White House said incredulously, 'that some kid scientist has set the whole world on its ear, weapon-wise? And that he's walking around loose, instead of working under lock and key with the entire British army guarding him?'

'The best kind of security,' the Director said, 'if you can get away with it. Like carrying a million dollars through the street in a paper bag.'

'We talked to the top men here in the U.S.' Head of Plans took over. 'What's beaten everybody on Shortchange, so far, is the fact that you need a new concept of mathematics. Up to now nobody's come up with it.'

'But you just need one man,' the Director said, 'if he's the right one. No equipment, no research team. That comes later. So officially you wind up your project on the grounds that you're wasting a lot of money trying to do what can't be done. You put the man that matters into a corporation hidey-hole, give him the use of a computer and let him get on with it. Safe as Fort Knox. Safer, so long as no one suspects, because officially the project's dead. That's exactly what the British did.'

Defence said, 'Except someone did suspect. The Russians. How? And what are they going to do about it, if all this is true?'

'Stu, it has to be true,' the Director said. 'It all adds up. If this isn't true, nothing's true, and if nothing's true, two computers lied and the President and the Russians are going to have some disarmament.'

White House said, 'All right. I'll buy it, but the President will have a hundred questions. So will the whole goddamed cabinet. How are you going to get the answers? The Russians didn't have to worry about spying on their closest ally. We do.'

The Director looked at his Head of Plans. He said, 'Henry, I think it's about time we had Charlie Osgood up.'

The head of the industrial intelligence section could have passed for a college professor. It might have been his mild, inquisitively clever face, his grey, thinning hair, his conservative dress or the fact that, before joining the C.I.A., he'd been a college professor.

After the introductions Osgood said to the outsiders, 'I'm sure you gentlemen know George Kennan's* thesis. There are only five regions of the world—the U.S., the U.S.S.R., the U.K., the industrial areas surrounding the Rhine valley, and Japan—that are capable of sustaining production of the kind of hardware you need to fight a modern war. Just five, until China joins the club.

'Because we can't afford to be second best in anything, technologically speaking, we have special intelligence groups working in these areas, collecting the data that's supposed to stay confidential. We're interested in everything. Even personalities and rumours. Knowledge of key people, their qualifications and the way they move around can often give you a good idea of what's going on secretly in a particular area. And you'd be surprised how often rumours turn out to be facts.'

He smiled almost shyly. 'It's a lot different than most folk imagine secret service work, but it's the kind that wins wars, these days.'

The Director said, 'Or loses them, if you don't do it.'

Osgood said, 'Our agents, too. They're a long way from the kind of people you read about in spy stories. Graduates, with doctorates, trained at reading between the lines in their special subjects. And they all have respectable technical cover in the countries they work in.'

White House said, 'Including the U.K.'

*U.S. diplomat and scholar; former American ambassador in Moscow; expert on Russian affairs and international power politics.

'That's where we have our most highly organized under-cover network. Those people do some of the most advanced and creative scientific thinking in the world.'

Head of Plans said, 'In a company like Pargeter Electromation, for instance. Do you have any answers to the question I asked you this morning?'

'How to take a look inside Pargeter? Yes, I do. I could have told you straight away if you hadn't been in such a hurry.'

Osgood sat back in his chair, interlaced his fingers and began touching thumbs in an unconscious rhythm. He said, 'I could give you six or seven ways straight off.'

Head of Plans looked round the table. He said, 'How about two or three, just to be going on with?'

Osgood's thumbs stopped kissing each other. 'All right. Pargeter currently holds three U.S. Defence Department research contracts. Data recording techniques, mostly. The terms of the contract give the right to send over an inspectorate any time we like. That's one. Here's another. Because of their minority interest in Pargeter, West Coast Radionics have a technical exchange agreement. There's a small Westcorad group already working with Pargeter's research people at Leatherhead, in England.'

The Director looked significantly at the others. He said, 'More fuel for Russian suspicions.'

Osgood said, 'Westcorad's board chairman, in case you forgot, is General Sewell. Ex-U.S.A.F. intelligence. If you wanted to slip a man into his group at Leatherhead he'd be glad to co-operate. Now, a third way—well, if you can work longer-term I could get a suitable man appointed directly to Pargeter's research staff. We have kind of a unique set-up in the U.K., as you know. Number four! I've already——'

The Director held up a hand. He was smiling at the expressions on the faces of the three outsiders. He said, 'Charlie, you're Exhibit A the next time we get one of those Senate investigations into the efficiency of the C.I.A. My immediate reaction is that we start moving on all three of your suggestions.'

Head of Plans said, 'I'll come and see you right after this meeting, Charlie. In the meantime, as I said this morning, we need to start a dossier on Pargeter.'

Charlie looked at him innocently. 'I know. I was going to tell you about number four. The London office of our Swiss-based operation. They're moving in right away to co-ordinate the whole thing.' He hesitated. 'It would be a big help if you could give me a better idea of what we're looking for.'

The Director hesitated in turn. 'I'll have to get clearance first. I'll let you know. Thanks a lot, Charlie.'

Osgood nodded, unoffended. He stood up. 'I'm available whenever you want me.'

When the door had closed behind him, State said, 'What's he mean, Swiss-based operation?'

The Director said, 'Jim, there're things even I don't know about.' State took the hint.

White House said, 'Well, I'm impressed. I admit it. At least I have something to keep the President quiet for a while. Which means until about this time tomorrow.'

That was another hint that didn't need to be spelled out.

13. SIR BEN—*Himself, but not himself*

SOME MEN, as English schoolboys could once recite, are born to greatness and some have greatness thrust upon them. Others, as the modern schoolboy is much more likely to know, are driven to greatness by the impersonal goading of deoxyribonucleic acid. Fused like projectiles, genetically programmed for the heights, nothing can stop them except such mid-course disasters as a sudden destructive blast of coronary thrombosis or some late-developing design fault, latent until it cripples.

With Sir Ben Pargeter it had been a case of drive failure in middle age. A slight variation in a supposedly replicated sequence of amino-acids, an unforeseeable cross-over during the production of gametes—the precise cause could never be known. But the shrewder experts had realized during the last ten years that the great man had flared out. His vital thrust was gone, leaving him to drift in a spectacular but empty orbit, his glory a reflection of past achievement, his life's ambition still unfulfilled.

In his sixty-second year and against all his own expectations, he had been presented with a second chance. His new friend, the Minister for Scientific Development, was as cold and slippery as an eel, an eel with a sense of direction that worked only one way—upward. Sir Ben had been more than happy to oblige the man on the assurance that his own reward would be a much-coveted seat in the House of Lords.

It no longer bothered him that he really didn't know what he was going to be rewarded for. Except, of course, that it involved whatever service to the state that queer bird, Tinn, was performing in his temporary hideout at Leatherhead. But Tinn cost Pargeter Electromation little more than a salary, an office and the occasional use of the computer, Sir Ben himself nothing at all. It was hardly a high price to pay for a peerage.

Forty years ago, back in the dawn of the radio age, he'd quit technical college in mid-course to start a back-street workshop turning out two hand-built one-tube receivers a week. The workshop had turned into Pargeter Electromation, with an annual turnover around £500 million. A knighthood had come comparatively soon, boosted by a flurry of wartime committee work. The peerage should have followed with the inevitability of a prize for regular school attendance, but somewhere along the way things had gone wrong. Sir Ben was still Sir Ben.

Until now! Or at least, until the first Honours List after Tinn finished whatever it was that he was doing. According to the Minister, that would be very soon.

It was just as well. Sir Ben didn't think he could last the pace much longer. Take this last week. The trip to Düsseldorf had been tiring, the days long on alcohol and rich food, the nights short on sleep. Ben Pargeter didn't need a doctor to tell him why he was feeling his age plus his golf handicap.

He'd wondered more than once lately whether the time had come for him to stop being his own chief executive, simply retaining the prestige and semi-retirement of the board chairmanship. The only thing that kept him going was the thought that retirement from the managing directorship would come better if it coincided with his elevation to the House of Lords. In the meantime he'd soldier on.

He sighed, signed the last of his letters, buzzed for his secretary and took a look at his engagement diary. A pretty clear day, thank God! Just these two fellows from Data Corporation of America coming later in the morning. One of them was flying across from their European headquarters so he could hardly have put them off. In any case, old Bradford had telephoned all the way from Boston to ask Sir Ben to see them himself and give them his official blessing. You didn't improve your stock by turning down personal requests from ex-U.S. ambassadors to the Court of St James's.

Apart from—he checked the names again—apart from Dobereiner and Simmons, then, his day was clear. He could lunch at the club, perhaps manage to get home early.

Miss Parry came in with his coffee. She put the tray on his desk, gathered up letters and said, 'Lady Pargeter rang. She asked me to remind you about Mr Jagger. She gave me the telephone number.'

He frowned, staring at her. 'Jagger? Do I know anyone called Jagger? Oh, yes! Now I remember. No, not yet. I'll let you know when.'

She poured his coffee and went. He added saccharin and stirred, still frowning. Myra had been unusually insistent. According to her, she'd only met the fellow once, when he'd brought Patricia home. But that was according to Myra.

He hadn't heard Patti's version. Attempts to make conversation with Patti were never very rewarding, anyway. But marijuana, even if Patti hadn't been directly involved! He sighed, sipping coffee morosely. Whichever way you looked at it, it was unpleasant. She'd narrowly escaped being picked up in a police raid that had made front page in the dailies. He was appalled when he thought of the publicity that might have resulted.

Then there was the fellow Jagger himself, nearly twice Patti's age, according to Myra. He sighed again exasperatedly. He knew why Myra was so anxious to renew the contact. She'd found the man attractive. That's why she'd suggested he should be invited back.

The fact was that Myra could do as she pleased, and she knew it. She'd divorce him tomorrow, given half an opportunity. It hardly encouraged her to be discreet in her own amusement. Sir Ben knew what was going on between her and Ralph Schramme. It would have to wait. He couldn't afford scandal at the present time. Once his peerage was in the bag he'd deal with Schramme. Myra, too, if necessary.

In the meantime he had to keep Myra happy, or at least, out of open mischief, but if it meant inviting this fellow Jagger round for a drink it could bloody well be at his club. He flicked on his intercom and said, 'You can get Mr Jagger now.'

Jagger said, 'Who?' but the efficient Miss Parry had already switched him through. Sir Ben Pargeter's voice was insinuating itself into his ear like something creamy from a tube.

In a sense, Jagger admitted to himself, he'd almost hoped for the call. Not particularly because he was interested in Brummagem Ben Pargeter but because the devious little man at New Strutton House had said he mustn't be. He wondered what Pargeter was up to that was so important.

Not that Brummagem Ben himself wasn't interesting. He was a sort of national figure, after all. His nickname referred to his Birmingham origins but as a corruption of Birmingham it had another meaning. It was used to describe the tawdry brilliance of the cheap costume jewellery that was one of the city's traditional products. It was used in the same way on Ben Pargeter. There were plenty of people who mistrusted his charismatic personality and the personal pyrotechnics he was apt to substitute for solid business ability.

If the nickname really applied, Jagger thought, Sir Ben

would be a great many things he disliked. But Sir Ben was suggesting a drink at his club and a mystery hovered invitingly about him. Jagger accepted the invitation. If the Master was going to behave like a suspicious old woman, he'd give him something to be suspicious about.

14. JAGGER—*Still himself*

MORTON stuck his head round the door. He said, 'Something interesting.'

The Master looked up from a report just in from West Berlin as if nothing less than divine revelation would justify the interruption.

Morton came into the room. He said mischievously, 'One of your prints is crooked. Monitoring has just reported that Jagger had a call from Sir Ben Pargeter, ten minutes ago.'

The Master marked something in his report, laid it carefully on the desk and stood up to study his row of flower prints. He made a minute adjustment to one of them. He said, 'Don't stop.'

'He's meeting Sir Ben for drinks at his club. Sir Ben wants to thank him. It all fits.'

The Master made another microscopic alteration to the offending print, one eye screwed up, his head tipped to one side. He said, 'Either that wall's out of true or my astigmatism is developing apace. Accepting the fact that Jagger met the Pargeter girl accidentally, and that Sir Ben has every reason to be grateful the chit was saved from a drugs charge, why couldn't he write a letter? It would be the appropriate thing.' He sat down again, closing his eyes.

He kept them shut so long he might have been asleep but he wasn't. Morton waited. He saw the faintest of smiles appear on that pink, deceptively Pickwickian face. He thought: He's pleased, so someone else won't be.

The Master opened his eyes and reached for one of his coloured telephones. In his silkiest voice he said, 'Get me the Minister for Scientific Development, will you? That's a good girl.'

He smiled again, an inward, secretive smile. He said to Morton, 'Stay. This may amuse you.'

Jagger walked quickly up the wide steps into the small lobby with its dark, well-cared-for woodwork and its upper-class English smell of fusty, unostentatious wealth. Intercepting him with unobtrusive skill, the porter said, 'Yes, sir?'

Jagger said, 'Sir Ben Pargeter?' Moments later, he and Sir Ben were walking into the tiny bar.

Sir Ben was pleasantly surprised. The voice had been reassuring. The appearance capped it. The man wore a respectable tie and a suit built by a master's hand.

But it wasn't so much the clothes as the man himself who impressed immediately. The thin, sharp face had a disbelieving, almost sardonic look, but it was intelligent, even clever, the eyes cool and perceptive. He stood well, self-possessed and with an outer stillness, yet his whole body suggested forces barely in balance, energies that would respond instantly and powerfully to the right stimulus. Sir Ben prided himself he knew a good chap when he saw one. He had no doubt at all that he was looking at one now.

They sat down on chairs of worn brown leather; chairs, Jagger thought, that had given uncomfortable support to the the patrician buttocks of generations of prime ministers. Behind Sir Ben the windows that gazed superciliously on St James's vibrated to deep, staccato harmonics of the traffic grumble. Sir Ben turned his charisma full on, ordered a pink gin for himself, Scotch for his guest and set about the familiar task of charming the bird out of its tree.

Ten minutes later, all he had learned was that Jagger had met his daughter once, by chance, and Myra simply because he had taken Patti home. In return for these meagre scraps Sir Ben had presented Jagger with his own de luxe edition of the rags-to-riches story, dropping as many illustrious names as a printer upsetting a chase of type for *Who's Who*.

At the end he returned to the subject of Patti, humorously inviting sympathy for his plight as a father with a wayward and unresponsive child. Unimpressed, Jagger smiled politely. He murmured, 'Fairest Cordelia, thou art most poor, being rich.'

Sir Ben stared, returning the polite smile.

Jagger said, 'Sorry. An inverted quotation from *Lear*.'

Sir Ben had stopped listening. He was looking towards the door. A moment later a familiar voice said, 'Now, Ben, I hope you're keeping out of mischief?' A hand rested lightly on Jagger's shoulder as if to reassure him that there was no need to prostrate himself.

Jagger looked round to see the round, professionally bluff face of the Minister for Scientific Development, all firm, calculatingly honest gaze, Bermuda tan and built-in benevolence.

Sir Ben said, 'Charles, my dear fellow, when did you get back? How nice to see you.'

The Minister said, 'Sorry to break up your little *tête-à-tête*, but would you spare me a moment?'

He squeezed Jagger's shoulder as impersonally as if it were a lemon and said, 'You will forgive us, won't you? Very rude of me.' He looked again and said, 'Hello! We've met, haven't we?'

Jagger stood up reluctantly, allowing his hand to be briefly mauled. He said, 'A long time ago.'

The Minister said, 'I knew it. I don't forget faces. Nice to see you again.' He made it sound like an apostolic blessing recited by a speak-your-weight machine, his sharp little eyes moving away before he'd finished. The thin hairs brushed horizontally across his scalp were jet black but Jagger caught a glimpse of grey at their roots, where the tint was growing out like the first glimmer of a false dawn.

Sir Ben said, 'Excuse us a moment, will you, old chap?' and followed the Minister as he walked out of the bar with his

95

famous stiff-armed stoop. Tipping back his Scotch, Jagger mentally brought the meeting to a close. He could hardly blame Sir Ben for giving precedence to a cabinet minister but neither could he bring himself to enjoy the way he'd been given a pat and told to amuse himself while the grown-ups had a little talk. He also thought that if the Minister really did remember the circumstances of their last meeting, only lack of practice could have stopped him from blushing.

When he saw Sir Ben's broad figure coming back, hair shining like antique silver, he stood up. Sir Ben pushed him gently but firmly down, signalling for another round. His attitude towards Jagger had changed, subtly but unmistakably.

Sir Ben apologized charmingly for his absence. The drinks came. The older man sipped his gin, leaned back and looked intently at Jagger.

'Well,' he said, his Birmingham origins lost under a landslide of first-generation breeding, 'secrets will out.'

Jagger said, 'If Ministers reveal secrets it's usually because they're looking for publicity.'

Sir Ben laughed. 'Such cynicism! Though of course, you're right. But I didn't mean his secrets. I meant yours.'

Jagger stared. 'Mine?'

'My dear fellow,' Sir Ben said, 'don't worry. I'm not in the habit of bleating things all over the place.' He swallowed gin, twinklingly conspiratorial. 'The Minister told me a little of your past. When you were—shall we say?—a civil servant.'

Jagger looked at his Scotch, drank a little and said, 'Oh.' The Minister really had recognized him.

Sir Ben nodded. 'Most commendable. I shan't press you. After all, a testimonial from a cabinet minister is just about as gilt-edged as they come.'

Jagger thought: Guilt-edged! But a testimonial from that source! It was like having your hand nuzzled by a crocodile.

Sir Ben said, 'He's a member here, of course. He just happened to see me when he peeked in.'

Jagger was still trying to resolve the implications. He said, 'I thought he'd been looking for you. He gave that impression.'

'Not a bit,' Sir Ben said. 'Pure coincidence. Anyway, after we'd talked over his own little thing he told me you're just the chap I ought to have.'

Jagger paused with his glass half-way to his lips. 'For what?'

Sir Ben leaned forward, cupping his drink with both hands between his knees. He dropped his voice. 'This is in strictest confidence. There's been a little trouble in my company. Industrial espionage. It's some time ago now, but we handle some pretty secret stuff on the research side. Old Charles, as the Minister most directly concerned, has been on at me to tighten internal security even more. I've been tending to resist overdoing it. The technical chaps don't like having snoopers peering over their shoulders. But the right kind of man—hm? Only where do you find him?'

Jagger said, 'You tell me.'

'I think you know. What about it? I'm making you an offer.'

'You mean the Minister suggested me?'

'Unprompted and unreservedly. On your past record. You must have made a good impression.'

Jagger was smelling fish. He said, 'I must have made some kind of impression.'

Sir Ben wasn't really listening. In his own mind, according to habit, he'd turned suggestion into *fait accompli*. He said, 'No use saying you're otherwise engaged. I know it isn't true.'

Still frowning, Jagger said, 'The Minister told you that too? Did he tell you why?'

'My dear fellow,' Sir Ben said blandly, 'I wouldn't dream of asking. You know, I don't mind telling you I took a liking to you as soon as I saw you. Picking out good men is one of my modest talents. Come and have some lunch and talk it over.'

He put down his glass and stood up, holding out a shepherding arm. 'Come along. Let's get settled before all the decent tables have gone.'

Jagger stood up too. He held out his hand. 'Sir Ben, I'm very sorry. I can't join you for lunch. Previous engagement. And I can't accept your other offer either, not even to please the Minister.'

Sir Ben had taken the outstretched hand automatically. He held on, pressing it tightly. 'My dear chap, forgive me. I should know better than to rush you. Think it over. I'll get my secretary to ring you in a day or two.'

Jagger liberated his hand. He said, 'I don't think I shall change my mind. And now, if you'll excuse me——'

He was still wondering about the Minister as he walked out into the pale, misty sunlight.

Behind him Sir Ben took out the small, leather-bound book in which he prefabricated his spontaneous *bons mots*. In his small, neat hand he wrote: *Any politician knows the surest way to publicise a thing is to tell it in confidence.*

An uncut diamond! It would need a lot of polishing, but it had possibilities. He hastened off in search of the Minister for Scientific Development.

15. JAGGER—*His own master?*

JAGGER watched the other car in his rear mirror. At the moment it was some distance behind, separated from him by a yellow delivery van and an ancient Austin hand-painted in psychedelic swirls.

Testing his theory, he slipped expertly from the middle to the inside lane and immediately took the next turning. Watching his rear mirror, he saw the grey Ford Zodiac continue on past the end of the street, trapped in the swirl of Piccadilly traffic as inextricably as a bead on a thread.

He crawled down Clarges Street and turned again. He idled, watching. The Zodiac reappeared in his mirror well inside five minutes. He was certainly being followed.

He turned north, Hyde Park stretching away to his left in a mirage of golden mist. A tractor clattered between the trees, towing a long-necked monster. The monster reversed a normal biological process, sucking dead leaves into its fundament and spewing them into a wire mesh cage from its gaping mouth.

Jagger made up his mind and took the slip road to the underground car-park. As he entered the tunnel the Janàcek string quartet on his car radio died abruptly, replaced by prickly bursts of static as he passed each overhead fluorescent lamp. The Zodiac had vacated his mirror. The concrete cavern stretched interminably ahead of him, a drab, cold world populated by lifeless metal. Behind him he heard the whine of the automatic barrier as another car came in, black, gleaming, noiseless.

He drove on, the radio treating him to regular spatters of static and occasional ghostly music. After zigzagging across the echoing desert with frequent changes of direction, he reversed into an empty bay and switched off.

Moments later, with the stealth of a cat in the night, the black limousine slid in beside him. Its uniformed chauffeur stared ahead as sombrely as a paid mute at a funeral. Ignoring each other, he, his passenger and Jagger sat like dummies in a tableau from 'Transport through the ages'.

Jagger found himself patting his pockets for his non-existent cheroots. It was time to make something happen. He went to the other car and peered through an immaculately polished window. The chauffeur's eyes swivelled like a chameleon's. Jagger breathed heavily on the glass and roughed out a crude face. He added polka-dot eyes with unnecessary force, opened the rear door and said, 'Styx car ferry service. Good afternoon. Have you a reservation?'

The Master opened his eyes briefly and shut them again. He said comfortably, 'This is the most tranquil spot in London. Why has no one told me?'

After a while, his eyes still peacefully closed, he said, 'Get inside and shut the door, there's a good fellow. This place smells like a mechanical morgue.'

Jagger got in. He tried to slam the door. It was like trying to slam the door of a bank vault. He said, 'What does this thing run on? Embalming fluid?'

Opening his eyes, the Master sat up a little. 'Your sense of humour verges on the tasteless. Also the juvenile. Have you no respect for craftsmanship?'

'For nothing,' Jagger told him. 'It restricts my freedom of action.'

The Master said stiffly, 'Absence of respect leads to anarchy, not freedom.'

Jagger said, 'Liberty as an institution is freedom by numbers. We sound like a double act.' He yawned. 'It's stuffy in here.'

The Master pressed a button. The window on his side lowered itself two inches with a faint shriek.

'So perish all enemies of the Queen,' Jagger said. 'Not to mention British craftsmanship.'

The Master said fretfully, 'They've already replaced that motor twice.'

Jagger said, 'Never mind. Your radio's working well.'

'Radio?' The other frowned. 'Oh, yes! Very well. We were already in Park Lane when our man in the Zodiac reported that you'd let him find you again. We saw you turn out of Curzon Street. After that it was easy.'

Jagger pressed the button that wound down the window on his own side. He said, 'Well?'

'Don't do that. You'll create a draught.'

'No draughts down here,' Jagger said. 'Only the cold winds that blow before and after Time. Or is Eliot too modern for you?'

'One prefers the Georgians,' the Master said reflectively.

'Drinkwater? Yeats? Graves?'

The Master shrugged delicately. 'Masefield has always seemed particularly apt:

> To get the whole world out of bed
> And washed, and dressed, and warmed, and fed,
> To work and back to bed again,
> Believe me, Saul, costs worlds of pain.'

Jagger laughed aloud, half jeering. 'You mean it's not so

much love as the secret service that makes the world go round?'

'That gives us reasonable assurance, from one day to the next, that we shall see the sun rise. Is it an ignoble endeavour?'

Jagger made his window close again. Ignoring the question he said, 'What do you want?'

The Master said, 'Don't do that. Trouble with one window is sufficient.' He sighed, folded his gloved hands on his lap and said, 'Sir Ben Pargeter offered you a job. I trust you will accept.'

Jagger tipped his head on one side reflectively. 'I didn't see you there. Unless—I know! You were disguised as a horsehair sofa. You needed restuffing.'

Looking a little pinched about the nose, the Master took a deep breath. Jagger pressed the button that wound down his window. He said, 'You're taking more than your fair share of air. And I'm not taking the job. My doctors advised against it.'

The Master leaned across him to button the window up again. 'We were talking about freedom. It can be abused.'

Jagger said, 'Yes. Or no, as the case may be.'

'One of the great contemporary paradoxes is that the greatest freedom belongs to those with the greatest power to restrict it.'

'People like you,' Jagger said.

'People like me. I restrict the freedom of the few in order to preserve the freedom of the many.'

'The greatest good for the greatest number. Something I don't believe in. It simply reduces everything to its lowest common denominator. You're going to lock me up?'

'Nothing so crude. I am merely hinting, if I have the expression correctly, that I am prepared to lean on you.'

'To what purpose?'

'In order to persuade you that you wish, after all, to accept Sir Ben's offer.'

'Otherwise?'

The Master made a small but comprehensive gesture. 'The only problem is one of choice. For example, you or the girl.'

'Which girl?'

'The one we could have brought in on a drugs charge.'

Jagger sat upright. 'You couldn't. She didn't.'

'To which occasion do you refer? We have people to swear that she did.'

Jagger said, 'The girl doesn't mean a thing to me, but, do you know, I don't think I'd like you to hound her.'

'No? Well, one could concentrate on you instead. One could make life exceedingly unpleasant for you. Do you doubt me?'

Jagger snapped his fingers. 'Of course! It was you. Your dear friend, the Minister for Scientific Development, *was* looking for someone. Me! He put Brummagem Ben up to asking me, but you put him up to priming Brummagem Ben. Am I right?'

The Master was looking pained. 'Not when you refer to the Minister as my dear friend. Any more than he is yours. I had some difficulty in convincing him that you were the man for the job. One had quite forgotten the unfortunate discovery you once made about him. However, being in many respects an overgrown adolescent he was not entirely reluctant to enter into a little conspiracy to place one of my staff on Sir Ben's payroll for security reasons.'

His voice flat, Jagger said, 'One of your staff?'

The Master reached out a small, gloved hand and laid it on Jagger's, gripping with surprising strength. His voice became sharp-edged, potentially dangerous, like a razor blade in a flimsy wrapper.

He said, 'At first I suspected you. But a few inquiries and the felicitous coincidence of your invitation to meet Sir Ben gave me a better idea. I mean to have you. I could lean on you until it hurts, and if necessary I will. But one prefers volunteers. So what if one says, "Please!"?'

The grip slackened. The hand was removed but the eyes glittered icily behind their contact lenses. The Master's features had subtly reshuffled themselves into something by no means unfamiliar to Jagger, something wholly ruthless. He was astonished. Never before had he heard the man beg. He began to take things seriously. He said, 'Tell me why.'

The Master took his time, Hyde almost imperceptibly submerging himself in Jekyll. 'One can't. That is to say, one can't tell you everything. Partly because there is some speculation. Partly because one wouldn't wish to have your potential value diminished by preconceived ideas.'

He considered. 'What I can tell you is this. Revolutionary weaponry, of the utmost importance to the future of this country, is at a crucial stage of development. For security reasons the work is being carried out under cover, but the most effective cover is sometimes no cover at all, particularly when one is dealing with an individual of some—let us say— eccentricity. The man of whom I speak is working quite openly at the Leatherhead research centre of Pargeter Electromation. Only the nature of his work is being concealed. It is, of its type, perhaps the most significant work ever carried out in this country. Possibly in the world.'

He stopped to study the effect of what he had said on Jagger. It was like trying to read the face of the Sphinx. Jagger flipped the window down, the electric motor whining unhappily.

The Master said, 'Some little time ago, quite unexpectedly, an attempt was made by a foreign power to secure details of the work. One wishes one could say that the attempt was frustrated by vigilance, by good intelligence work. In fact, the situation was retrieved only by the sheerest good fortune.'

Jagger said, 'A foreign power?'

The Master appeared not to have heard the question. He said, 'Retrieved. One might, I believe, even say stabilized, in the sense that the power concerned was warned off, indirectly but unmistakably. However, that power is now confirmed in its suspicion that something is afoot, though it may not be aware of the exact nature of the work being completed. It is hardly in a position to make another direct attempt at espionage, and in any event, certain discreet precautions have been taken.'

'The man's still working for—with Pargeter?' Jagger asked.

'He is. To move him at this stage would be to confirm what may only be suspicions. However, one's anxious to forestall any further attempt to interfere with the work, no matter how unlikely. Nor—and this is of almost equal importance—dare we chance any kind of open confrontation, deliberate or inadvertent. Do you follow?'

Jagger said, 'I'm not sure. Why not open confrontation? We've arrested spies before.'

'Certainly, but the entire nature of espionage is changing. Becoming more subtle,' the Master added after a brief hesitation. 'What was once, by definition, a secret activity is increasingly being used to achieve long-term and sometimes highly camouflaged aims.'

Jagger said innocently, 'The Department of Disinformation and Decomposition in Moscow, for example?' He laid the lightest stress on Moscow.

'Just so,' the Master said smoothly. 'For example, to apprehend a spy is to give official recognition to the fact of espionage. In the present instance such recognition might force our hand before we are ready, even lay us open to diplomatic blackmail of a type which might be difficult to resist.'

Jagger shifted impatiently. 'You have an organization, trained men. I don't see where I come into it.'

The Master seemed to relax a little, as if sensing that he had negotiated a major obstacle. 'You'd come into it precisely because, although trained, you form no part of that organization.' He searched for the right simile and said, 'An irregular. An outrider. The mere presence of outriders sometimes prevents accidental escalation. You understand me? The enemy has the option of turning away instead of fighting it out.'

Jagger nodded reluctantly. 'How do you know that's what he'd do in this case?'

'I can assure you,' the Master said emphatically, 'that in this case he would retreat. But I have something more in mind.'

Once again Jagger found himself feeling for cheroots that weren't there. Irritably, he said, 'I thought you might.'

'Sometimes, when an enemy is compelled to retreat, he must abandon his own outposts.'

'And you've someone in mind?'

'One. Possibly more. When prepared positions are abandoned strange things come to light. That might be for you to discover.' He peered slyly at Jagger. 'You would be on your own. There would be no contact—no open contact—between us. None whatsoever. Your appointment as temporary security adviser to Pargeter would be the outward, plausible explanation for your presence. The adversary is clever enough to take the hint, as well as being thrown off balance. He would almost certainly accept discretion as the better part of duty.'

Jagger said thoughtfully, 'Well, it certainly makes a change.'

'Indeed. Idleness is no way of life for a man of your parts.'

'I didn't mean that. I meant, to be asked, instead of tricked or bullied. It's unlike you. Where is the deviousness of yesteryear?'

'The matter is too important, the dénouement too imminent to permit the luxury of finesse.'

'I didn't say finesse. I said deviousness. How would we communicate?'

'That you must leave to me. You will have to trust me.'

Jagger opened his door and got out. 'That would be the hardest part.'

The Master craned out of the open window. 'Would?'

'All right. Will. I'm not exactly a patriot but I find slightly less to dislike in this country than in any other.' He wasn't really sure why he'd agreed. Unless it was the shock of that 'please'. Or vulgar curiosity. Or boredom.

He said, 'You want me to get in touch with Sir Ben.'

'If you will. Concern yourself only with Pargeter's research establishment at Leatherhead. Sir Ben will understand. Incidentally, have you ever heard of a man called Schramme? Ralph Schramme?'

Jagger remembered Patti's gibe at her mother about someone called Ralph, the night he had taken her home.

He said, 'No, should I?' He took it for granted that the Master was keeping things from him.

'It will keep, for the time being.' The Master pressed the button to close the window. It made a noise like a vacuum cleaner with hysterics and stayed open. After several attempts the Master abandoned it, his face slightly pink. It might have been due to the effort. The man in chauffeur's uniform opened his door and came round to help.

Jagger slid into his own car, ostentatiously hand-wound his window down and up again and drove off. As he emerged on Park Lane a thought surfaced in his mind. Had he been influenced in whatever it was he was going to do by the possibility that it might bring him into contact with Patti Pargeter again? The idea was ludicrous. He pushed it under. Though there could be no harm in asking her who her Ralph was, given a suitable opportunity.

16. D.C.I.—*Them or us*

HEAD OF PLANS pushed open the door labelled D.C.I., crossed the suite to room 74706 and entered the big office quietly, trailing smoke from his pipe like an old-fashioned steam locomotive. He slumped his lanky frame in an easy chair. His posture would have horrified a physiotherapist.

He said, 'Well?'

The Director said, 'I just got back. No more meetings in the Statler-Hilton coffee shop. The comrades aren't interested. The only thing left is to prepare data for their computer, to show we'd be worse off than Moscow if the British pull it off.' He massaged his face wearily and looked at his hands as if he expected to find that something had rubbed off.

Head of Plans rearranged himself until his weight was entirely concentrated on his left sacroiliac. It didn't seem to bother him. He said, 'What if their computer disagrees? Anyway, I'm not surprised they don't believe us. Supposing we knew the East Germans were working on the ultimate weapon, just when we were trying to negotiate some kind of disarmament. We go to the Russians and say, "What the hell?" The Russians shrug their shoulders and say, "Nothing to do with us." Would we believe them?'

The Director didn't even bother to answer.

Head of Plans said, 'I'm going to say something stupid. I suppose we've considered a direct approach to the British?'

The Director said, 'The cabinet consensus is that it isn't even a starter. The British made a hell of a big contribution to the development of the atomic bomb. When the war was over we shut the door in their faces and left them to go it alone. They may have forgiven us, but they'd treat us the same way now. Look what they have to gain! It puts them back in the big league overnight. In a league by themselves! All the rest of us will be able to do is work and worry ourselves stupid until we've caught up. Henry, the arms race has only just begun and the parity issue may drive the President to do something foolish. He's scared blind of that Senate sub-committee.'

Henry nodded. 'I can just imagine the British reaction to a direct approach. Those politely raised eyebrows they're so good at. A bland denial they'd ever heard of Shortchange. Well, the only thing we can do is what we've agreed to do, penetrate Pargeter six ways from Sunday and see what we can find out. If they won't deal us in we may end up by having to steal it. Or try.' He rapped his pipe three or four times in an ashtray. 'If Charlie Osgood does his stuff I'll have more electronic gadgets in that Pargeter research place than they turn out in their goddammed factories.'

The Director's secretary opened the door. 'Mr Osgood wonders whether you gentlemen can spare him a little time.'

The Director said, 'Right on cue. Have him come in.'

Osgood perched on the edge of a chair and said, straight-faced, 'We just heard that production of chopsticks in the Canton area fell by seventeen per cent last month. Good or bad?'

The Director smiled a little. 'You tell us, Charlie.'

'Bad. That production came from a small factory in the Shameen district. They switched girls away to retrain for a new plant that will make silicon wafers for micro-circuits. The circuits are intended for missile guidance systems. What I really wanted to tell you is that we've made first base at Pargeter. Alex Bradford helped by telephoning Sir Ben Pargeter direct from Boston. Give us a little time to get organized and you can slip an extra man into the team. It should last some while. Part of a general survey of the British electronics industry for U.S. financial analysts and investment houses. Sir Ben was pretty anxious to get a good showing for his company.'

The Director said, 'Fool-proof?'

'So long as we tread warily. Long term, if there is a long term, I've a much better bet, as I mentioned before. We have this man in London—Henry knows about him—who could probably put a properly qualified man right into one of Pargeter's research teams. I gather they're always advertising.'

Head of Plans said, 'This is Schramme, right?'

The Director had been looking puzzled. Now his forehead smoothed itself. He said, 'Oh, I'm with you! The headhunter who approached our London embassy about moving to New York and setting up business.'

Head of Plans said, 'That's the one. The opportunity was too good to miss. Charlie's been having him work his passage. But if the British took him now they might crack open the whole nut. It could be embarrassing.'

Osgood was shaking his head. 'Embarrassing, but nothing more. He might tell them the nut existed, but he doesn't know where it is or what it looks like. Incidentally, something I just remembered. Pargeter was the company Bohm thought was——'

He stopped, his mouth opening a little wider. He shook his head. He said, 'The trouble with this business is that you get to imagining things.'

The relaxed atmosphere dispersed as if whisked away by the air-conditioning. Head of Plans let his pipe slip through his long, spatulate fingers. He ignored it, letting it lie in a light spatter of ash on the thick pile of the carpet.

The Director said, 'Don't stop, Charlie.'

Osgood said doubtfully, 'It could be nothing at all.'

Head of Plans said, 'Try us.'

Osgood shuffled thoughts in his tidy academic mind like a bridge buff arranging his hand. He coughed twice, dry little coughs that gave him time to think. 'Well, Bohm was one of my field men in the U.K. Nominally a stringer for a New York technical magazine. A man like that can learn a heck of a lot if he moves in the right circles, cultivates a reputation for discretion and keeps his eyes and ears open. Bohm was good at it. One day he turned up what looked like a case of industrial espionage at Pargeter Electromation.'

He stopped, fumbled in his pocket and pulled out a small packet. He took two white tablets from it, chewed them methodically and patted his stomach. They waited. He belched, politely, behind closed lips.

Head of Plans said, 'Boy, Harvard sure gives you the edge in the social graces!'

Osgood sighed in relief. 'Where was I? Oh yes! Bohm got the idea that one of Pargeter's research men, a fellow called—' he frowned—'Lusty! That was it! That this man Lusty was trying to sell technical information to one of Pargeter's European competitors, through an intermediary.'

He chewed another tablet and went on. 'Bohm wanted to follow it up. His group head checked with Simmons, as head of U.K. operations. Simmons told Bohm to lay off and stay off. Taking it any further or reporting it to Pargeter might have jeopardised our whole position in the U.K., especially if the thing had gone to court and Bohm had been called as a witness. That's how I came to hear about it. There was a mention in one of the summaries.'

Head of Plans and the Director were watching Osgood as if trying to commit him to memory pore by pore. He said apologetically, 'That's it. I told you it wasn't much.'

Head of Plans said, 'When was this?' Osgood told him. He did sums in his head. 'That just could have been the start of it all. Where's Bohm these days? Still in the U.K.? It might be worth talking to him.'

Osgood said, 'He's dead.'

Head of Plans was feeling for his pipe with one hand and his tobacco pouch with the other. He stopped as if he'd pulled a muscle. 'Dead?'

Osgood shook his head. 'See what I mean, Henry? Maybe you don't notice. You've been in it longer than me. People die every day without sinister implications. Bohm's family came back to Sioux City, Iowa. There was a boy going to West Point and Bohm only had about three months to go to the end of his tour in England. He was in his forties, a bit overweight, more blood pressure than was good for him. Living on his own in London, with the kind of wining and dining he had to do as part of his cover activity, didn't help too much. He had a heart attack one night, driving his car out to——'

He didn't finish the sentence. He gave a short, embarrassed laugh, looking away from Head of Plans and back again. He said, 'Seriously, you can get too suspicious. You'd begin to suspect your own wife.'

Head of Plans had forgotten about his pipe and tobacco. He said softly, 'Where was your wife when Bohm died, Charlie? Or were you remembering something else?'

Osgood gave a couple more meaningless coughs. 'Oh hell! I taught for a spell at the London School of Economics. I know the London countryside pretty well. The place they found Bohm wasn't too far from Leatherhead. Where the Pargeter research place is located.'

Head of Plans said, 'What do you think, Mart?'

The Director, playing with a silver paper-knife, said, 'Let's dig.'

Osgood was beginning to worry about something. Sitting there, increasingly unhappy, he could hardly bring himself to say it. He tried. 'Look, if Bohm was—knocked off because he knew something he shouldn't, it would mean that someone —that the British——'

The Director pointed with his paper-knife. The metal flashed icily under the ceiling lighting panels. 'Bohm might have died naturally. Or if he was killed, it might not have been by the British. It could have been the other side, the side that was in the market for Pargeter's secrets. But, Charlie, it *could* have been the British.'

Osgood started to protest. The Director cut in pitilessly. 'Be honest with yourself, Charlie, or you don't belong here. We have allies, people we like, and we're loyal to them. More loyal, sometimes, than they are to us. But in the last extreme, if it's a choice between the United States—between your wife and kids, Charlie—and any other country in the world, whose side are you going to be on?'

He let silence point the question, then said, 'When it comes to the crunch, and it sometimes does, that's the way every country feels. Including the British. We're none of us that far out of the jungle. We're all prepared to put friendship before national interest some of the time, but not when the chips are really down. Not when it's their kids or yours.'

He laid the paper-knife on the desk-top with an air of finality. 'And certainly not if you could preserve both your national interests and an alliance simply by tidying away one unimportant, overweight, middle-aged man called Bohm.'

17. PATTI—*His and hers*

THERE WAS once a time, Jagger thought, when all you needed to start a restaurant was food and somewhere to sit. Now it took Sean Kenny, out-of-work actors and enough cheek to be able to call stewed shin *boeuf à la bourguinonne*.

From a velvety, pungent darkness lights glowed red, green and amber. A coffee machine whistled and hissed against a background of guitar music. The Regretful Virgin was like a railway siding on a dark night. A railway siding in Seville.

He stood in the doorway, accustoming himself to the blackness, the noise and the smell. An androgynous voice sidled into his ear and said, 'Yes, sir?'

He said, 'Good evening,' and fumbled his way a little farther in. From some abysmal alcove a voice, brittle with high-pitched contempt, said, 'He couldn't write copy for a Soho tart's come-on card. He thinks soft sell's a brand of toilet tissue.'

The manager floated after him, saying, 'Just the one, sir?' The question was as ambiguous as its poser. He said, 'I'm looking for someone.' The heteroclitic breath in his ear murmured, 'Of course, sir. Just a teentsy bit ace-of-spadesy but you'll soon adapt.'

Jagger was beginning to see faces, faint blobs of colour under the primordial glowings. He recognized a pale green one in a dark corner as Patti's. He shook off a touch that was half a caress, thanked his guide and sat down. He said, ' "And the earth was without form, and void; and darkness was upon the face of the deep." I call it blackmail when the price of giving a message to your father is being taken out to dinner.'

She said, 'I'm ruthless, really. We all are. You'll learn. The curse of the Pargeters.' She sounded bitter.

He looked at her thoughtfully, remembering something from his last conversation with the Master. 'No backlash from the other night? From your parents, I mean.'

'Backlash? No. Why on earth should there be? I wasn't involved. You told Myra yourself.'

'True. But I gather you like to be involved. Have you, ever?'

'I don't understand.'

'Have you ever tried pot, for instance?'

'No, I haven't. I'm sorry. That's not really true. I tried, once. All it did was hurt my chest as if I'd swallowed a nail. Never again!'

So it could hardly have been that. He tried again. 'A trip?'

Her eyes began to stammer. She fiddled unconsciously with the check tablecloth. 'A trip?'

'Oh, come on! You know what I mean.'

She began a denial and changed her mind. She said

defiantly, 'I don't see that it's any of your business, but once, yes. You should do everything once. I told you before, I believe in making things happen.'

'Taking acid is making things happen?'

'I wanted to know. How can you judge if you don't know?'

'All right. How did you judge?'

She hesitated. 'Well, it was marvellous, at first. I couldn't begin to describe.' She broke a bread stick into fragments and decided to try anyway. 'I knew everything. I mean it. Absolutely everything. You know? The reasons why everything's what it is. And it all seemed so obvious, so simple. But later on it all changed. The—other thing came up from somewhere deep down inside me. You couldn't understand. Like a sort of black, icy spring. And suddenly I was in a sort of endless labyrinth. Just me, millions of miles under the earth and no way out. Darkness and cold rocky walls, wet and slimy. I screamed and cried for hours.'

She glared defiantly. 'All right! I had a bad trip. You have to do *something*! We'll all be dead soon enough, won't we? And nothing to show we've ever been. Everything just as it was before. Don't worry. I shan't do it again. Not that. But there must be—something, mustn't there? The one big thing to do that makes it all worthwhile. I mean there *has* to be!'

She was studying the tablecloth as if it were a complicated game, her face desperate with frustration. She took a deep breath. 'I'm glad I told you. I haven't told anyone else.'

Remembering the Master, he thought: But someone else knows. A waiter put a menu on the table. Jagger said, 'Shall I choose?'

'Please. I like everything.' She brightened a little.

He ordered Italian food and a bottle of Bardolino. When the wine came he poured immediately. She gulped down half a glass. 'You think I'm stupid. Boring. Someone who needn't be taken seriously.'

'None of these things.'

She smiled but she appeared to have become uncharacteristically shy. It made him feel curiously tongue-tied. He said, idiotically, 'Is your mother well?'

It was the wrong thing. She went very still. 'Why?'

He retreated before her latent aggressiveness. 'Politeness. That's all.'

'She's attractive, isn't she? To men, I mean.'

'So I suppose.'

She drank the rest of her wine. 'You suppose? Or you think so?'

Their first course came. When the waiter left, Jagger said, 'You've no need to be jealous of her.'

She flushed. It was visible even in the wan light. 'I'm not. She's pathetic, really, when you think how old she is.'

'You are. Does she try to steal your men?'

'I haven't any *men*. Don't talk down to me by trying to talk up to me, for Christ's sake.'

He came to his own point. 'You said something about Ralph last night. Who is he, or shouldn't I ask?'

'Why shouldn't you? Ralph Schramme. He does things for Daddy.' She caught his eye and began to laugh. 'I could have put that better, but who cares?'

'What kind of things?'

She pulled a face. 'I knew you'd ask that. All very boring. He's a sort of talent scout for industry. Top people, especially scientists. He's quite well known.'

Jagger was beginning to remember. 'How to make money by insulting people. Is that the man? Tell me some more.'

She groaned. 'Oh God! Must I? He calls it stress probing. I can't stand him, as if you couldn't tell!'

She had eaten quickly, with absent-minded application. She put down her fork and began to play pointedly with the stem of her wine glass. Jagger refilled it.

He said, 'Any reason in particular?'

'Yes. No. I don't know. It's just that—well, in some ways he's not what he seems and in others he is. That's not very clear, is it?'

He smiled. 'What you know of him you don't much care

114

for, and what you don't know you think you wouldn't like if you did.'

She laughed. 'Is that what I mean? I suppose it is. It sounds like me.'

'What don't you like?'

'Well, to start with he's lechy. One woman at a time isn't enough. He'd like me, as well as Myra.' She stopped, seeing his eyes arch. 'Now what? Some people happen to think I'm attractive. There was this pukey man who offered me the earth if I'd spend the night with him. Don't look like that!' She kicked him, hard, under the table. 'Did that hurt? Good! Anyway, when I give I'll give. I don't wear a price tag. What are you giving, after all?'

He started to say, 'It isn't the gift that matters. It's the thought behind it,' but she might have thought he was joking. The waiter brought their second course, veal piled high with chopped peppers, aubergines and tomatoes. She attacked it at once.

'What about the things you only suspect?'

She stopped, fork in hand. 'Oh, Schramme! Well, I don't know, do I? I mean, it's just that on the surface he's always trying to be polite, friendly, but there's another man inside who isn't a bit nice, who's cold and watchful and gives nothing away. I expect that's the one who does the interviewing.' She frowned. 'Do we have to go on talking about him? You don't even know him.'

'I'm sorry. But if I'm going to work for your father I'll probably meet him.'

She dropped her fork on the plate with a clatter. 'Work? For him?'

'You don't think it's a good idea?'

'I think it's a bloody awful idea. You must be mad!' She flushed, blinking fast. 'I suppose you think I'm a real bitch, running everybody down, parents included. That's what comes of acquiring your dazzling polish at a posh finishing school, rubbing shoulders with minor royalty. They all hated their parents. Everybody did, except my best friend.

She was the daughter of the U.N. Secretary-General, which ought to prove something. Still, it was the happiest year of my life and that proves something, too.'

'There's no law that says you have to like your parents.'

'What about loving your neighbour?'

'Loving doesn't always mean liking, and anyway, it's less a law than a pious hope.'

'Socrates corrupting the young. Can I have some more hemlock?'

'Should you? You've had nearly half a bottle.'

'Oh, God! Now you're really being your age! What are you? President of the Y.W.C.A.? Or haven't you learned your first lesson in seduction?' She helped herself, poked the tip of her tongue at him and began to eat again as if nothing had happened. Her mouth inelegantly full, she said, 'What are you going to do for Daddy?'

'Look at one or two things.'

'Very informative. What sort of things?'

'Who earns twenty quid a week and comes to work in a Rolls.'

She looked at him shrewdly. 'Is that your line?'

'In a way.'

She was still staring speculatively. 'I know practically nothing about you, do I? Is it about those two men?'

He was lost. 'Two men?'

'My, we *are* cautious, aren't we? The burglary or whatever it was.'

He remembered Sir Ben's mention of industrial espionage. 'What do you know about it?'

She wrinkled her forehead, trying to remember things. 'Well, it was a while back, wasn't it? At the company's research centre. A man was killed falling from a window or something, and another was burned to death in a car smash, trying to get away. Don't say I told you. I'm not supposed to know.'

'How do you, then?'

She looked mischievous. 'I listen at keyholes.'

'I'm sorry. I asked for that.'

There was a flash of insolence. 'Oh, but I meant it. I do. You have to, if no one tells you anything. I expect Ralph does, too. He's the type. He's the one you should keep an eye on.'

He poured a good deal of wine into his own glass and what was left into hers. 'Why?'

She considered. 'I suppose I was joking. I'm malicious, you know. He was a refugee. He was in some kind of German prison camp during the war.'

He said, 'Something else, or shall we just have coffee? Isn't it a bit hard on a man to suggest he's bent just because he's a refugee?'

She agreed instantly. 'Yes, it is. I told you I don't like him. But remember who gave you the tip when you find he's a—a Russian agent stealing secrets for Moscow. No! That's not it! It's—I know! He recruits all these brilliant people for key positions in industry, but they're all Russian master spies. Taking over the country bit by bit until—pow! Who cares? Now I want to talk about you.'

The waiter reprieved him, bringing her a huge confection of ice-cream, fruit, chopped nuts and whipped cream. She dug her spoon into it and poked it at his face. 'Have some. You need fattening. Who's the woman who cares for your simple needs?'

He refused. He said, 'There isn't one and they aren't simple.' He signalled for coffee.

She said, 'In that case, perhaps——' and changed her mind about something. Instead she said, 'But of course you're going to be a cog in the grrreat grrrinding Pargeter machine. You'll be much too busy to notice women. You're like that, aren't you? You think you don't need them. Has he told you about Tinn?'

Once again she'd left him behind. She saw it. She said derisively, 'He's the one, I bet. The human computer. The Tinn Man.' The wine shone in her eyes like a Tuscan summer. 'I could help you, you know, more than you'd think. Daddy never really talks to me. He com-*mun*-icates. So I have to find out for myself. You'd be surprised how successful I am. You haven't met the Tinn Man, have you?'

He said, 'No,' feeling that one word in response to so many was a kind of verbal usury.

'The resident genius, doing something no one's supposed to know about.' She laughed. 'I expect those two men were trying to steal him, like Aladdin's lamp. He fell for me, you know.'

'No,' Jagger said helplessly. 'I didn't. Who?'

'Jack, of course. Right from the start, when Daddy brought him to the house. Myra thought it was hilarious. She would, poor little man. Then I met him again when Daddy took me to Leatherhead during one of his ritual attempts at communication. All he did was sort of *moon*, like a love-sick robot. Jack, I mean.' She looked contrite. 'I'm a bitch. I told you. He stammers. You might guess. He h-h-hoped we'd m-m-meet again. The smallest encouragement and he'd have told me the story of his life, all in figures and complete with working drawings.' The contrition returned, switching off lights at the back of her eyes. 'I shouldn't laugh. He's probably just like me inside, doing what he does because it's all he knows. Little causes for the lack of big ones.'

Watching her, Jagger realized that her biggest fear was of not being taken seriously. That was why she hid her obvious intelligence behind a smoke-screen of apparent inconsequentiality.

Now her mercurial temperament was plummetting towards zero again. Eyes cloudy, she propped her face between her hands, her elbows on the table. Her voice muffled by the pressure of her fists at the sides of her mouth, she said, 'So bloody pathetic! Schramme, hiding behind his image like a big cat in a small bush. Daddy, spending half his life fooling other people and ending by fooling himself. The Tinn Man— equations for everything, meanings for nothing. I could twist them all round my little finger if I wanted. Oh yes I could! Don't bloody well doubt it! And then there's you——'

Her voice almost inaudible she muttered, 'In your case it wouldn't be her so it bloody well had to be him.'

She turned towards him, throwing back her head angrily so that her hair flew about her face like a ragged halo. 'We're a pukey lot, Jagger, us Pargeters. You'll probably wish you'd never met us.' She walked out of the restaurant.

He paid the bill hastily and went after her. She was far down the street. He slipped into his car and drove after her. She got in without a word. When they arrived in Cheyne Square a fine drizzle was falling, drifting across the lamplight like heavy smoke. The rain brought out the pungent smell of autumn, sooty earth and fallen leaves. She made no attempt to get out. She simply sat, her head turned away from him towards the yellow street light. He switched off the engine.

He said, 'May I dare to give you a little advice?'

In a flat, dispirited voice she said, 'Why not? It seems to be the custom where I'm concerned.'

'Leave home, Patti. As long as you stay you'll be half daughter, half furniture. On your own you'll be somebody, first to yourself, later, perhaps, to them too. Sooner or later you'll find——'

She cut across him, her voice as bitter as quinine. '—a nice young man who'll accept me for what I am and not what my parents are. Marriage, children, happy ever after! That's it, right?'

'As a matter of fact,' he said resignedly, 'no.'

She turned abruptly towards him. 'Insensitive, patronizing, bastard prig!' she said. One hand went round the back of his neck and pulled him forward. His teeth met hers jarringly, then her mouth forced itself on his; warm, soft, fierce.

For an instant he was taken by surprise, even though a part of his mind had been peering myopically at risks without actually identifying them. He felt her breasts against him, smelled her fresh scent. He found civil war breaking out inside him. After a moment, reason won. He put up his hands to remove hers.

There was no need. She pulled away, fumbling for the door

release. Her right fist, small and hard, reached out and struck the side of his jaw none too gently. 'Go to hell!' she said.

The car door slammed. Footsteps hammered up the pathway towards that solid, arrogantly exclusive front door. He wiped his mouth with a handkerchief, looked at the pale shadow of lipstick. He said aloud, 'Prig! Bastard! Fool! Oh, damn, damn, damn!' The drizzle was thickening. He switched on his wipers and drove away.

18. SIR BEN—*Himself*

AUTUMN IN LONDON can be warm flat beer, cold stagnant water or iced champagne. Today the wine flowed freely. Clear yellow light fizzed and bubbled almost audibly in the inverted glass of the sky.

Jagger was driving to meet Sir Ben at the Pargeter Tower. From the Victoria Street corner of Parliament Square he glimpsed the crude anti-art of the Board of Trade building, dragged lengthways to the ground by sheer weight of architectural platitudes. Above it the topmost storey of New Strutton House peered at him, symbolizing the omnipercipience of the Master. He turned towards the Foreign Office, its archways like haughtily raised eyebrows, and veered left again towards the exquisite green-and-gold miniature of St James's Park.

On the parade ground of the Wellington Barracks guardsmen stood in ten-pin rows while a termagant-voiced drill sergeant tried to bowl them over with sheer volume of sound. The Palace squatted glumly between the twin towers of the Hilton Hotel and Portland House like a squat, condemned tenement in a high-rise development area.

At Hyde Park Corner, traffic rioted round Apsley House. Jagger remembered how the Duke of Wellington had caused its windows to be shuttered against the violence of the mob. Following His Grace's example of ignoring what couldn't be controlled, the shutters were going up on Britain's windows on the world. In spite of a city full of symbols, the imperial bubble had been finally pricked and with it the spirit, the self-respect of a great people.

Now, according to the Master, one man, one eccentric technologist was on the verge of an achievement that was supposed to restore the lost greatness. But greatness rested on something more than military power or was the new national ethos based on a belief that lack of power demoralizes, and absolute lack of power demoralizes absolutely?

Jagger was a cynic but like Pitt in an earlier age he felt instinctively that only when Britain had saved her soul by her own efforts could she hope to save the world by her example.

And in that case, what the hell was he doing now?

Was his motivation no better than Patti's; the need to do something, anything, rather than nothing at all? In a sense he could answer with an immediate yes. What meaning was there in the whole idiotic confusion, beyond what each man chose to give it? And wasn't one man as likely to be right as another? According to Nietzsche, if you had your *why* of life, you could get along with almost any *how*. But what if there was no why?

The champagne had gone flat. He nosed down the ramp into the basement parking area of the Pargeter Tower, relinquished by the Knightsbridge traffic torrent as suddenly as a stick into a river backwater. Even as he thought his doubting thoughts he was swept aloft to Sir Ben's penthouse suite overlooking Hyde Park.

Sir Ben, seeing out two earlier visitors, greeted him effusively and introduced him. The two men just leaving were Americans. One, a big man with bright blue eyes and a broken-veined, whisky-battered face, was the European regional director of Data Corporation of America, based on Geneva. He had a mannerism of heaving his shoulders convulsively every time he laughed, which was often. His name was Dobereiner. The other was young, soft-voiced and earnest, with the shop-window neatness of a Saks Brothers display dummy offset by a look that beat as it swept as it cleaned. His name was Simmons and he was Data Corporation's London manager.

They had the trick of getting Jagger's name first time, using it often and leaving him with the impression that he had been photographed, finger-printed and documented from then to eternity. He gathered they had been there to continue earlier discussions on a survey to be made by Data Corporation of the British electronics industry.

Once the visitors had left, Sir Ben changed his manner, treating Jagger with the judiciously blended mixture of affability and respect he might have shown to a very senior police officer of high reputation and impeccable breeding. He had received further instructions from the Minister. The Minister in his turn had had them skilfully implanted by the Master.

Sir Ben didn't pretend to understand them. So far as he could see, he'd been presented with another Tinn, though Jagger was altogether more prepossessing than Tinn. Like Tinn, Jagger was to be on the staff of Pargeter Electromation in name only. After an initial introduction to Leatherhead he was to be left to his own devices, coming and going as he pleased.

Sir Ben wasn't the kind of man to enjoy living with secrets he wasn't allowed to probe. But like a great many other people the Minister had learned to deal with, he was only too willing to abdicate real power for its empty symbols.

Miss Parry brought in coffee. The two men sat away from the broad desk, a low table between them and the autumnal panorama of the park stretching away across the mirror-still glitter of the Serpentine towards Bayswater and the Marble Arch. On every side, Jagger thought, staring through the wide expanse of double glazing, lay the bastions of privilege, as if the park were a parade ground enclosed by tower-defended curtain walls. Only geography and ideology had experienced an apparent reversion. The Russian embassy lay to the west, in the millionaires' row of Kensington Palace

Gardens. To the east were the millionaires and the American embassy, in the crumbling bastion of Mayfair.

Preliminaries out of the way, Jagger said, 'I have to start somewhere. Who's Ralph Schramme?'

Sir Ben looked surprised, then wise, anxious to show his perspicacity. 'Of course! You have to begin somewhere, and a good many people who've joined us over the last few years started with Schramme. You obviously know his line of business. He has an exclusive contract with my company, covering all senior staff appointments below board level. It doesn't entirely prevent us from finding our own people, but if we do he's supposed to screen them, just to observe the letter of our agreement.'

'What about me?' Jagger asked.

Sir Ben was briefly puzzled. 'You? Oh, I see. Well, technically speaking I suppose we should let him pass you. But naturally——'

'Why?'

'Why? I'd have thought you'd be the first to see why. After all, you're not really joining the company. And the very nature of your responsibilities argues against normal treatment.'

'Would Schramme see it that way?'

Again Sir Ben hesitated. 'He would if he knew why——' He stopped. He'd just had the germ of an idea. Or rather, Brummagem Ben had just had the germ of an idea. It grew in size and attraction the longer he looked at it.

He was bound to Schramme by contract and long association, but the publicity value was gone. That apart, the relationship between Schramme and Myra had lasted long enough. Sooner or later the scandal must break. He made up his mind. Myra could never let Schramme go willingly. But he might well be frightened away.

Jagger unwittingly helped the embryo plot along. He said, 'I'd like to meet the man. You said that sometimes you only observe the letter of the contract. Presumably with people you're going to hire whether Schramme likes it or not.'

Sir Ben saw Jagger's drift. What he saw he liked. He said, 'Ah, now I'm with you. But how much could I tell Ralph about the reasons for signing you up?'

Jagger considered the question in the light of some ideas of his own. They'd started some while back, after he'd taken Patti out to dinner. 'You wouldn't be the first firm to appoint a security officer. You could say I came complete with impeccable references from high quarters. The kind he couldn't very well query. And you could give him the chance to save face by agreeing to a pseudo-interview. He'd know it was just for appearances. He might even guess that I knew, too, but he'd probably go through with the act.'

Sir Ben refilled the coffee cups and sowed the first seeds of his private project. 'He would. Not only that but——'

'Yes?'

The pause had been deliberate. Sir Ben timed it carefully. He said, 'I haven't actually thought of it this way before, but in a sense I suppose quite a lot of our technical security depends on Ralph.'

Jagger sensed something. He thought: You use Schramme but you don't really like him. Because of your wife? He said, 'I suppose so. And not only yours. How much do you think he gets out of this—what does he call it?—stress probing? You've never had reason to doubt it?'

Sir Ben edged another step along his private path. 'Doubt it? Not a bit! At least——' and another precisely calculated delay.

At the end of it he said, almost reluctantly, 'There was *one* incident. I'm not entirely sure one would be fair to blame it on Schramme.'

Jagger said, 'Tell me.'

Sir Ben gave himself his mid-morning cigar and tormented Jagger by pushing the box across the table. Jagger shook his head, feeling anything but virtuous. Sir Ben took a little time to light the cigar. 'You might as well know, if you don't already. We had a chap called Lusty. Brilliant scientist. We thought he might eventually take over from Arnold Parsons, our research and development director. Schramme found Lusty for us.'

He drew luxuriously on the cigar, turning a barbed blade in Jagger's self-inflicted wound. 'You know how these head-hunters work? Schramme has a list of possibles for any given vacancy. Most of 'em are already in jobs, so he rings 'em up at home, in the evening, sometimes at the weekend. Tells a chap there's a chance he might be suitable for a post much better than the one he's in. Tickles his curiosity and self-esteem, eh? Chap thinks he hasn't anything to lose by finding out a bit more and that's the beginning. That's how Schramme latched on to Lusty.'

'What happens then?'

'Oh, some fall by the wayside. The good ones get pro-gressively more searching interviews until they end up hooked. After that comes the really tough stuff, the kind Schramme made his name on.'

'Why on earth,' said Jagger, 'are people willing to go through with that kind of thing?'

'My dear fellow!' Sir Ben said, 'Ever watch television? The incredibly intimate questions folks'll answer, just between themselves, the interviewer and several million people? With Schramme's methods, by the time they get to the bit that hurts they already smell money, success. There's no more powerful persuader.'

The whole idea was as repugnant to Jagger as starring in blue movies, but he saw how it might work. *Did* work! He said, 'About Lusty.'

'To cut a long story short,' Sir Ben said, 'Lusty started selling technical information to a competitor but he wasn't very good at it. He was caught, panicked and tried to bolt. Broke his neck falling from a fire escape. It turned out that Lusty had a wife who was spending faster than he could earn. He was infatuated with her. That's why he tried the spying thing. But the point is that Lusty had had the full treatment from Ralph Schramme. According to Schramme's claims, the facts about Lusty's wife and the fellow's infatuation with her should have come out, not to mention his moral flaw. But they didn't. In fact he couldn't have recommended Lusty more strongly.'

He stared at Jagger through a sunlit nebula of cigar smoke, his eyes narrowed. 'You take my meaning?'

Jagger took several meanings. He didn't know which, if any, was Sir Ben's. 'Schramme isn't infallible, so any check on personal security should take account of the fact. That's why I'd like to meet him.'

Sir Ben was satisfied. It was near enough. He could add the finishing touches afterwards. In the meantime it might be best to back off a little. He didn't want to overdo things. He said, 'Don't get the wrong idea. Ralph's a good chap. After all, you might say I was the one who discovered him.'

Jagger suddenly realized. He was going to be used to put the wind up Schramme, on the theory that once you had a security inquiry under way, anything could come out and probably would. Including sleeping with your client's wife. He said, 'Who discovered Lusty? You said he was caught.'

Sir Ben made it vague, falling back on the official story. 'I wasn't there when it happened, of course, but it was some Ministry nark. We didn't pursue matters. After all, the fellow was dead.'

Jagger took the chance. 'Who, the Ministry investigator?'

Sir Ben was caught off balance. Obviously Jagger knew more than he was admitting. 'I was talking about Lusty, but of course, the other chap as well, later. Had a heart attack or something, and wrecked his car.' That's how Sir Ben himself had been fobbed off, though a couple of very private chats with Parsons had left him with certain doubts. Still, you didn't argue with the Official Secrets Act. And you didn't get peerages for querying official explanations.

Jagger seemed satisfied. He said, 'May I leave it with you to fix something with Schramme?' Sir Ben was thinking: You can, my dear chap! You certainly can! 'And I'd like to take a preliminary look at your place at Leatherhead,' Jagger finished.

Sir Ben had an idea. 'Could you go tomorrow? Splendid. In that case I'll take you there myself, if you don't mind being left with Parsons. I've business elsewhere.'

Jagger stood up. He had enough to be going on with. More than enough, especially if he added it to what he'd been thinking on his way to the Pargeter Tower.

When he'd gone, with an arrangement for a rendezvous in Cheyne Square the following morning, Sir Ben buzzed Miss Parry. 'Get hold of Ralph Schramme for me, will you? If his secretary says he's interviewing, tell her it's important.'

Now he'd given Jagger a shove in the right direction he couldn't wait to spoil Schramme's morning.

19. HEAD OF PLANS—*Definitely them*

THE BIG MAN, his wide shoulders hunched against a raw cold that had blown in from the sea since nightfall, crossed Park Avenue and went through the side entrance of an apartment building as discreetly prosperous as a Swiss bank. All about him the lid was coming down on the Manhattan jewel box as cleaners and janitors switched off the lights in deserted skyscrapers, floor by floor. Winking like a firefly, a helicopter lifted slowly from the roof of the Pan Am building.

The big man took the service elevator to the fifth floor and stepped out into a long, softly lit corridor. Rows of smooth, blank doors reflected the light in a respectful, almost religious sheen. Behind one of them a television huckster pushed dentrifice with the febrile, synthetic excitement of an evangelist offering eternal salvation for a dollar down and twelve easy payments. In the wall-to-wall carpeted silence it was like a drunk bawling dirty words in church.

The visitor went silently down the corridor. It occurred to him that in over a score of visits to this place he'd never met a living being once he had crossed its threshold, never heard a human voice except from a loud-speaker through a closed door. For all he knew the building was tenanted solely by robots and even they, he felt sure, never spoke to each other.

He pushed a key at the lock of the door. A sharp spat of static electricity between knob and key made him jump a little. He turned the key, went through and closed the door gently behind him. Before he could turn the corner into the long sitting-room a voice said, 'Hi, Dob! Right on time. Want to mix yourself a drink before you sit down?'

Dobereiner headed for the kitchen, waving his hand to the man sitting on the king-sized sofa. He said, 'Hi, Henry! Be with you.' Behind Head of Plans the blinds of the windows on to Park Avenue were still open, dividing the night outside into horizontal strips of light and dark like a trick photograph.

Dobereiner took down the bourbon, clinked chunky ice into a chunky glass and baptised it in alcohol. He came back into the room. The only light was a parchment-shaded standard lamp. Dobereiner pulled up an easy chair and sat under the lamp like a sunbather. The light shone through the lobes of his ears so that they glowed pinkly.

He drank a little bourbon, sighed and said, 'Every time I come in on that damned chopper I know it's going to quit, ten feet short of the roof.'

Head of Plans said, 'Pan Am has fifty-nine storeys. You'd have time to think of something before you hit bottom.'

Dobereiner said, 'A storey for every day of my life and a few over.'

Head of Plans, his arms folded, his eyes closed, his pipe fuming like a dormant volcano, said, 'A man like you has a story for every day of his life and a hell of a lot over. What's the story for today? How's the climate in the tight little isle?'

Dobereiner said, 'Anti-American.' He swirled whisky and ice-cubes round his glass several times and drank. 'That Air Force major flew me here so damn fast my feelings didn't catch up with me until Fire Island. Now I have the only supersonic thirst in Manhattan.' He finished his drink and went back to the kitchen.

Raising his voice a little, he said, 'You were right.'

Head of Plans nodded to himself, though Dobereiner couldn't see him. He said nothing, his eyes still closed. Dobereiner came back and sat down again, his glass refilled. He said, 'There's some things you don't see unless you look. Then you wonder how you ever missed them.'

Head of Plans said, 'Did you have time to put it all in writing?'

Dobereiner slapped the briefcase at the side of his chair. 'It's all here.'

Head of Plans said, 'Give me the highlights.'

Dobereiner slid down in his chair until his body pivoted on the base of his spine. He yawned cavernously and said, 'Augustus wanted his three legions back. I'd settle for my six hours. Bohm was killed.'

Head of Plans said, 'Proof?'

'Circumstantial.'

'Convincing?'

'Overwhelming. They took him at Pargeter's research complex at Leatherhead. It was the last time he was seen alive. There's hours missing in between.'

'Who's they?'

'The special outfit. You know? The super-secrets.'

Head of Plans said lazily, 'I know the little guy. He's one smart hombre.'

'You can say that again. And again. The official story is that Lusty was selling secrets and Bohm working with the British. Incidentally, that's——'

His eyes still tight shut, Head of Plans cut in. 'That's how the Russians got their final proof that we were in cahoots with the British. Because——'

It was Dobereiner's turn. '—Lusty was working for the K.G.B. Which means——'

Head of Plans took over again. It was like a verbal tennis game. '—that we should take a look at Lusty's background. And we already did.'

'With what result?'

'Lusty came to Pargeter from another British electronics

company. But before that he'd worked on the British Short-change project, down in Wiltshire.'

'With Tinn?'

'With Tinn.'

In the long silence that followed, traffic swished past, somebody in the street below argued with a cab driver and the siren of a prowl car wailed across the darkness from somewhere in the East Thirties. A light patter of rain flurried at the glass of the windows.

Head of Plans tapped his teeth with the stem of his pipe. 'All hushed up, huh?'

'You bet it was. The heart failure was genuine enough. They called in the embassy doctor to help with the post mortem. But the body was too badly burned in the phoney car crash to show anything else. Not that our man would be looking for anything else.'

After another silence, Dobereiner said defensively, 'I don't believe you can hold anything against Simmons. So far as he was concerned, Bohm had accidentally run up against industrial espionage. Simmons told Bohm to drop it and made a routine report to Charlie Osgood. It should have rested there.'

'But it didn't.'

'It didn't.'

In the kitchen the refrigerator motor burst into life. The silence made it sound like the start of a Grand Prix. The siren of the prowl car, or another one, keened again, much nearer. From the East River a tug shouted back in the bass clef, once, twice, three times.

Head of Plans opened his eyes and shifted his long legs. Clenching his pipe between his big, white teeth, he pushed himself up with both hands, his fists sinking deep into the sofa cushions. He said, 'I'm having a whisky sour. Should I prescribe for you?'

Dobereiner looked at his empty glass. 'Straight, on the rocks. The giant economy size. My economy. Your whisky.'

Head of Plans went through to the kitchen. Dobereiner

followed him. Head of Plans, lining up glasses, looked round and nodded. He said, 'It's a big lonely world and sometimes you feel it.'

Dobereiner, in a husky, whisky-and-smoke-filled-room voice, sang. 'New York! New York! It's a wonderful town! When you've time to spare, money in your pocket and nothing on your mind.' He took the bottle from Head of Plans, doubled his own measure and said, 'Bohm was a nice little guy.'

Head of Plans said, 'Our very good friends and blood brothers! I wonder?'

'How much Bohm spilled?'

'Was made to spill. Let's give him some credit.'

Dobereiner hoisted himself up on the smooth work surface at the side of the big double sink. 'Not too much. He was controlled the same way everybody else is.'

'What about a phone trace?'

Dobereiner shook his head. 'They couldn't have got that far. We'd know.'

Head of Plans tugged the cord that closed the slats of the window blind behind him. It was a symbolic action, but they both felt better for it. He leaned against the tall refrigerator. 'They'll think Bohm was working under instructions. I know that little guy in London. He's too careful to want a direct confrontation but short of that, anything'll go. He won't have Bohm on his conscience. He'll remember what happened to those two British S.I.S. men who were too nosy in Mayaguez. And that unfortunate fire at the Hotel Theodosia in Istanbul.'

Dobereiner said, 'He's using a stalking-horse already. A guy called Jagger.'

Head of Plans said, 'What about Tinn? How tight is the security since Bohm?'

Dobereiner hesitated. He said, 'Look, I could be wrong about this, but suppose they think they have everything under control? Lusty dead, so out go the Dzerzhinsky boys. Bohm dead, in circumstances they know we have to accept

131

as an accident. So, like I said, I could be wrong but I kind of feel they're keeping the whole thing cool. Tinn's still living under minimum surveillance and working under none. At least, unless this guy Jagger's going to move in real close. It also suggests something else.'

Head of Plans was absentmindedly opening and closing the refrigerator door. 'That Tinn's pretty well at the end of the trail?'

'That's right. So building electrified fences and calling out the army would only advertise the fact. After all, but for Fifth Ace and Bohm doing what he'd been told not to, we'd never have known, even now.'

'But the Kremlin would. There ought to be a way of giving Bohm some kind of medal for disobeying orders in the line of duty. Has Simmons moved in?'

'Out at Leatherhead? Yes. He's had one of his people take a house. We're making the first official visit to the Pargeter place the day after tomorrow but they've already done some phone tapping.'

Head of Plans appeared to be concentrating on seeing how nearly he could close the door of the refrigerator before the light went off. He said, 'Jagger. You know, I seem to remember something about a man with that name. And if what I recall is correct, he quit the British service quite a while back. Or, more exactly, he was invited to quit. Dob, do you know for sure he's official?'

Dobereiner blinked. 'Well, he's official with Sir Ben Pargeter. We were introduced in Sir Ben's office. Apart from that, how would I know?'

Head of Plans nodded to himself. 'How would you? How would anybody? That little guy in London doesn't even talk to himself in case he says something he shouldn't know. If we wanted to do ourselves a good turn we'd get the Ford Foundation or somebody to build a new college at Oxford just for him to go back to.'

Dobereiner finished his drink and put the glass tidily in the sink. He said, 'When are you going back to Washington?'

'Tonight. The boss'll want to see me. What time do you take off?'

Dobereiner pulled a wry face. 'Dawn plus thirty. Guess what Uncle Dob's going to do in this jumping town between now and then.'

Head of Plans opened and closed the door of the refrigerator for the last time. In a dreamy voice he said, 'When I was a kid I took everything out of our Kelvinator, shelves and all, tucked myself inside and pulled the door to, to find out just what did happen to that little light. If my ma hadn't happened along right that minute, I'd have been the coldest kid in Lancaster County. Give me that report and I'll leave you to catch up on your sleep.'

At the door of the apartment he said, 'Spread the word to play it cool, Dob, and if anybody should suddenly close the door, mind you're on the right side.'

20. SCHRAMME—*Theirs*

HE HEARD a faint buzz from the room next door. He guessed what it meant. The typing stopped. There was a moment's silence, then Schramme's secretary came in. She said, 'Mr Schramme will see you now. Will you come this way, please?'

The corridor was as hushed as a catacomb. He supposed discretion was the very essence of this business. It wouldn't do to be seen by other applicants. One of them might turn out to be your boss.

He thought of repeating the joke to Schramme's secretary but she'd probably heard it before. She opened a door, smiled, standing aside for him to go in. She closed it behind him as if he were already dead.

The room was small and featureless. He found the lack of a window oppressive. He took the chair in front of the plain, bare desk. There was no sound at all. He could have been in orbit.

Just as the fuse of his patience was burning short, the door opened and the man framed against its brightness said, 'Mr Jagger. Please forgive me for keeping you waiting.' He shook hands with a cool, precisely measured grip and went behind the desk to the other chair.

Jagger's first impression was of a fastidiousness of dress verging on the unnatural. The man's clothes appeared to grow on him in a kind of wrinkle-free perfection. Dazzling white linen showed at his neck and wrists. His tie and the handkerchief in his breast pocket had been positioned with theodolite and spirit level.

Schramme's eyes, metal grey, like nail heads, dominated his sallow, slightly Slav-looking face. Their colour was repeated in hair brushed straight back from the broad smooth forehead. Jagger remembered Patti's description. There's another man inside him who's cold and watchful and doesn't give anything away.

The man took a leather cigarette-box from a drawer, opened it and pushed it towards Jagger. Jagger shook his head.

Schramme said incuriously, 'You don't smoke?'

'Not any more.'

'You are opposed to the habit?'

'For me. Not for others.'

'What others do does not concern you?'

'Oh yes, so far as it affects me.'

Schramme raised his eyebrows ostentatiously. 'So far as it affects you? That gives an impression of selfishness.'

'I can only judge other people's actions in terms of my own.'

'And if their viewpoint appears to differ from yours?'

'No "if" about it.'

Schramme was drawing invisible masterpieces on the top of the desk with his forefinger. 'This produces conflict?' He still sounded disinterested.

Jagger thought: He can't be taking the interview seriously. Or can he? He said, 'Not necessarily. A point of view is only an opinion.'

'But the meaning of life is something more than a series of

points of view. Or perhaps you don't believe in absolutes?'

'Not ethical absolutes.'

Schramme sketched out a series of parallel straight lines, then carefully bisected them. The backs of his hands, sallow like his face, were covered with a dense scribble of black hair. The man's body, Jagger thought, would be white, white all over with a black pelt from chest to crotch.

Schramme said, 'You are your own judge and jury. Doubtless a stern one.'

Jagger said, 'How stern is stern? Is there some point to all this?'

For the first time, Schramme looked at him directly. He said, 'Do you know the methods on which my practice is based?' His lips were slightly compressed.

Jagger said, 'I think so. Much the same as some people use to break a man down so that they can put him together in a different way.'

Schramme appeared to consider for a while. He said, quietly, reasonably, 'No man knows himself, Mr Jagger. How then can he know which is the proper way for him to be put together? Even a psychiatrist? Possibly least of all a psychiatrist. Each of us has a simulacrum which he knows, but he plays God, modelling the simulacrum in the image he would like to consider his own. It is my function to lay bare the true man, either by guile or force.' He paused before adding, 'Verbal force. The force of shock.'

Jagger said, 'Why should a man's behaviour under artificial stress tell you whether or not he's suited for a particular job?'

'Concentrated, yes. Artificial, no. And a particular job. There you have the point. Not any job, but a job at the top, where stress is the everyday order of things.'

'Stress is the everyday order of life. We all adapt to it.'

'Indeed, but some, you will agree, far better than others. I am only interested in those who have adapted well. Any interviewer looks for a man's weak points. I, when I have found them, press upon them to see whether he will endure. When I break through, it is to the truth.'

'Yes, well that's something else I'm not sure I believe in,' Jagger said casually. 'Truth's like beauty. It exists in the eye of the beholder.'

Schramme now had his whole attention concentrated on Jagger. He was breathing a fraction more audibly. 'You believe you would be able to resist?'

Jagger thought he'd found one of Schramme's weak points. He pressed on it. 'I'm sure,' he said with deliberate bumptiousness.

It didn't work. Schramme said imperturbably, 'I don't believe it would prove impossible to penetrate your guard, Mr Jagger. And once through—well, every man has a little mud in his make-up. From clay we come and to clay we return. One must not be surprised if some of it sticks.'

Jagger tried again. 'Isn't dirt-digging a rather despicable technique?'

'Without dirt-digging, as you call it, and as any psychiatrist will confirm, it is impossible to uncover the real man. But in any event, is this not what you yourself are to be employed for?'

Schramme's eyes took on a faintly mocking sparkle.

Jagger revised his initial estimate of the man. Schramme pressed his advantage. 'Security is a dirty business, is it not? Little to do with beautiful women, fast cars and similar Hollywood stupidities. A good security man constantly digs for dirt. He trades in moral depravity, sexual aberration, any form of human weakness, for where there is weakness there is temptation, guilt and the ever-present possibility of betrayal.'

For a moment Jagger had the curious sensation that Schramme himself had changed, that the man inside, the real Schramme, had taken over and was speaking openly, frankly. It was only for a moment. Schramme lowered his eyes. When they looked up again the veiled mockery had returned and the smile showed genuine amusement.

Schramme said, 'I will perform a cheap trick, without looking at your palm or feeling the bumps of your head.

136

You ride yourself like a man on a tiger, Mr Jagger. You have trust neither in others nor yourself. You are perpetually afraid of betraying yourself or of being betrayed, in small things as well as great. You seek to avoid such a betrayal by withholding yourself, by living within yourself, and yet it is precisely there that you are on your weakest ground. Stendahl, you may remember, warns that a man living in such a fashion will eventually strangle in his own emotions. Every man's strengths are his weaknesses seen in a mirror, Mr Jagger, and you are no exception.'

He stood up. 'But you and I are in the same occupation and should not quarrel. We should be allies, not enemies.'

He took a cigarette from a slim gold case, coming round the desk. He lit it with a matching gold lighter, inhaling deeply. The acrid smell of cheap Balkan tobacco drifted across the room. Schramme smiled again. He opened the door and waved to Jagger to pass him. He said, 'The interview is over, if indeed it ever took place. Let us continue the conversation in somewhat less forbidding surroundings.'

They went the length of the corridor and Schramme opened another door. It led into a large, bright room with windows on two sides. Furnished with flair, it would have suited a leading designer or a film director with unusually good taste. It should have looked out on Stockholm or Helsinki.

Schramme waved Jagger to a seat altogether more comfortable than the first and sat down in its twin. He waved his cigarette so that its pale smoke drew an evanescent arc across the still air. 'I smoke only two things. The best Havanas money can buy, to convince me of what I have become. And these, to remind me of what I once was.' He indicated his cigarette.

Jagger said, 'And what were you?'

Schramme said, simply, 'Nothing. The poor son of a poor father. The heir of a hundred generations of nobodies. A conscript worker in Germany during the last war. An industrial slave, living in a camp where the only difference

137

from an Auschwitz was that one received a little encouragement to stay alive. As to what I have become——'

He waved his hand again, embracingly and at the same time contemptuously. Suddenly, astonishingly, he dropped his cigarette on a superb Finnish rug and ground it out with the sole of one gleaming, hand-sewn shoe. It was, Jagger thought, the first genuine and unpremeditated act of their encounter.

Schramme stared at the ugly black mark and the crushed fragments without seeming to see them. He said, 'Be so kind as to accept my apology for anything which I may have said to offend you. What can I do to help you?'

Jagger took his time. He had the feeling that something of major significance had just taken place but it was beyond his power to understand it. He had come here with the intention of making things happen. He might have succeeded, but if so they were no longer under his control. Of all situations it was the kind he liked least.

He said eventually, 'How many of Pargeter's research staff came through your hands?'

Schramme nodded quickly, as if he had been waiting for the question. 'Four of the seven most senior men in the last nine years, and approximately half of those in the second echelon. Below that, we are not interested. Of recent years, as this business has expanded, my two associates have handled all except the most senior appointments.'

Almost as an afterthought, he added, 'Of course we do not and could not assess their scientific qualifications except in the most general sense. Only their human qualities.'

'And never the twain shall meet,' Jagger said. 'What about a man called Tinn?'

Schramme sounded almost bored. 'He was not recruited by this organization.'

Jagger made a mental note. The face-saving process that acknowledged the letter but not the spirit of the contract hadn't applied in Tinn's case. He said, 'There was someone you did recruit. His name was Lusty.'

138

For a fleeting moment, someone behind Schramme's metallic eyes put up the shutters. He leaned forward, prodding at the burned rug with the toe of his shoe. He said, 'Lusty. Yes.'

When he lifted his head his face was washed clean of expression, as if the space behind his eyes had been put up for sale. 'There would be no point in concealing this from you. Lusty is my failure. It is better to say that honestly, rather than to call him the exception that proves the rule. Lusty had faults which were revealed during the stress interviews, but they were what I term positive faults. Negative faults rule a man out. Positive faults are recorded and reported to a prospective employer but, properly used, may be considered advantageous.'

Seeing Jagger's frown he said, 'Take a man who has the fault of being aggressively sceptical, who questions everything, who is satisfied with no answer until he has taken it to pieces like a watch. A difficult man. But ideally qualified to question negative findings, no matter how authoritative their source. Ideally qualified, for instance, as a research leader.'

'Lusty?'

'Lusty.'

'And yet you missed something.'

'I did. His wife. We invariably probe deeply into family background, marital relationships and so on. This is fertile ground for the seeds of human weakness. But Lusty, as I have explained, was very aggressive. He resisted questions about his wife most strongly, on the grounds that it was he, not his wife, who was a candidate. This is an argument I can respect. In view of his other qualifications I recommended him. I erred. I thought his attitude no more than a commendable regard for marital privacy. In fact it concealed a fierce infatuation with a woman who, though she'd left him, was bleeding him to death, financially and emotionally.'

He drew a deep breath, his nostrils pinched. 'I do not believe the mistake has been made again, but even one failure cuts deeply.'

Jagger said, 'I believe he was killed, falling from a window.

Presumably he was being blackmailed to spy on his employers.'

Schramme seemed lost in the recollection of his failure. He said, almost disinterestedly, 'So I believe.'

He stood up and went round the back of his desk. He must have pressed some concealed button. His secretary came in. He said, 'Janice, Mr Jagger is to have access to the Lusty file any time he wishes.'

She said, 'Yes, Mr Schramme.' She had several dazzlingly white hand towels over one arm. She pointed at the door behind Schramme's desk and said, 'May I, please?'

He nodded and she passed behind him. As she opened the door Jagger saw that it led into another room, half-tiled, with a washbasin and mirror partly visible through the gap.

Schramme looked questioningly at Jagger. He said, 'What else can I tell you?'

Something floated vaguely at the back of Jagger's mind, something that hadn't been there a short while before. It refused to come into focus. He abandoned his attempt to pursue it. He said, 'Nothing. For the time being, anyway. I mustn't take up any more of your time.'

Schramme smiled. He made a deprecatory gesture with his beautifully manicured hands, revealing gold cuff links in restrained good taste.

Janice came back from the washroom, closing the door behind her. Schramme said, 'Janice, will you show Mr Jagger out?' He held out a hand. '*Au revoir*. Please consider me at your disposal whenever you wish. Perhaps we might have lunch once you have settled.'

Jagger took the hand. Once again it squeezed his own with a meticulously calculated precision, as if Schramme were operating some kind of machine. Jagger followed Janice into the anechoic stillness of the corridor. The ghost at the back of his brain reappeared as if at a doorway, and as quickly vanished. He allowed himself to be shown into the lift.

Schramme sat down once more. He sat for a long time, his

140

hands resting on the arms of the chair, his body motionless except for the almost imperceptible rise and fall of his chest. They had played a game, he and Jagger. It was a game in which Schramme was supposed to be the acknowledged master, but it was Jagger who had won. Had won, Schramme thought bitterly, because, though each had defined the weak points of the other, only one of them had dared press home his advantage. Jagger knew!

He stretched out an arm and slid Jagger's file from the top of the desk. It held nothing other than a photostat of a letter establishing Jagger's credentials beyond any power of Schramme's to query. At the foot of the letter was the sprawling, steeply angled signature of the Minister for Scientific Development. But there was more to things than that. There was the tersely worded warning from Geneva.

Sir Ben, making Jagger's appointment, had dropped veiled hints. Schramme's lips curled at the recollection. Brumma-gem Ben was cunning enough, but to a man like Schramme his cunning was transparent. Ben Pargeter had meant to frighten Schramme away from Myra. In itself the motive was convenient enough, from Schramme's point of view. He and Myra had come to the end of their relationship. All that remained was to tell her so. But Sir Ben had alarmed Schramme in another way entirely, leaving Geneva barely enough time to confirm a hastily transmitted query. Jagger, according to Sir Ben and his precious Minister, was in business for himself on the basis of a not too explicit background in government security. Schramme had thought otherwise, and Geneva had agreed. Jagger had a long record as an active and dangerously experienced agent. There was no reason at all to think that things had changed.

So a part of Schramme's life had come abruptly to an end. His instructions were explicit enough. He was to safeguard his long-range position at all costs, to take whatever steps would best serve that purpose. And the time to take them was now.

He looked at his watch. The day was almost over. He

buzzed Janice and told her to leave when she was ready. She said goodnight, her pleased eagerness showing in her voice. That damned priapic clerk! If things had been different——!

Schramme worked quickly, now that he had made his decision. He passed through the mirror and spent half an hour emptying the files. He stacked their contents neatly on the wall benches. He destroyed the spare gamma pads sheet by sheet. He took every magnetic tape from its tin and erected cylindrical towers of tape around the stacked files. He took down the cameras from their mounts behind the air grilles of his interview room and added them, with all the spare film, to the collection on the bench.

Finally, he pulled out the heavy wooden chest from its position against the wall beneath the bench. He unlocked it, activated the radio-controlled fuse, closed and locked the chest and heaved it back into position. The time to trigger the fuse might be days away, or it might be tonight. In either event, he would be ready.

He returned through the mirror, took his contact book from his desk and found the name he had decided upon. The man was a First Secretary at the embassy. They had met often enough, the last time for lunch. He dialled the number on his direct line and asked for the extension. The matter took a little time to explain but once he had made the position clear, picking his words carefully so as not to be more explicit than was essential, he had no difficulty in making his appointment.

Finally, he rang Myra. This time he was quite explicit. He took a taxi to his club. There would be time for a drink and an early dinner before he kept his appointment.

On the other side of central London, Ida read the transcription of Schramme's two telephone calls for the second time and smiled a smile that was at the same time amused and dangerous. 'This,' Ida said, 'should be really interesting.'

21. PATTI—*Us?*

HE HAD STARED for more than an hour through his big dormer windows, watching the light leach slowly from the high, cirrus-ribbed sky. Outside, starlings manœuvred in tight patterns, like dots before the eyes as they gathered for the nightly return to the electric warmth of the city. An elm, tall on the fringe of the dingy open space, dropped leaves in reluctant ones and twos, like a miser parting with coppers.

He had been thinking about Schramme; expert at provoking indiscretions, dealing daily with ambitious men seeking key positions in British industry. It would be easy to misread the situation. Yet, after all, Schramme was only an extreme version of the commonplace. Every day, in London alone, a score of management consultancies interviewed key men, probing, pressing, encouraging them to talk about themselves and their jobs. By nothing more scientific than the law of averages, indiscretions would be committed, secrets revealed, confidences broken.

But how many led a man to fall to his death from a high window? Or another, so far nameless, to be killed in a car crash allegedly due to heart failure?

He prepared a meal mechanically, chasing thoughts in circles. Schramme, for all his vaunted skill, had failed to discover Lusty's susceptibility to blackmail. Lusty needed money. Someone had employed the classic technique. Something harmless and well-rewarded to begin with, the tasty bait. Afterwards, the man had found himself trapped between the carrot of gain and the scourge of exposure.

He ate slowly, scarcely tasting the food. Given that this was what had happened, where had the pressure come from? Not through Schramme. As Sir Ben had said, Schramme hadn't even found out——

He stopped, incredulous at his own stupidity. He had one man's word for Schramme's error and it wasn't Sir Ben's. Sir Ben had simply repeated what he had been told. The confession of failure had originated with Schramme himself, and it was totally out of character. Recollecting that immaculate façade, that smooth and unshakeable confidence, there was only one possible explanation. Ralph Schramme would admit professional error only if the alternative was something utterly inadmissible.

He cleared away dishes and switched on his high fidelity equipment, taking his time over the choice of a record. The room flooded with the astringent sadness of Schoenberg's second string quartet. He stretched full length on the sofa, surrounded by books and pictures; his fortifications against a world in which he found little to like. He let his eyes walk from picture to picture—his Nolan, the Picasso sketch, his Staël, his mortuary Bacon.

The twisted, bloody carcase in the Bacon seemed, suddenly, brutally, to present him to himself—warped, tormented, isolated. Not so long ago he had been trying to recollect a single act to justify his existence. Now he felt himself faced with a choice of decisions. The right one might give him some small significance.

But which?

Schramme had placed Lusty with Pargeter. And Schramme, if Jagger had deduced correctly, had known Lusty's vulnerability; known it and concealed it. The only possible explanation was that Schramme himself had made use of it. Schramme, not the dead Lusty, was the real security threat. On the other hand, the more he considered the implications, the less he liked what was threatened, the greater his regret that boredom and curiosity had led him to accept the Master's suspiciously open request for help. The United States and the Soviet Union between them might—just might—keep humanity in being as a going concern, might even reach an eventual accommodation with the Chinese. But a super-superpower, especially one that seemed at least temporarily to have lost its sense of moral purpose, could do infinite harm.

His personal conflict was between training and inclination, between instincts and belief. For the ferret the scent of the quarry was sufficient. For the man there was the old and arrogant presumption of attempting to distinguish between the right and the wrong, not merely for himself, or even the times, but for all the ages to come.

While he was still contemplating his choices, someone rang the bell of the street door. When he opened it, he found himself looking at Patti.

She looked as enchanting as moonlight, but the instant she saw him she switched on a supplementary, artificial brilliance. She said, 'Hello, Jagger!' marched past him into the bare hall and turned, waiting. Half amused, half impatient, she said, 'Well, is it all like this? Do you sit on the floor? I know you didn't expect to see me, but there's no need to make it so obvious.'

He led the way upstairs, explaining that the top floor was all he occupied. She wasn't really interested in his eccentricities. She came into the big third-storey living-room with the smile still fixed immovably on her lips, as if she'd borrowed it and was afraid it might break. She looked about her, but nothing was registering. There was something she had to get through first. Like a first-time skier, she wasn't prepared to run the risk of being distracted.

She wore a light coat. She unbuttoned it, throwing back her head so that her hair danced shiningly. She said, too gaily, 'I've taken your advice.'

He stared. 'My advice?'

'You're like all the rest. You scatter advice like confetti because you don't have to sweep up the mess afterwards. Hey! That's quite good, isn't it? Don't worry. I forgive you. In your car, the other night. After "The Reluctant Virgin". Remember?'

He remembered with an effort. 'You're leaving home.'

'Not leaving. Left.'

He made a desperate attempt to tune in on the same wavelength, helping her off with her coat.

She rattled on as if a sluice had been opened. 'What a strange place to live. Not just this house, though staying on the top floor's a bit like living in a sort of fortress. I've never

145

really been in this part of London before. You don't think of people actually living here. I like your pictures. All except that one, anyway.' She wrinkled her nose at the Bacon, still taking care not to dislodge her borrowed smile. 'Not because it's bad. Because it's too good. It's just the way people are, isn't it?'

He was still trying to keep up with her. 'Is it?'

'Well, some are good and some are bad and most are a bit of both, but whatever mixture they are, they're stuck with it. Sentenced to life for things they never did. No escape until they die but never a moment's rest from trying. Isn't that what the artist's trying to say?'

He said, 'I don't know. Perhaps.' He was half astonished that she should be so close to his own view, half appalled that she'd arrived there so soon. He made an effort to redirect his thoughts. 'What's brought you slumming?'

She bounced down on the sofa with a flash of long legs, a glint of aureate hair. 'I like the music, but that's sad too, isn't it? Listen, that's *Lieber Augustin*, but it's just like your picture. It's had something uncomfortable done to it.'

She sang, '*Ach, du lieber Augustin, Augustin, Augustin; Ach, du lieber Augustin, alles ist hin.*' Then she said, 'I told you.'

'Told me what?'

'Why I'm here. I've left them. Walked out. For good. At least, I won't go back to live there.'

He said, 'Does this call for a drink, perhaps? Where are you going to live?'

She said, 'Juice is a trip, man! A down trip! Dubonnet, if you have it.'

'With lemon? You still haven't answered the question.' He went out to the kitchen to slice lemon. He called out, 'Keep talking. I can hear.'

She said, 'Here.'

'That's what I said.'

'You don't understand. I mean, here. With you.'

He came back, fast. 'I hope I still don't understand.'

She was standing. She looked calm, determined. 'You do.

146

You understand very well.' The smile had fallen off. Her eyes showed something he didn't want to look at.

After a moment's awkwardness he went back to the kitchen. Very matter-of-factly he said, 'It's out of the question. You know it, Patti.'

She followed. 'I don't. Do you remember something else I told you?'

'Quite a lot of things. Which one is this?'

'That I'd give, not trade. No price tags.'

He gave her the drink, trying to think fast enough. 'You also said it wasn't much to give. I think you undervalue it.'

' "An ill-favoured thing, sir, but mine own." No one else has had the offer.'

He put a hand on her shoulder, pushing her gently before him back to the living-room. Thin ice cracked ominously on every side. He said, 'Which I shall take as the greatest compliment ever paid me.'

Sharply, she said, 'Stop it! You're being priggish and patronizing again.' Her smile had half-returned, but the muscles beneath the soft skin were taut, the eyes wary against hurt.

He thought agonizedly: If it be possible, let this cup pass from me. He said, 'Patti, whatever became of the generation gap?'

She said, 'I jumped across. So could you.'

He said, 'Not me. For me it would be strictly a down trip,' but she had him on the run because he was so desperately afraid of wounding her.

She pressed her advantage instinctively, standing close, her head tilted so that her eyes locked with his. She said, quietly, 'I'm offering myself, Jagger. Count ten before you refuse. Count a billion.'

The Schoenberg had reached the transcendental fourth movement. The soprano voice sang *Ich fühle Luft von anderen Planeten*. His mind was paralysed. There was nothing to say that wouldn't be the wrong thing.

Patti put down her drink. She came up against him. He

147

could smell her scent, innocent as orchard blossom. She put both hands on his shoulders. She held up her mouth. Someone kissed her while he watched helplessly. Her eyes closed.

When she took her mouth away she stumbled dizzily, clutching at him for support. Her voice thick, dazed, she said, 'Lie to me if you have to, Jagger, but don't lie to yourself.' A part of him stood aside, watching. It said maliciously: Five minutes more and you're cooked.

Feeling as absurd as if he'd been cornered by a Pekinese, he said, 'Patti, wait!' She shook her head like an obstinate child, her eyes still closed. She tightened her arms. His unsympathetic *alter ego*, brutally amused, said: Go on. Tell her she's only a kid.

Then she opened her eyes suddenly, smiled and said, 'Poor old Jagger! Did I frighten you? Don't worry. Now I know, I can wait. For a bit, anyway.' She let him go. She said, 'I want to look round, get used to things. Oh, your record! It's still turning. Hadn't you better stop it?' She went into the kitchen, happy as a house-hunting newly-wed.

He took off the record and switched over to the radio, desperate for something to fill the silence. How was he going to tell her? The last bars of a banal love song made a tasteless joke of what had happened. A voice fizzing with spurious excitement said, 'How about *that*, pop pickers? And now, a break for the news.'

The news was Geneva, all the way. The British Foreign Secretary, blandly offering his widow's mite, had said the British delegation would do everything in its power to bring about a lowering of tension and an end to the arms race. The Secretary-General of the United Nations, due to open the conference, had given a message to member nations. He begged them to do everything in their power to reduce world tension and end the arms race. He sounded sad, Jagger thought, perhaps because the brief rôle he would play in Geneva in two days' time would have all the impact of Miss World opening a sale of work.

The head of the American delegation was hopeful, but. The

Russian Foreign Minister was optimistic, but. The B.B.C.'s diplomatic correspondent was optimistic, no buts. He hadn't the same sources of information. Patti turned off the radio. She sat next to him, very close. Retreating down the sofa like a nervous-spinster, he wondered what to say that wouldn't hurt.

From the wall his Bacon jeered. He thought of the other Bacon, the one the Master was so fond of quoting. 'He that hath wife and child hath given hostages to fortune.' It applied equally, so far as he was concerned, to would-be mistresses.

She said, nostalgically, 'Oh, Geneva! I told you I went to school there, didn't I? The happiest days *et cetera*. Until now.' She squeezed his arm. 'It's one of the best times, you know, October. Lamplight, lovely old streets and marvellous little places to sit and drink wine. The Bourg-de-Four, flowers round the fountain, lights in the water.'

She sighed into a long silence while he thought his own cowardly thoughts.

After a while she said, 'If they made this agreement it would be history, wouldn't it? Disarmament! It doesn't even sound real, as if it had been banned from the dictionaries.'

He had to start somewhere, though he couldn't bring himself to make the first blow the *coup de grâce*. Without thinking, he said, 'There won't be any agreement. Or at least, if there is, it won't mean anything.'

She looked puzzled. 'Oh! But they say——'

Previous thoughts came back into his mind with a rush. 'You want to see history made, an end and a beginning? Why bother with Geneva? It's all happening on your doorstep.' Bitterness at his doubly intolerable position overflowed into his voice.

She stared. 'What do you mean?'

Partly to postpone something else, partly because he couldn't help himself, he found himself telling her about the past two weeks.

At the end she said, 'There you are! Schramme and Jack

Tinn! What did I say? But what exactly is the Tinn Man doing?'

He said, 'I only know what I've told you. And I shouldn't have told you even that.'

'Why don't you ask him?'

'Ask him? Haven't you heard of the Official Secrets Act? Don't you know what they can do with people who ask awkward questions?'

'I don't suppose I do. But neither does Jack. If you'd met him, you'd understand. Why don't you go down to Leather-head?'

'I am, tomorrow.'

'Then you'll see. But could it really be just Jack? One man?'

'Apparently.'

She made an impatient noise. 'You've been finding out the wrong things. And for the wrong people. Does it matter what Ralph Schramme does? It's Jack who's the important one.'

He thought: You put the ferret down where they've gone in, not where they'll come out.

She said, 'Would you like me to find out?'

'Find out what?'

She kissed him, lightly, before he could escape. 'I love you, but you're being just a tiny bit thick. I told you once. I could make Jack jump through hoops.'

He thought grimly: I believe you! After all, you nearly did me! He said, 'He's not my business. Schramme is.'

She squeezed his arm. 'That was before this evening. I'm your business now.'

He felt his thoughts must show in his face, his eyes, his voice. Hating himself had ceased to be a hobby and become a full-time occupation.

Suddenly he was alarmed. He must have been insane even to have mentioned it. It was all of a piece with a disastrous evening. He said, 'Look, Patti. This is big. Bigger than you could possibly imagine.'

She gripped his hands. 'Big things need big measures. Big! Big! You have to do something and this is something worth doing, isn't it?'

She read his silence with disconcerting accuracy. 'I shan't talk. I want to help.'

That was what he wanted least. He said, 'No! Forget it. It's all out of our hands.'

'The hell it is,' she said indignantly. 'Anything's better than nothing. Isn't that your great philosophy? Don't let things happen, make them?'

He felt trapped, helpless, like a fly caught on wet paint. He said, 'Please! Please forget it.'

She was still holding his hands. She shook them fiercely. 'There must be something! Bloody hell! You can't let one man do this to the world! *My* world! That's the trouble with your generation.' She'd forgotten her earlier attempt to equate their years. 'You've had half your lives. We're only just starting. You think we've accepted things the way they are? Just because we don't shout all the time? It's there!' She rapped her forehead, so hard that white marks appeared and reddened before fading. 'We've learned to live with it, but sometimes I think that's the wickedest thing of all. Now there'll be something else, something worse, and all you can say is stay out.'

Her face brimmed over with the strength of her feeling. 'If one man could destroy the world, and you knew, would you stay out? Or would you——'

'What?' he interrupted starkly. 'Kill him?'

It stopped her. She was too honest to accept the idea without thought, and the thought repelled. But she was also too honest to give up. She said, 'No. I don't know. There *must* be something. The government——'

'Is sponsoring it.'

'The newspapers, then.'

'Official Secrets Act. You'd be in jail before you could turn round.'

Her eyes glittered with angry frustration. 'He's the one

who should be in jail! Jack Tinn! No, that's not fair. You don't know him. He's a baby with brains. In need of care and attention.' Her anger changed to a kind of exasperation, then her eyes widened. 'Care and attention! The United Nations! Don't look like that, you silly bloody man! What's the U.N. for?'

'Patti!' he said. 'Patti! Listen!'

'No! You listen! I went to school with his daughter. The Secretary-General's daughter. He's going to Geneva the day after tomorrow and she's going with him. Now do you see? I could see her. I could tell her, and she would tell him. At least that would be *something*. Anything's better than nothing.'

She jumped up, hair flying, eyes alight. 'Come on,' she said, 'We've got things to do.'

He still sat there. This was the classical confrontation—youth and 'Why not?' versus disillusion and 'Because——!' with all its maddeningly, crushingly spelled-out reasons.

The light drained from her face. Her outstretched hands dropped limply to her sides. She said, 'You won't.' It was a statement, not a question.

He said, unthinkingly, the terrible words. 'You don't understand.' She read the rest in his face, far, far more than he had been ready to reveal.

'Yes, I do,' she said eventually. 'Oh yes, I do, now.' He sat as motionless as she stood, neither of them able to do or say one more thing that would change matters in any way except for the worse. The telephone rang like a tocsin.

It was by her side. Automatically, she reached out and picked it up. She said, 'Yes?'

Her face changed again as she listened. She held it out. 'It's for you.' Her voice sounded anaesthetized.

He recognized the voice on the phone at once. It was Myra's, soft, intimate and at the same time coldly dangerous, like Chaucer's smyler with the knyf. She said, 'Mr Jagger? Michael. It's Myra Pargeter. I want to see you. The sooner the better. It's important.'

Behind him he heard Patti say in a voice she struggled to control, 'Goodbye, Jagger. You were right. You're too old.'

As he turned his head, the door closed behind her. In his hand the telephone was making sharp, interrogative noises.

22. SCHRAMME—*Whose?*

SCHRAMME'S TAXI put him down in the dreary forecourt. The home-going rush was over. A scatter of buses stood in the open bays. Their brightly lighted interiors almost empty, they looked forlorn, like a collection of parties nobody'd come to.

He looked about him uncertainly. The days when he had eaten in station buffets were so far behind that he felt as awkward and inexperienced as a boy in a brothel. He saw the illuminated sign, pushed open the swing door and went in.

A handful of people sat at plastic-topped tables, each as far as possible from the other in a kind of mutual quarantine. Unoccupied tables gleamed wetly or carried a sad debris of soiled plates and abandoned wrappings.

He walked straight through into the station concourse and waited a minute or so to make sure he wasn't being followed. Satisfied, he went back in and bought a cup of tea he had no intention of drinking. He took a corner table and waited.

Not long afterwards a man came in by the station entrance and bought coffee. He looked around, came across to Schramme and said, 'Mind if I sit here?'

Schramme said nothing, staring briefly before nodding. The man sat. He said quietly, 'What's on your mind, Mr Schramme?'

He had a soft American accent, a thin, anonymous face and eyes crinkled as if he'd spent all his life staring at bright lights. He was dressed in an American idea of the English style, but the cut of his suit, the lie of his shirt collar, the knot of his tie were all small betrayals.

Schramme said, 'It would help if you did not use my name, even here. I presume this tomfoolery is necessary?' He knew it was, but he had a part to play.

The other sipped coffee, grimaced and pushed it away. He said, 'It is. It didn't seem like a good idea to have you come to the embassy.'

Schramme pretended to sigh, the sigh of a man in deep trouble. He let his face muscles limber up on a mixture of embarrassment, reluctance, resignation and a carefully measured touch of fear. He said, 'Very well. As I explained to the First Secretary, I am prepared to put my trust in your country's understanding and magnanimity.'

The other said meaningly, 'Hope's a great thing. You understand?'

With a suitable pause, Schramme said slowly, 'I understand.'

The man with the crinkly eyes said, 'Okay. Shoot.'

Schramme looked at the other's elaborate watch, fully displayed as he propped the side of his face on his left hand. He smiled faintly. He said, 'Very well, if your recorder's switched on.'

Without so much as a blink the American eased the cuff of his shirt down the wrist so that the watch was a little more fully exposed. He said, 'It is. Please tell your story.'

Schramme told his story while the tea and the coffee grew cold. He told it well and left out nothing. Virtually nothing.

Afterwards they sat in what might have passed for companionable silence, like a pair of chess players. A coloured girl was serving two naval ratings with sausages and chips. From the concourse loudspeakers made cryptic statements in the language which is understood, if at all, only by other station announcers.

The American stirred and looked at Schramme. 'All those years.' he said. A Pakistani cleaner cleared tables, pushing a loaded trolley as if he had nowhere to go and all his life to get there.

Schramme said, 'Nine. Nearly ten.'

The Pakistani hovered briefly over their cold and brimming cups, faced with a decision of immense difficulty. They ignored him. He gave up and moved on. An abandoned newspaper fell from his trolley. The American picked it up and went through the motions of reading it. When the Pakistani was out of earshot he said, 'You've never seen them. Never had any direct contact with them.'

'Never. All instructions were passed in the manner I have described. All information was transmitted by dead drop.'

'Cloakrooms, left baggage offices. That kind of thing.'

'Exactly.'

'You never attempted to find out who was collecting?'

Schramme hesitated. The American turned a page of his paper. The sailors emptied a bottle of tomato ketchup, turning their plates into surgical operations. Schramme sensed that the answer to the last question was important, but he didn't know in which way. He decided on the truth. 'Once. In the early days. The lobby of the Regent Palace Hotel. I had to leave a cloakroom ticket in an envelope. I thought I could not be seen but no one turned up to collect. I received a telephone call warning me against such tricks.'

'You never tried again.'

'Never,' Schramme said flatly.

'And this voice? Ida's voice?'

Schramme shrugged. 'A woman's voice. Devoid of expression, devoid of accent. All routine information was passed through a recording device, as I have explained.'

The other had apparently found something of particular interest in his paper. He turned sideways to Schramme to get the fullest light on the page, the wrist with the watch microphone prominent. 'Then why should you think this organization is Russian? Or Russian controlled?'

Schramme tapped his cup of cold tea gently with the nail of his forefinger. The surface of the liquid broke briefly into concentric circles of light. He permitted himself to look surprised at the question. 'Surely that is obvious?'

'Why?'

'Only the Russians could have been aware of my background. Only the Russians could want the kind of information I have—was compelled to supply. Unless——' Schramme broke off, letting his face generate a sour smile.

'Yes?'

'Unless you wish to believe that Ida is American. Or that the British are spying on themselves.'

The American began to fold his newspaper with meticulous care. He was equally careful not to speak until he had finished. The sound of paper being crumpled can sound like a major forest fire through a sensitive microphone. He said, 'But in fact, most of this is surmise?'

'What I think may be surmise. What I have been doing is not.'

'And now the British are on to you.'

'If they are not, it is only a matter of time. This man Jagger is a British security agent. He is also highly intelligent.'

'Surmise again.'

'I think not.'

The other appeared to look at his watch. 'You realize decisions of this kind don't rest with me?'

'Of course.'

'And that things may take a little time?'

'Naturally.'

The American stood up, looking casually about him. 'We take a lot of trouble to stay friendly with the British.'

Schramme said, 'I came to you voluntarily. Surely that is worth something?'

'After nine years? Nine years of betraying the country that took you in. You say you were blackmailed. You could have gone to the British then in the same way you've come to us now.'

Schramme tried playing an ace. 'Perhaps it would be wiser, even at this stage.'

The other dropped his paper. He stooped to pick it up, his face close to Schramme's. He said. 'I wouldn't advise it. Not now. No promises, but I might be able to work something.

Maybe even U.S. citizenship, if that's what you want and you play your hand the way you're told.'

Schramme's face was impassive, the smile hidden deep inside. He had already played his hand. He had a feeling it was going to prove a winner.

The American said, 'You have a virus infection. Something slight. Stay home a couple of days. We'll contact you. Give me a few minutes and leave by the other door.'

He left.

Five minutes later Schramme found a taxi and went home.

In the refreshment room the Pakistani slow-coached his trolley round to the vacated table. His face expressionless, he picked up the untouched coffee and tea and tipped them into the slops bowl. He had long since given up trying to understand Westerners.

23. MYRA—*No one's*

MYRA WAS WAITING for him in her look-but-don't-touch drawing-room. In spite of her strained face and the dark smudges under her eyes she immediately put on a touch-but-don't-look act, practising a smile that flickered on and off like a faulty light bulb.

Patting the settee for him to sit next to her she said, 'It may come as a surprise, but I have a certain feeling of responsibility towards my daughter.'

He said, 'Of course. What could be more natural?'

'She was there, wasn't she? She answered the phone.'

'I didn't invite her. She left immediately after you rang. Did she come home?'

Myra shrugged, pulling a face. 'How would I know? One's children come and go. It's normal, isn't it?'

She took a cigarette from a Wedgwood box. She pointed at a silver table lighter. He flicked flame from it. She held his hand unnecessarily while she lit her cigarette. He saw through her smooth porcelain-thin sociability. Tightly controlled rage showed in her eyes. He knew instinctively that it was directed at someone else. She said, 'I won't ask you what Patti was doing.'

He said, 'Good.' He disliked elaborate and devious conversational manœuvres.

Her look switched from his mouth to his eyes. 'My God!' she said wonderingly. 'I do believe you're a bit of a prig.' He thought wryly that the idea of his priggishness must be hereditary on the distaff side of the Pargeter family.

'Or you have an old-fashioned sense of honour,' she went on. 'I hope it won't complicate our conversation.'

He said politely, 'I hope not.'

She drew hard on her cigarette, so that it burned like a fuse, and detonated a small, carefully calculated explosion of feeling. 'Christ!' she said. 'You're determined not to help, aren't you? I know about you. That's why I wanted to see you.'

He said, 'Well, here I am.'

She took a deep breath, rearranging her ruffled poise like a swan trying to preen in a high wind. 'What do you propose to do? Follow me around? Hide under the bed with a camera and notebook?'

He realized then. Everyone was using him. But everyone! It had begun with the Master and spread. Sir Ben had aimed him at Schramme and pulled the trigger. Schramme had deflected the shot towards Myra. Now it was ricocheting wildly.

She said, 'I don't care, you know. I'd give him a good run for his money.'

He said, 'Who? Your husband? Or Schramme?'

Viciousness curled the edges of her composure like a flame scorching paper. 'Either! Or both!'

He said, 'You don't have to tell me, you know,' hoping she would ignore the caution.

She did. She said, 'Why is it always the men who're most afraid of scandal these days? It used to be the woman's reputation that had to be protected at all costs. Is this what they mean by equality of the sexes?'

'Schramme's walked out on you?' It had to be that, to account for this smouldering, barely damped-down anger.

'Run, ducky! Run!'

She reached across him to crush out her cigarette. It brought her much closer. He knew what kind of bargain she'd consider making for anything she thought worth the price. She must be almost twenty years younger than Sir Ben, but the only thing he wanted from her was information.

She was looking at him with a curious, half-regretful smile. She said, 'Michael dear, you can't fool me. You're a representative of that almost extinct species, the honourable man.'

He said, 'I'm sorry if I disappoint you.'

She chose not to answer. Instead she said, 'I could tell you a lot about Ralph Schramme.' The sparkle of rage flared in her eyes again, bright and hard as diamonds.

He said, 'What makes you think I want to know?'

She ignored him. 'The man's a peasant. Savile Row suits. Jermyn Street shirts. Shoes from St James's and ties from the Burlington Arcade, but underneath it all—a peasant. He's saved me trouble. I'd become bored.'

He was flicking the lighter on and off.

After a while she said, 'You learn a lot you're not meant to know when you've slept with a man a few years. He has secrets, and some of them keep him awake at night. I've seen it in his eyes. And in his face, when he thought I was asleep.'

She turned to face him. 'Let's stop playing games. He may think you're just a private detective, but I doubt it. And Ben's as cryptic as a comic strip. You're after something a bit more important than evidence for divorce proceedings, even if you won't admit it. Well, so am I, now.'

She was looking drawn, bitter, some of her composure gone. 'Ralph and I began our affair in Rome. You've seen those cats, among the ruins? Fighting for scraps? I've often thought: I'm a Roman cat, ducky. Fighting for scraps in the ruins. Guess what ruins!' Her voice had become ugly, her fingers attacking each other until the knuckles showed white. 'Ben and Ralph are cats too; but sleek, well-fed cats. Ben was neutered years ago. Age and success. Ralph's an alley cat who's struck lucky. Nothing neutered about him and he'd claw if he was cornered. I want to see it. I want to see his fur fly. Do I disgust you? Shall I go on?'

She didn't wait, or didn't want to wait, for his answer. 'Have you ever thought how much information he must get from all those interviews? He says some of them'll say anything when they're rattled.'

'What are you suggesting?'

She wouldn't face him now, knowing she'd exposed an aspect of herself that wasn't attractive. 'I don't know. Blackmail? Secrets to sell? You tell me. It's your business, isn't it? He's scared. He rang me after you'd been to see him. He wouldn't even meet. Finished! Now! This minute! I don't know what you did, but you put the fear of God in him, ducky.'

Jagger said, 'If I did, he kept it a very closely guarded secret.'

'Not from me. I call it sixth sense. He was scared! I like that!'

He thought: Hell hath no fury. . . . He said, 'What exactly do you have in mind?'

She stopped twisting her fingers together. 'He's hiding something.' In the moment that she said it, vague thoughts at the back of Jagger's mind coalesced into something solid, as if she had pulled a verbal switch. He knew what it was that had been tickling his subconscious ever since his visit to Schramme.

She was saying, 'I know what you're thinking. I've known for a long time that he was up to something, but so long as he—amused me, it didn't seem to matter. Everybody's up to something these days, aren't they? Exploit or be exploited. The survival of the lousiest. Well, he's built to last but I'm damned if I'll let him.'

She picked up her handbag. It was crocodile. It seemed

entirely appropriate. She snapped it open, fished around and found a latch-key.

She said, 'The very sign and symbol of *le cinq à sept*! I shan't be needing it any more, shall I? It's his. The key to his offices in Charles Street.'

She slipped it into his breast pocket with a swift, unpreventable movement. She put a hand on his arm to stop him from retrieving it.

'We used to meet there sometimes. But you'd probably find it more useful when he was out. Keep it. Think it over. After all—' there was a tincture of bitterness in her tone— 'it's free of any obligation.'

She took away her restraining hand. She said, some of the life seeping from her voice, 'I expect you'll want to go now. There's really nothing much to keep you, is there?' She reached for another cigarette and lit it herself.

She said, 'Show yourself out, ducky, unless you want to ring for the housekeeper. I'm feeling frail. And watch out for Patti. She's fallen for you. Let her down lightly. She's only a baby.'

He winced. It was salt in a wound Myra knew nothing of.

24. D.C.I.—*Who?*

HEAD OF PLANS said, 'Come!' as soon as he heard the knock on the door. He went on staring out of his window to where death flamed gorgeously through the encircling woodlands. He said dreamily, 'This time last year, Charlie, I was on a fishing trip in Wisconsin. Lake Onapotasi, you wouldn't find it on a map. I caught ten nights of deep, dreamless sleep, a slight chill and some of the biggest lake trout you've never seen. They had the first big frost the day we set back.' He watched a small, slow flight of leaves settle like red and orange birds at the edge of the nearest parking lot, seeming to die at the very instant that they passed from bright afternoon sunshine into deep blue shade. He sighed.

Osgood said, 'The fishing in London is pretty good this fall. Or if not good, unusual. They caught the screwiest fish you ever heard of.'

Head of Plans started to turn, stopped, put his arm through Osgood's and drew him to the window. 'Before we talk about your fish, join me in snapping up an unconsidered but very worthwhile trifle. That ash-blonde from Research would handle her car better if she pushed it around by hand, but watching her get those long legs in or out——!' They watched her get them in with quiet pleasure. She over-revved her engine and backed into the car behind.

Both men winced. Osgood said, 'Her bumpers have more dimples than——'

Head of Plans said, 'Married men shouldn't know how many dimples she has in her bumpers. What kind of a fish?' He waved Osgood to a seat and took his own. He put one thumb over the bowl of his empty pipe and blew down the stem to produce a series of thin screams.

Interestedly, Osgood said, 'You should be able to play some kind of a tune by tonguing and varying the thumb pressure.'

Head of Plans tried, failed ingloriously and said, 'Let's get back to the fishing.'

Osgood said, 'You remember saying Schramme would probably talk if the British picked him up?'

Head of Plans shot forward in his seat as if his office were a Mustang and the ash-blonde had just stood on its brakes with both feet. He said, 'Oh no! Why can't I just sit and think about Lake Onapotasi? They picked him up? When? Does the D.C.I. know?'

Osgood said, 'They didn't do a thing. He gave himself up, less than an hour ago.'

'*Gave* himself up?'

Osgood smiled, almost demurely. He timed his pause nicely and added, 'To us.'

Head of Plans carefully laid down his pipe. He put his hands together and played a silent game of pat-a-cake, his head bowed religiously. He stopped, looked up and repeated, 'To us,' as if making sure he'd heard properly. Osgood nodded.

Head of Plans drew a deep breath and made gimme signs with the fingers of both hands. 'Okay! Tell!'

Osgood summarized the report just in from London office. At the end, Head of Plans said, 'The *Russians*! He said for the Russians?'

'That's what he said. The whole thing was recorded. We'll have the tape in the overnight bag. Incidentally, Schramme knew he was being taped.'

'You think he really believed it? About the Russians?'

Osgood said mildly, 'Look, we use wrist-watch tape mikes. They haven't given us portable mind-readers yet. If we brought him over here, now——'

'Which is what he wants.'

'That's what he wants. He was blackmailed into industrial spying for the Russians, so he thinks. He's always wanted to break away, but he couldn't see how. Now he's sure the British are on to him, through this man Jagger. He wants out fast and he'll play any game we like in return for admission to the U.S.'

'Which is how it all began, way back.'

'That's right. He went to our embassy in London about the possibility of immigration. Some years ago. I forget how many. He was already in his fancy consultancy business, he told us what we found out were lies about his European background and London office saw he was a natural for us. The technical intelligence operation was just getting off the ground at that time. Anyway, they put the bite on him and he had to co-operate. He could have been deported by the British for a list of false statements as long as your arm. He decided to play. He's been playing ever since.'

'But he thinks he's been working for the opposition.'

'We didn't identify ourselves to him one way or the other. There's been no direct contact from that day to this, just telephone and dead drop. He even confessed he once tried to spy on a pick-up, back at the beginning, but nobody turned up. That's true and it's why I think it's safe to assume the rest of his story's true, too.'

Head of Plans was screwing his mouth cruelly between thumb and forefinger. 'Well, if that isn't the goddammest thing! It opens up one heck of a lot of possibilities, whichever way you play it. He'll have to be pulled out fast, before the British take him. We don't want another Bohm.'

Osgood winced very slightly. Head of Plans said, 'Charlie, your conscience is showing. Come on. Let's go talk to the chief.'

The Director was on the phone. He glanced in their direction and jerked his head to signal them in. He said into the phone, 'The cooing of doves? Maybe, allowing for the Russian accent. It's more likely they've been thinking over the stuff we fed them about the Wuyuan tests. If their spy satellite pictures were as good as ours they'll show up that burn-off like the Fourth of July.'

He put his hand over the receiver and said, 'White House. The Russians want——' He hadn't time to finish. He took his hand away and said into the phone, 'You bet we will. We'll have the place wired for pin drops, so mind your table manners. Okay. Goodbye.'

He replaced the telephone. He said, 'Henry! Charlie! Take a seat. Well, it's not over yet, after all.'

Head of Plans stretched out his long frame. He said, 'Who was it? Our good friend, the President's security adviser?'

The Director said, 'Right! I thought we'd seen the last of those clandestine meetings at the Statler-Hilton. It seems I was wrong. One of the Amtorg* people met a man from State last night. Accidentally, of course! He mentioned that our old friend Gregoriev had allowed as how he'd admire to meet a real live Presidential security adviser in private for once, so's they could talk about this and that. The dinner party's tonight.'

*The Soviet Union's export-import centre in America and also a cover for Russian intelligence operations.

164

Head of Plans said, 'The Chinese gambit paid off, huh?'

'It looks like it.' The Director turned to Osgood. 'Charlie, we slipped your news about the successful rocket motor test at Wuyuan to a certain gentleman who believes in Russo-American co-operation and proves it by working for both sides. At least, the Russians think he does. What we give him, he gives them and we've been feeding him a lot of worrying news about the Chinese of late. Moscow's just worked out that Peking's a year ahead of forecast in developing its I.B.M. system. It's made the Kremlin think twice about discontinuing private discussions on matters of mutual interest.'

The Director picked up his paper-knife and pointed with it. 'That's my side. What's your bad news?'

Head of Plans grinned crookedly. 'That's always a safe bet. Nobody in this place ever seems to drop in just to tell you things are great. Burst your bombshell, Charlie.'

Osgood told his story while Head of Plans enjoyed watching the Director's changes of expression. The Director repeated most of the questions Osgood had been asked already. At the end he said, 'Well, we'll just have to wait until the full report and that tape arrive. Then we'll talk again. Thanks anyway, Charlie. Henry, can you spare another couple of minutes?'

When Osgood had gone, Head of Plans said, 'About that private dinner party. The Geneva conference opens in two days' time. What does Moscow expect between now and then? Miracles?'

The Director said, 'Are you suggesting they don't know how to stall for time? Once the Secretary-General's opened that conference it could take a month just to iron out points of procedure if time is all we need. But Schramme is another thing entirely.'

Head of Plans said, 'Are you thinking what I'm thinking?'

'That's something I'm never too sure of.'

Thoughtfully, Henry said, 'I think on balance we should invite Schramme Stateside. But the alternative is mighty tempting.'

The Director nodded. 'It was the alternative I was thinking

about. It could solve a lot of problems. It looks to me as i Osgood's British operations are crumbling. If we could dump the whole thing on the K.G.B.'s doorstep when we pulled out we'd be settling a few old scores with the Department o Disinformation and Decomposition.'

Henry said, 'To do the thing properly we'd have to give the British Schramme.'

'Complete with his confession.'

'That tape could take care of the confession.'

'It could, so long as Schramme didn't change his story.'

'What I had in mind would be to make it difficult for him to change his story.'

'Dead men—'

'—tell whatever tale suits best. At the worst it'd throw the British into a state of confusion. At best they'd be off our backs.'

'Which is what I'd prefer,' the Director said. 'If we have to have allies, they're the ones I choose, Henry.' He wa trying to balance the heavy-handled paper-knife on hi finger-tip by the point. 'On the "Us" list, not the "Them". The knife toppled. He caught it dexterously.

Head of Plans said, 'Balancing acts can sometimes be dangerous, but on balance I agree.'

The Director said, 'I have two alternative views abou Schramme. The first is that he's a smart operator.'

'And the second,' Head of Plans finished, 'is that he's a very smart operator. Recognizing the time to get out is smart Being smart by pretending to be foolish would be very smart Why don't you try balancing that thing on your nose?'

The Director said, 'What do you take me for? A per forming seal?'

'That,' Head of Plans said, discovering a loose button or his jacket, 'is a view I leave to members of the general publi and congressmen. Incidentally, what's the news from th Hill?'

'The senator you have in mind,' the Director said, 'ha read the confidential position paper the President had prepared for him. It won't stop him. Some time soon he'll announce he's advancing the date for the commencement of hearings. He figures the Geneva conference will abort, so he plans to take the gloves off.'

He drummed his fingers on the table, accelerating the rhythm to end with an angry thump. 'Damn it, Henry!' His restraint broke briefly. 'I keep my politics to myself but I don't have to take party sides to see that the President's right in this one. Nuclear superiority doesn't mean a thing when you're talking about the U.S. and the U.S.S.R. It doesn't matter a dime's worth which has the more megatonnage, the more missiles, warheads or diversionary gadgets when you're dealing with supersaturation. The plain fact is that each of us is capable of destroying the other several times over. Of taking all that he can put into a first strike and still destroying him. Parity or no parity, what we have is stalemate. Arms limitation is the only thing that makes sense. We know it. The Russians know it. Only people like the senator and his friends can't see it. Or won't. He wants to go on spending dollars by the billion to save what he calls the American way of life and all the time the American way of life is being eaten away at the heart because we're spending money on overkill that should be spent on houses and jobs and schools. We're like a man inside a suit of armour, dirty, lousy and in a fair way to dying of suffocation, but we won't so much as unscrew a bolt in case we're caught with our goddamed steel pants down.'

He pounded a fist on his desk top. 'The senator will quote Washington, Lincoln, Stephen Decatur, Teddy Roosevelt and Barbara Frietchie, and all the time he'll be plugging away at the fact that we've reduced our nuclear stockpile by forty per cent of total megatonnage while the Russians have gone on increasing theirs.'

'Even though the reduction was approved by Eisenhower,' Head of Plans said softly. 'On the recommendation of the Joint Chiefs of Staff. Initiated by Kennedy and backed up as good military common sense ever since. And even though we still have enough striking power to wipe out every man, woman and child on the face of the planet.'

'So,' the Director said even more softly, 'I want arms limitation. It doesn't mean I have to like the President or his party just because he wants it too. I want a cautious, fool-proof, fail-safe accommodation with the Russians. I want it as Director of Central Intelligence, as a private citizen, as a man who wants a future for his kids and as a democratic American. With a small "d"!'

Head of Plans was still playing with his loose button. Almost idly, he said, 'Which leads up to what in particular?'

'Which leads up to this. I hold two and a half billion lives to be more important than any one, and don't give me the quotation about the sparrows, or the very hairs of our heads being numbered. The human race is more important than any one man, British, or Russian, or American.'

Head of Plans gave his button a final careless twist. It came off in his hand, slipped through his fingers and rolled out of sight. He went down on his hands and knees.

The Director said, 'Why would any sane man take on this job? Or have I begged the question?'

Head of Plans found his button and straightened up, a little red in the face. He said, 'You could take a vacation. Wisconsin's great at this time of year and you don't necessarily have to fish. No, I guess you couldn't, at that.' He stood there looking at the Director.

The other man's eyes were bleak, introspective. He said, 'Taking a man's life to buy time for the rest. I guess you could make out a moral argument against it.'

Head of Plans said, 'There was one before, remember? He was supposed to die to save us all, but up to now nobody knows whether it worked. Who's your candidate for cruci-fixion?'

The Director said, 'An innocent man, Henry, like as not.'

Head of Plans flipped and caught his button, spinning it like a gambler with a lucky silver dollar. He said, 'Isn't that the primary qualification?'

168

25. TINN—*Himself*

THE HELIPORT projected into the river like a concrete T, small and unspectacular. The tide was at full ebb. Glistening banks of mud, littered with flotsam, exposed themselves to the early autumn chill, a parade ground for strutting gulls. Across the sluggish flow Fulham power station unfolded thick, steamy billows that merged into the morning haze. A tomcat odour of coal gas warred with the rank stench of ooze.

The helicopter squatted at the centre of the damp pier like a goggle-eyed bug on a lily pad. Everything was ready. The safety-man saw them stowed either side of the pilot. The hatch closed with a soft thump. The engine fired, drowning the chug of a barge-toting tug as it surged downstream, its bow wave glistening in the pale sunlight like the wings of a grubby angel.

They were airborne almost at once, the clatter of the blades rising to a roar as the safety-man waved them away. The pilot eased up the collective and fed power. The machine quivered as it clawed for the lift. Quite quickly, the scruffy horizon began to retreat, as if blown away by the down-draught. A gleam of smoke-soiled sunshine crept through the fishbowl of the cockpit. The grey disc of the flying rotors became a glimmering halo.

Below them the Thames was uncoiling itself like a sluggish serpent, changing from oily brown to shining pewter. All about them the metropolis sprawled like a town-planner's model of how not to.

Sir Ben raised his voice to overcome the teeth-jarring clamour. 'Takes about twenty minutes this way,' he said, 'even though we have to follow the river out of the built-up area.'

The great bend at Barnes was rolling beneath. From Kew Gardens the pagoda poked up among brilliant green and autumn motley like the centre-piece of a Japanese trough garden. Beyond were the West London reservoirs, sliding towards them like cracked, irregularly-shaped pieces of looking-glass peppered and salted with birds.

Soon they were thrashing south-west, the eyots and small-boat reaches of the Thames below, the bracken-covered slopes of the North Downs corrugated to port like crumpled sisal matting. The rattle of finely-chopped air altered in pitch as the pilot increased rotor revs.

Jagger shouted, 'Does Tinn know about me?' but at the first mention of the name Sir Ben twisted round in his seat to peer down at the Vickers factory at Weybridge. Jagger let his question die.

The helicopter changed course, leaning gently into the turn. The green countryside spun across its nose like a revolving stage-set as suburbs dwindled among Mondrian patterns of fields. Ahead, a small town stretched out red and yellow spatters of new, raw brickwork from a dark, ageing nucleus, like a petrified amoeba. A small river, silvery, eel-like, sliced it in two. Sir Ben shouted, pointing. 'A big brick and glass building, just at the end of that service road. Got it? Other stuff to the west of it. We're coming down by those trees.'

The helicopter sank in a steep spiral, rotors screaming. Trees and fields ballooned up like a zoom shot. They hung motionless, forty feet up, then swept foward and down like a swing to settle lightly on the turf. The pilot cut the engine. Jagger unfastened his safety-belt. Outside, a man sauntered towards them.

Sir Ben nodded. 'There's Arnold Parsons. Research and development director. Rough diamond! I'll just introduce you, then I'm away to the Midlands.'

Parsons got in the first word. He said, 'This the security king? How do you qualify? Is there a course?' He was around fifty, with an air of aggressive, unabashed cheerfulness and a habit of twitching his nose jerkily between remarks. He wore a shabby jacket and trousers creased in unorthodox places. A forest of ball-points and pencils sprouted from his breast pocket. One of his shirt buttons was missing.

Sir Ben shot a sideways, slightly malicious glance at Jagger and made introductions. At the finish he said, 'I'm off now, Arnold. You'll take care of Mr Jagger?'

Parsons said, 'I thought it was his job to take care of us.' He laughed noisily and took Jagger's arm. 'Let's get away from that thing before they wind it up. Mustn't lose our heads before we've started.'

They watched the helicopter bear Sir Ben impressively aloft. Parsons said, 'The apotheosis of St Benjamin of Brum. Come on, mister. This way for the guided tour. You have to earn your lunches down here. We're not like those layabouts in London. Have you done any homework on Pargeter, or am I supposed to be wet nurse as well as guide?'

It was impossible to take offence. The man had as much social grace as a drop-out but his obvious lack of ill will took most of the sting out of his manner. For the next two hours they went from building to building, all of them, Jagger noted, enclosed behind a high steel fence. The only entry was through double gates controlled by a guard-house. Visitors were booked in and out.

Although he knew that Pargeter's own research work was probably irrelevant, Jagger soon found himself absorbed. Parsons talked, cheerfully, almost mockingly but with a high degree of intelligibility about everything they saw. He switched from industrial lasers to system control, from data processing to automation without faltering. Beneath his frequently jarring facetiousness flowed a steady current of absorbed interest and dedication.

At the end he said, 'Well, there you are, mister. A personally conducted tour of the ivory tower. You've only skimmed the surface but you've seen all that matters in Pargeter Electromation. We run the think tank. We do the creating. All the rest is like the old joke, nuts, screws, washers and bolts.'

They were coming out through the gate-house. Jagger said, 'And all the secret work's inside this compound?'

'All the work, period!' Parsons pointed at the big, five-storey building they were approaching. 'That's administration, not work. Clerks, typists, paper-pushing. No, let's be fair. The computer section's there, too, and the research library. The rest? So much waste space so far as I'm concerned.'

'But that's where Lusty fell,' Jagger said. 'It must be. The only building with more than one storey.'

Parsons stopped, his nose twitching, his eyes bright and faintly derisory. 'Danger! Brains at Work! That's where Lusty fell. And where everything else happened.'

'Such as?' Jagger prompted.

Parsons said, 'Oh no, mister! Not me! I've been signed up under the Act. I've said all I'm saying. And anyway, you know a lot more than I do.'

Jagger heaped silent invective on the Master. *Where ignorant armies clash by night as on a darkling plain!* Matthew Arnold had been another Oxford man. He said, 'Refresh my memory.'

It didn't work. Parsons grinned and punched Jagger roughly on the shoulder. 'I don't like snoopers, but if ever I have to try, I promise to start with you. Look, mister, we're not secret agents, we're scientists. We're paid to turn up the truth, not hide it. If that isn't what you want, you'll have to look somewhere else.'

Jagger followed him towards the administration building, mulling over the bit about hiding the truth. It didn't surprise him. He said, 'If that's the end of the tour, haven't you left something out?'

Parsons stopped. 'A million things. Which in particular?'

'Tinn. I'd like to meet him.'

Parsons said, 'Tinn? Why not? You're the boss.' They turned the corner of the administration block. Several cars were parked between V.I.P. markings. Among them were a big blue Chevrolet and a white MG sports. Parsons was looking at the white car.

He said, 'Hello! An unexpected visitor,' but nothing more. They went up the steps. Parsons nodded callously to one side. 'That's where Lusty bounced. I expect you know.' He pushed through a door, characteristically letting it swing back in Jagger's face. They took a lift to the top floor, stepping out in a long, window-lined corridor with a row of glossy doors painted in a variety of primary colours. The last one was blue. Parsons stopped, raising his hand to knock. Jagger noticed the door was fitted with a very special lock.

Parsons still hadn't knocked, though his arm hovered. A voice was clearly audible from the other side. There was no possibility that it belonged to Dr Jack Tinn. Jagger recognized it at once. Parsons opened the door.

Patti, jacketed, booted and all but spurred, turned her golden head, throwing the switch on a blinding smile before she saw Jagger. The smile faltered like a light in a power failure. It came back almost instantly as she cut in the reserve supply.

She said, 'Hello, Arnold. I came to see me old man.'

Parsons said, 'You'd better start flapping your arms, birdie. He left for Stafford, two hours ago.'

She said, 'Oh! Damn!'

Her surprise was as unconvincing as if someone had told her she was pretty.

Parsons said, 'This is Mr Jagger.'

She said, 'We've met,' glancing at him for the time it would take light to travel from head to tail of an under-sized rat. Jagger was looking beyond her, at the other occupant of the small office.

Jack Tinn could have been a very young thirty or a very old ten. He blinked at them through huge, round, steel-framed lenses that turned his eyes into a pair of blobs, like oysters on the shell. He had short, sandy hair and a flat-crowned head that turned through a right angle at the back and gradually became his neck.

His face was pink, the skin more flawless than Patti's. His ears projected like cupped hands. His nose was small and slightly upturned. His wide mouth had cupid's-bow lips that would have gone down well in the thirties, on a girl.

Parsons said to Jagger, 'This is Dr Tinn.' Now his amusement was open, mocking, saying: And what are you going to do about it?

Tinn peered at Jagger. His glasses slipped. He wrinkled his button nose to hold them, prodding them back with the tip of his thumb. The myopic oysters behind his lenses swam incuriously from Jagger to Parsons and back to Patti. Tinn nodded and muttered incoherently. He seemed chastened, as if Patti had been saying something to scold him.

Patti said, 'Bloody hell! I thought he was here for the day. My father, I mean. Well, you'll just have to invite me to lunch. You wouldn't turn me away empty-tummed?' She looked at Tinn. 'We were just finishing, weren't we? We've had a lovely chat.' Under the downpour of her radiant energy Tinn's torpid soul reacted visibly, like a tortoise drawn out of its shell by spring sunshine. Once again he wrinkled his nose in a huge, unconscious grimace, thumbing his glasses back into position. Belatedly reacting to another external stimulus he nodded several times at Jagger and said, 'H-h-how do you do?'

There was something hectic, febrile about Patti. She slid from the top of Tinn's desk, hugged Parsons's arm and said, 'Well, when do we eat?'

Parsons stepped quickly into his rôle of lovable buffoon. He said, 'Don't you come the crown princess with me, my girl. I don't give a tinker's cuss for your old man. Still, I dare say we could give you some bread and cheese if you behave yourself.'

Patti squeezed his arm. 'Oooh, he's *lovely*!' she said. 'Go on, then. Pour me a drink. I'll be down in five minutes.' Once again her eyes skittered across Jagger so quickly that he wasn't sure whether he was meant to notice.

Parsons shoved Jagger out of the small office. When they were in the lift he said, 'Go on. Admit it. He's not what you thought, is he?' He pressed the button for the basement floor.

Jagger smiled. 'Putting it briefly, no.'

Parsons nodded. 'If you'd said anything else I'd have

called you a liar, mister. He's not what anyone thinks. I don't know exactly what he's doing down here. Nobody does, but I know where he came from and he's out on his own, believe me!'

The lift stopped. They stepped out. Parsons held Jagger back, pulling at the sleeve of his jacket. 'We've guests for lunch. A couple of Yanks from Data Corporation of America. We don't talk about Tinn in front of other people.'

Jagger disengaged his sleeve. 'As a matter of interest, how old is he?'

'Twenty-nine, physically, Ninety-nine, scientifically. Nine, behaviour-wise. He's—what was that thing about Hamlet? Can't remember, but Tinn's only daft when the wind's in the wrong direction. Which, mind you, it invariably is when it's a matter of unimportant things like eating, sleeping and knowing what's happening beyond the great, wide world of radiation physics.'

It reminded Jagger of something. 'Where does he live?'

'With us, mister. Me and my missus. He's not fit to be out on his own. Parents dead and no relatives to speak of. My lad's grown up and married. Jack has his room. Not a scrap of trouble, really. Give him his telescope—he's a mad keen amateur astronomer—his stamp collection and his classical records and he'll cause you as much trouble as a caged canary. No security problems there, see? Come on, I'm supposed to be host to these bloody Yanks.'

They went through a door. Parsons said, 'Senior management dining-room. Not bad grub, if you're keen on that sort of thing.'

A recess at one end was fitted out as a bar, mirror-backed and brightly lighted. Two men talked quietly. As he expected, Jagger had met them before. Dobereiner looked round first. He raised a glass and said, 'Hi! The mad scientist himself! How's the boy, Arnold? They told us to help ourselves. We did.' He saw Jagger. He said, 'Well! Small world!'

Simmons, neat and self-effacing as before, rolled his blotting-paper glance over Jagger, absorbing him instantly. In his soft voice he said, 'Michael! Good to see you again.'

Parsons, noisily good-humoured, said, 'Oh, if you buggers have met you can look after each other while I give myself a drink. Help yourself, Jagger. We've everything except unicorn's piss.'

The door behind them opened again and Patti came in. Parson's smile widened, then jammed between gears. She led Jack Tinn behind her, holding his hand as if he were a shambling small boy arriving for a party. She said, 'It didn't seem fair to leave Jack behind. I knew you wouldn't mind.'

For a moment, Parsons lost his grip. Dobereiner stepped in with the smooth aplomb of a bank president. His silver crew-cut, dark suit, dazzling white shirt and mirror-bright shoes made him look the part—the kind of man photographed drinking Chivas Regal or wearing a Rolex hewn from a block of solid gold. He said, looking at Patti while Simmons looked at Tinn, 'Hey! Why did nobody say? Arnold, you dog, you've been holding out on us.'

Parsons made introductions like a nervous newly-wed at her first coffee party. Patti played up beautifully to Dobereiner's sugar-daddy act. Her eyes swept across Jagger briefly, but long enough to say: Try and stop me! She glanced at the table. She said, 'You'll need two more settings. I'll ring.' She did. Parsons got himself between Tinn and Simmons, trying to control an unease that Simmons, at least, had defined. Patti led Tinn to the bar. She said, 'Jack drinks Coke. Would somebody like to pour one?' A waitress came in to set extra places.

Lunch turned out to be a battle of wits. Parsons struggled to keep the conversation on a strictly business plane. Dobereiner was skilful in refusing to respond. Instead he concentrated his rugged charm on Patti, drawing her out, laughing at her feverish, quickfire inconsequence. She seemed determined to suppress every trace of her normal sharp intelligence. Dobereiner played up to her like the straight man in a comedy act, trying hard to involve Jagger.

Simmons, sitting between Jagger and Tinn, concentrated his studious politeness wholly on Tinn. He had to work hard.

Tinn, shyer than ever, answered in stammered monosyllables, wrestling his glasses up the bridge of his nose at sixty-second intervals, like an ocular Sisyphus. Before they were half-way through the second course, Parsons realized Simmons was hoeing a rock-hard row. He began to relax a little. He said to Jagger, 'These people are going to be in my hair for weeks, just to put together another bloody survey nobody's going to read.'

Dobereiner said, 'Arnold, we'll be like mice, I promise.'

Simmons said, 'Arnold, is Jack here on our interview list? I'm not too sure just what he does.'

Parsons and Patti spoke together. Parsons said, 'No, he's not.' Patti said, 'Sums.'

Dobereiner reeled off the feed-line as if he'd written the script. 'Sums? What kind of sums?'

Parsons said loudly, 'More vino, anyone? There's plenty left.'

Patti said, 'Does anyone happen to know the *day* he was born on? Not many people do.'

Simmons said, 'Yes, I do, as it happens. A Sunday. Why?'

'And the year? Not the date, the year.'

'1938.'

Patti said, 'Jack?'

Tinn made his first unprompted statement, also his longest so far. He smiled worshippingly at Patti and said, 'That w-w-was the twentieth of March. Your b-b-birthday's on the twentieth of M-m-march.'

Simmons stared, astounded. 'Say! If that isn't the darnedest thing! That's right!'

Patti said, 'He can do a lot of things like that. Can't you, Jack love?'

Tinn went very pink, dropped his fork, wrinkled his nose violently and pushed up his glasses with his thumb. He mumbled agonizedly, wrenched between embarrassment and pleasure.

Patti, radiant and enchanting, was also as merciless as a Gorgon. She said, 'What's—oh, let me think!—I know! What's 365 six times in a row, all multiplied by itself?'

Tinn stared at her as if transfixed. His mouth began to twitch, his glasses slipped almost to the end of his nose and behind his thick lenses his oyster-eyes rolled wildly. They all stared back, uncomfortable yet unable to look away, like people watching a man throw a fit in the street.

Tinn's clumsy hands were trembling. Perspiration appeared on his face. His mouth worked as if it had a wife and ten children to keep. Suddenly, in a loud, choked voice, he said, '133,491,850,208,566,925,016,658,299,941,583,225.'

There was an utter silence. Tinn was gazing at Patti with something that reminded Jagger of the dumb devotion of a dog.

The silence unnerved him. His eyes fell, he fumbled for his fork and began to eat discarded scraps from the side of his plate.

Patti said to Dobereiner calmly, 'You didn't write it down so we can't prove it, but he was right. He always is. Shall I ask him to do another?'

Dobereiner blinked, shaking his head slightly as if to clear it. He said, 'No, honey. You don't have to convince me. I'm a believer.'

Parsons grabbed the remainder of a bottle of château-bottled claret and said, desperately, 'Can't waste good plonk.' He jumped up and went round the table in a diversionary frenzy of pouring.

Simmons said quietly, 'But that's incredible. Really incredible. I take it maths is your line?'

Tinn shook his head, blinking embarrassedly. Before he could answer, Parsons said, 'It's his party trick. We don't ask him to do it every day.' He looked edgier than ever.

Dobereiner said, 'I should hope not! Why don't you buy the guy a computer?' He heaved his shoulders in his silent mime of laughter.

Parsons tried to change the subject. 'There's one here already. Jack uses it. So do a lot of other people.'

Simmons said, 'What exactly is Jack's line of work?'

Parsons chose insult as the best form of spoiling tactics.

Deliberately aggressive, he said, 'A British computer, mind. None of your second-rate Yank stuff.'

Patti sighed. 'What a nice world it would be if we only had people. No Yankee this or Limey that. No white supremacy or black power or yellow peril. Just people.'

Dobereiner said, 'No glory that was Greece or grandeur that was Rome?'

Patti said, 'Glory! *Je m'en merde!*'

Simmons said gently, 'But it's people who're the trouble, surely? Not countries, human nature.'

Patti said sarcastically, 'And you can't change human nature. It wouldn't do if we were all the same.'

Parsons said, 'You can't change human nature yet, but give us time.'

Patti said, 'Test-tube people? Bloody scientists!'

Parsons rounded on her. A combination of nerves and hastily gulped wine had made him a little drunk. 'Bloody woolly-minded idealists! Who's given you nearly a quarter of a century without a major war? The amoral, dirty-fingered, illiterate, Philistine bloody scientists!' He lifted his glass. 'I'll give you a toast, girl. The *pax atomica*! Long may it last!'

Simmons said, 'How long can it last, do you think?'

Dobereiner said, 'Oh, a long time, unless someone dreams up a way to beat the bomb.'

Simmons looked surprised. 'Make it obsolete? You think that's likely?'

Dobereiner shrugged. 'Sooner or later.'

Simmons said, 'How soon? Twenty years? Ten? Five?'

Patti said bitterly, 'This year, next year, sometime, now.'

Tinn had been quiet ever since his astonishing feat of mental arithmetic. Now, mumbling to himself, he said, 'No, n-n-not now. But soon. V-v-very soon.' He seemed quite unaware that he had spoken aloud.

Five faces turned towards him. Parsons went a little grey. Dobereiner's face was curiously blank. Simmons looked quietly attentive. Patti's first reaction was one of surprise but as Jagger watched it changed to cool satisfaction. For the first time since they had met in Tinn's office she looked directly at Jagger and held his gaze, a kind of meaningful triumph in her eyes. In her brightest, most innocent voice she said, 'Why, Jack! Whatever do you mean?'

Parsons pushed his chair away from the table. 'Good God!' he said, his voice a shade too high-pitched. 'That bloody meeting! Excuse me a couple of minutes. Jack, you're supposed to be there too.'

Tinn stared, thumbing his glasses up the bridge of his wrinkled nose. Parsons swooped down on him. 'Come on,' he said. 'I shall have to tell 'em I'll be late but there's no need for you to be.'

Patti had brought Tinn like an unwilling child to a party. Parsons dragged him out like one who didn't want to go home. In the silence that followed, Jagger said, 'What a pity! I've always wanted to know what day I was born on.'

26. THE MASTER—*Cat's-paw*

MORTON, as Briggs showed him in, said, 'Sorry to intrude, but I felt I must. Complications.'

The Master looked up from his official reading. 'So I gathered from your message. Come and sit down.'

Morton took the chair on the opposite side of the Adam fireplace. The big, slightly old-fashioned drawing-room with its massively constructed furniture, flock wallpaper and sombre colouring reflected tastes indelibly patterned by more than a quarter of a century's association with Oxford. From the walls photographs of undergraduate, don, colonel in army intelligence and Master of college looked down, four of the seven ages of man.

Briggs hovered, white, wispy hair radiating from his pink scalp like a dandelion clock. From the hearthrug before the crackling blaze of a coal fire the Master's three Burmese cats watched him with lazy indifference. The Master said, 'A drink? I can recommend this port.'

Morton smiled. 'Scotch, please. I dined more meagrely than you. One course, between two slices of bread.'

Briggs shook his head in silent sorrow and left to fetch whisky. He chirrupped at the cats through pursed lips as he went out. The Master reached down to rub Isun-Kyankse behind her left ear. She stretched out a white-gloved paw and rolled languidly on to her back but the Master was already looking away. He said, 'Well, he went to Leatherhead and was paraded for inspection?'

'He was. He also lunched with Dobereiner and Simmons.'

The Master shuffled reports together and laid them at his side. Briggs returned, Morton's whisky balanced in the very centre of a chased silver salver. He watched reproachfully as Morton took the glass, before departing as silently as a wraith through a wall.

'I've upset Briggs with my mention of sandwiches,' Morton said. 'He still hankers after ivied walls and gracious living. There was another guest for lunch. Pargeter's daughter. She claimed she'd driven out to see her father.'

The Master snorted derisively. 'She drove out to see Jagger. The foolish child appears to have fallen for him.'

Morton savoured his Scotch appreciatively. 'Perhaps. But if that's true, she had a funny way of showing it. She brought Tinn down to lunch with her.'

For a man who prided himself on disciplining his emotions, the Master reacted gratifyingly. 'Tinn!'

Morton nodded. 'I gather Parsons had a somewhat trying time. Particularly when the conversation took a serious turn and Tinn all but said outright that the H-bomb had had its day.'

The Master was better prepared this time. He took up his port, gave himself time by sipping reflectively and said, 'Now why would she do a thing like that?'

'Parsons seems to think he detected a certain coolness between the girl and Jagger. He thinks she may have dragged Tinn down on the spur of the moment, just to annoy him. I gather Tinn's putty in her hands.'

The Master's face was eloquent. He opened his prim mouth, changed his mind and stared into the fire. After a while he said, 'You're familiar with games theory? The technique of "minimax"? An admixture of random, totally irrational actions to a logical plan, in order to confuse the opposition? If Dobereiner and Simmons are the ones——' He broke off again.

Morton said, 'If those two are our men they certainly took a liberal dose of confusion. But they may also have had their suspicions confirmed.'

The Master sniffed delicately at this Croft '35. He said, 'Yes, they may have had their suspicions confirmed, but if they think we have something to hide, they can hardly know what, can they? Or, at any rate——' He halted, sighed, and said, 'I deceive myself, Morton. Or I try to. Somehow the secret is out. From Lusty to Bohm. And through Bohm, in the shape of a riddle they have begun to resolve, to our allies across the Atlantic. Who says dead men tell no tales? What about the others? Jagger was taken over the full course?'

'Oh, yes. The grand tour. The Westcorad joint research team, including the new man who arrived this week. The U.S. Bureau of Ships inspector, if that's what he really is. Parsons made a point of introducing our man all round, as well as dropping portentous hints about his function.'

The Master said pensively, 'It's not so much like looking for a needle in a haystack as finding a haystack full of needles and having to decide which is the right one. Data Corporation is a long-established, highly-respected organization, West Coast Radionics no less so. And the Bureau of Ships, as a U.S. Navy department, is fully entitled to send over an inspector under the terms of its research contract with Pargeter.'

Morton said, 'Inspector or not, he really does understand marine radar technicalities. Parsons vouches for that.' He stopped smiling. 'It's hotting up.'

'It is indeed. The Geneva conference opens tomorrow. Our American friends are obviously aware that they could be wasting their time if Tinn's work leads to practical results. I propose to bring Tinn in. The time for orthodox security measures appears to have arrived.'

Morton said, 'I thought a major factor was that he's not amenable to working to order, let alone under close supervision.'

'Perfectly true. But if, as one understands, his work is almost ended, it no longer arises. In any case, it is totally outweighed by the need for maximum precautions until he's put his results in a form that others can understand.'

'Good God! You mean that it's all in his head?'

'In effect, yes. His mental abnormality includes what I'm told is called an extended eidetic imagery. You and I would call it photographic memory.'

'That makes it more dangerous than I realized. You don't think they'd try anything overt?'

The Master finished his port. 'One doesn't know what to think. It seems unlikely. There are limits to the extent to which one can stretch an alliance. But something else is required.' He looked meaningly at Morton. 'Jagger has made a good start, considering his free-lance function. Now the time has come for something more direct.'

Morton said, 'In what way?' The bleep of his pocket transceiver interrupted, its electronic clamour high-pitched, hysterical. He silenced it and acknowledged.

A voice said, 'Relayed call from Alpha Four, sir. Go ahead, please.'

Another voice, fainter, said, 'Alpha Four to Hydra. Cat's-paw has left home, direction north, repeat north. Am in attendance. Over.'

Morton said, 'Thank you, Alpha Four. Advise destination as soon as apparent. Over and out.'

He slid down the whip antenna and tucked the transceiver away. 'You were saying?'

'Spoiling action,' the Master said. Beyond the heavy drapes at the windows a wind was rising, blowing across Regent's Park from the east. It passed through the trees outside with a sound like distant surf. In the London Zoo, less than a quarter of a mile away, an unknown beast howled mournfully at the rising moon.

'Spoiling action,' the Master said again. 'Schramme, so to speak, is the end domino in the row. We must make Jagger jostle him.'

Morton was showing signs of impatience. He said, 'I thought the time had come for orthodox measures. I can have a couple of men going through Schramme's place within the hour.'

The Master bent forward to scoop up Jade Princess. He put her on his lap, encircled her with his arms and began to stroke her head. He said, 'This is not an area for orthodoxy. You miss the point, Morton.'

'Not in the least,' Morton said. 'I understand your nice sense of diplomacy very well. Schramme made open contact with the C.I.A.'s London liaison section. That confirms long-standing suspicions. Now we have to smoke out their under-cover group, but with every regard for their tender feelings.' He couldn't prevent sarcasm from creeping into his voice. 'So we hammer on the front door but we make it ostentatiously clear that the back's been left unguarded. Honour served, friendship preserved, old friends march forward, arm in arm, towards those broad, sunlit uplands where——'

'That is sufficient,' the Master said with a hint of acerbity. 'Churchill's oratorical style may seem a fit subject for parody in these stark and unadorned times, but twenty-five years ago —After all, no one mocks Demosthenes. And there's something you appear to have overlooked.'

Almost rudely, Morton said, 'Have I? What?'

'Bohm.'

'Bohm?'

'There have been inquiries, as you well know. Discreet, but thorough. They will have no doubt what happened to him.'

'I'm sorry. I don't understand.'

The Master said quietly, 'The C.I.A. thinks we killed Bohm. If we give them the chance, they might feel inclined to settle the score. A silent but mutually recognizable token of the fact that we are sometimes driven to hurt those we love most. There are precedents.'

'Istanbul. The Hotel Theodosia.'

'And elsewhere. An eye for an eye, a Bohm for a Bohm.'

Morton's face, orange in the fire-glow, suddenly showed his realization. '*That's* the real reason why you——'

'Why I prefer to use Jagger?' The Master was still stroking Jade Princess, his small, neat hand as light in its touch as a lover's. 'Of course!' He met Morton's eyes and said, as if it were the most reasonable thing in the world, 'If someone should be killed, I would rather it were Jagger than a member of my staff. Than you, Morton, for example.'

The bleep of Morton's autocaller saved him from the difficulty of finding a suitable response. He took out his transceiver and acknowledged. The distant, relayed voice, a little distorted, said, 'Alpha Four to Hydra. Cat's-paw is at Echo Dog 3259 and has gone in. Repeat, has gone in at Echo Dog 3259. Instructions, please. Over.'

The Master had put down Jade Princess. He was already sliding transparent plastic rules over a map of London on the nearby table. Morton stood up to watch. The transceiver said, 'Alpha Four to Hydra. Are you receiving me? Over.'

Morton said, automatically, 'Loud and clear. Wait, please. Over.'

The Master made the final precise adjustments, but there was already no doubt in Morton's mind. He raised the transceiver. 'Hydra to Alpha Four. Wait and watch. I am joining you. Over.'

The reedy voice said, 'Thank you, Hydra. Message received and understood. Over and out.'

Morton put away his transceiver. As he headed for the door he said, 'Sometimes I suspect you of supernatural powers.'

The Master smiled faintly. 'In the old days, one of Jagger's more trying characteristics was his unpredictability. Now one begins to appreciate its advantages. You're to keep clear, Morton, you understand? That's an order. A watching brief. No more.'

Morton said, 'But——'

The Master said, 'An order.' He restored Jade Princess to her warm throne. Morton went. With no need to retain his pose of imperturbability for Morton's benefit, the Master forced Jade Princess to abdicate. There was just time to get back to New Strutton House. He rang for Briggs. While he waited, his eyes went back to the map. The point at which the two Perspex rules intersected was just west of Berkeley Square, on the south side of Charles Street.

27. WHITE HOUSE—*Only us and them*

'He doesn't want to know,' Head of Plans repeated, more in confirmation than surprise.

'That's right.' The President's security adviser looked tired, his face a diary of the past few weeks. 'He said, and I quote, "If the C.I.A. can't find a way out of this foul-up on their own, we'll hand over national security to the Daughters of the American Revolution." '

'Pontius Pilate,' Head of Plans murmured, perhaps to himself.

The White House aide took off his glasses, slowly, deliberately. He pressed the tips of his fingers against his closed eyes head bowed. He said, surprisingly, 'Maybe Pontius Pilate did what he thought was for the best, even if he knew it was going to be tough on one guy in particular. It's the kind of decision you're paid to take when you're running a country. Heaven protect us from men who can't see when it's right in the long term to do wrong in the short.' He replaced his glasses, staring out of the window to where a tour guide was trying ineffectually to stop a bunch of children from running across the scorched lawn.

Head of Plans thought about things for some time before breaking the silence in the room. He said, 'It's a comforting justification. Is it too comforting?'

The Director said, 'Well, the Russians left the ball in our court all right.'

'Sure they did,' White House said. 'What did you expect? They haven't asked us to do a thing. They've simply made it crystal clear where things stand if we do nothing.'

Polishing the warm bowl of his pipe against the side of his nose, Head of Plans said, 'Wisdom after the event, but I'm not sure it was good thinking to give 'em COMSTAR'S last review. Proving that a British-developed version of Shortchange gives us a lot more problems than it does the Kremlin isn't exactly bidding from strength.'

'Too late!' White House said, yawning openly. 'We started off playing this thing by computer. The way I understand it, computers are only infallible so long as we're infallible. Since when did we change? No use having doubts now. And even if we do, the comrades won't.' He yawned again. 'Sorry. I'm bushed. Chewing the fat with expert dialecticians until four in the morning is like being beaten all over the skull with tiny hammers. The effect is slow but cumulative.'

Head of Plans picked out the piece that mattered to him. 'They won't what?'

'They'd been putting in some overtime on their own computer, Henry,' the Director said. 'They'd come to an independent conclusion about who stood to lose the most. It was one of the reasons they arranged the meeting. They're right, too. We'd have to spend more time handling London than Moscow.'

'What about the other aspect?'

'The fact that we both know that Shortchange *is* possible? It's a chance they're prepared to take. If we get it, it'll only be a matter of time before they get it, and *vice versa*. New weapon systems are a risk we live with from day to day, and the race is pretty even. What matters most is that no one else wins it. Not just the Chinese. Nobody.'

White House stretched, shutting his eyes tightly and pulling his head down between his shoulders until his neck muscles quivered. He yawned again. 'Look! We're going to be in a posture of conflict with Moscow for at least another ten years. Maybe twenty or thirty. But privately the area of agreement grows. I don't say we'll ever trust each other, but chances are we'll learn to live with each other, barring accidents. Short-change won't change things in the long run, whether we get it first or they do. The only thing that can change it is other countries. Left to ourselves, we and the comrades will pull faces, wave fists and call each other dirty names but we won't come to blows. The danger's when other countries come to blows and we have to take sides. So, Russian or Yankee Shortchange—*si!* British Shortchange—*no!*'

'Which brings us,' Head of Plans said, 'back to one man. Did you see Dobereiner's report?'

'Yes, I did,' White House nodded. 'The British are practically home and dry. I don't see how you can read it any other way.'

'Unless the whole thing was meant to fool us,' the Director said thoughtfully.

Head of Plans said, 'Mart, I see your point, but I doubt it. I spoke with Dobereiner right after he arrived back in Geneva. He said it was an obvious slip-up. He said the guy who arranged the lunch nearly wet his pants trying to shut Tinn up and get him out before he spilled any more. And Simmons's check-up shows Tinn's had the reputation since way back of doing his problem solving in his head and then having to be coaxed to put things on paper because he couldn't see the need.'

The Director made a gesture of submission. 'Okay, okay! So we have all the confirmation we need. Deal with Tinn and you've dealt with the whole problem. Temporarily.'

'Temporarily,' White House said grimly, 'is good enough to be going on with, so far as this particular problem's concerned.' He looked significantly at his watch.

Head of Plans took the hint. 'All right. Let's recap. The President doesn't want to know, and we know exactly what it is he doesn't want to know. We're already planning to take Schramme out of circulation. Tinn comes next, so long as everybody realizes that it may take time. The kind of accident this has to be just doesn't happen accidentally.'

'Time,' White House said, 'is running out.'

Head of Plans said firmly, 'Schramme first. It won't take long but until it's done there'd always be the chance that they'd link us too positively with anything that happens to Tinn. Without Schramme, and knowing that Lusty worked for the K.G.B., they could never be sure. Not sure enough, anyway. They're great realists when it comes to the crunch.'

White House stood up. 'Do it your own way. Just make it fast.' He went with them as far as the door. 'I never forget,' he said as he opened the door for them, 'that 1945 gave us a whole new situation. Up to then it was people who ran out of time. Now there's always the chance that time will run out of people first.'

28. JAGGER—*On his own*

THE MOONLIGHT made the highly polished brass plate reading MANAGEMENT SEARCH LIMITED pallidly phosphorescent. The street was deserted. Jagger slid Myra's key in the lock. In the basement area of the next house the wind whispered cold comfort among tubs of autumn-shrivelled shrubs. Light glowed treacly-yellow through drawn curtains and a radio not quite tuned in played *Smoke gets in your eyes*.

The key turned easily in the lock. The heavy door floated open. He stepped into darkness. As he closed the door a car moved out slowly from a parking place fifteen yards down the street, switching on its lights. It slid into a vacant space almost opposite Schramme's office, its light dying instantly. Its occupants settled down once more.

The blackness of the lobby smelled of lavender-scented floor polish, stale cigar smoke, centrally heated dust. Jagger switched on the small cadmium cell torch, the tight beam thrusting through the dark like a sword blade. Its brilliant tip glided over furniture and leaped gaps like an agile will-o'-the-wisp. Ignoring the lift, Jagger went up the stairs. His target was the top floor.

Even now he wasn't sure what had brought him here. If he was working for the Master it was because he suspected Schramme was a spy, but that was all irrelevant, all on the surface. If offered explanations but not reasons, *hows* but not *whys*.

So he was here because he was here, because he had made up his mind to meet stimulus with little more than reflex. The last thing he intended to be influenced by was any concern for what was alleged to be right, or even important. His one certainty was the impossibility of knowing or ever being able to know what was right or important.

He reached the topmost floor, shut off from the stair-well by glass-panelled swing doors. Once through them, he found himself in the corridor leading past Schramme's elegant office to his interrogation cell. He went there first, pacing the distance from the door to the wall behind the desk. As he came back along the corridor, he opened the remaining doors.

The first was a small store, filled with stationery, minor office equipment and the smell of pine shelving. The next was a filing room, lined with grey cabinets like silver-buttoned soldiers rigid at attention. Both rooms were equal in length to the interview room.

The third and last door led into Schramme's office. As he opened it the smell of cigar smoke mingled with the ranker odour of Schramme's Balkan cigarettes. Again he paced the distance from corridor to far wall. Reaching the entrance to the washroom he went through, taking the four extra paces that carried him to the exterior wall of the building, but what he had suspected was already a certainty. It was something that had nibbled at his subconscious like an important but maddeningly forgotten name, ever since his first meeting with Schramme. Then Myra had said, 'He has something to hide' and the lost knowledge had come back.

The interview room, the store, the filing room all equalled

Schramme's office in length. The rear of the building ran straight, but beyond Schramme's room was the washroom. Where was the missing space behind the three smaller rooms?

On the wall of the washroom that should have been contiguous with the filing room, but wasn't, was a full-length mirror. It took him four or five minutes to discover the trick.

The long, narrow space beyond the mirror was windowless. It sprang from blackness when he found a light switch. Here, too, were filing cabinets, empty, their contents heaped on benches running the length of the wall. There were stacks of recording tape, removed from their tins and beginning to unwind like released watch-springs. Beyond them was a built-in recording machine from which leads ran towards Schramme's interview room.

He took a chair and climbed up to peer through the ventilating grilles into the interview room. The white spot of his torch beam moved across the chair in which he himself had sat. Behind the grilles were neatly fixed camera mounts, the cameras lying among unused film at the end of the bench. Operated by remote control, they were positioned to give right and left profiles and a full-face portrait as anyone occupying the chair moved his head.

As he stepped down another thing caught his eye. He bent to rescue it from its dark corner. It was something he recognized instantly; a red deciphering sheet torn from a 'one-time' or gamma pad. Its scores of printed, five-digit groups were used to convert a gamma-coded message into English. He corrected himself. Into whatever language it had been sent in. He slipped the sheet in a pocket and went back to the heaped files. There were two categories. One concerned people, the other, companies and research organizations, government and private.

He looked among the personal files for his own name. It wasn't there. He looked for Tinn and found him. The file held only a four-page personal data sheet. Its sparse entries could have been compiled from a variety of sources, none of them Tinn.

191

He tried again, searching this time among the L's. His quarry proved to be LUSTY, Hector Lionel. He raised ironic eyebrows. Someone's hopes had come to a sad end. He opened the file.

The first item, once again, was Management Search's four-page record sheet. He glanced through it and stopped when something caught his eye. Lusty had gone to Pargeter Electro-mation from another well-known electronics company, but before that he had been employed at the Ministry for Scientific Development's advanced weapon systems research centre in Wiltshire.

It was a new fact, so far as Jagger was concerned, and the first indication that Lusty's spying might have begun long before Tinn went to Pargeter Electromation. According to understandably brief notes in both Tinn's and Lusty's folders, the unspecified projects on which each had been engaged had been wound up as part of a cut-back in govern-ment spending.

It didn't take much intelligence to conclude that they were one and the same project.

Once someone, who might or might not be Schramme, had realized that Tinn was still working on the project, Lusty had been ordered to follow him to Pargeter. And who was in a better position to place them there than Schramme?

Jagger worked forward through Lusty's file. There was one item of proof still to be found. It was hardly essential but it would be the clincher. Lusty's disqualifying character weaknesses had not been reported to Pargeter. The reason was obvious enough. But this was Schramme's private dossier. The truth about Lusty would be recorded here if nowhere else.

It wasn't.

The reports on his stress interviews simply confirmed what Schramme had already told Jagger. They listed what Schramme had called Lusty's 'positive faults' but there was nothing about his basic vulnerability.

And yet, in the light of everything that lay around him,

Jagger refused to believe Schramme had been telling the truth.

He put down Lusty's file, shuffling quickly through the others. They were clearly hand-picked from the hundreds Schramme must have compiled over the years. Complete with secretly taken photographs, they all listed inadvertently revealed and skilfully pursued character weaknesses, some squalid, some pathetic, all invitations to blackmail. Each record was up-to-date so far as the subject's employment was concerned. All held positions of significance in the British technological hierarchy. Several occupied key posts in government research establishments.

Jagger was baffled. Lusty's ruthlessly exploited defects had driven him first to espionage, finally to death. Why had Schramme made an exception in failing to record them?

The second group of files, listed by organization, consisted of dozens of items of highly confidential information disclosed over the years by hundreds of individual interviewees. Properly pieced together and expertly evaluated against a broader background, they were the very meat of modern strategic espionage.

It seemed clear that the whole of Schramme's material had been accumulated on behalf of an outside organization. Schramme himself couldn't have controlled a fraction of his blackmail candidates. Painstakingly collected information about dozens of secret research projects was valueless unless passed on. A photocopying machine provided confirmation. Who had received the copies? The answer seemed obvious.

He'd seen enough, and the signs suggested that Schramme was preparing to shut up shop. The proper thing now would be to turn over his findings to the people at New Strutton House. Well, to hell with them! He was no more interested in what was proper than in what was important. They'd chosen him because they had him in the book as 'rogue.' If that was the way he was listed, that was the way he'd play.

He went back through the mirror, checked Schramme's home telephone number and dialled. Schramme had offered co-operation. The offer was worthless, but there were times when bad faith was better than none. At least it gave you an opening.

Schramme himself answered the call. After the preliminaries, Jagger said, 'You hoped you might be able to help me. I think you can.'

Schramme said, 'Why not now?'

He said, 'I'm on my way,' and rang off.

He patted himself over the heart. The shoulder-holster had been developed for the double-breasted jacket but he still preferred it. A pistol stuck in a belt or trouser-band was too much like playing pirates. It had been almost an afterthought but, recalling Schramme's cold eyes and what he'd just seen, he felt all the better for having it. He listened at the street door, waited for footsteps to pass, let himself out and walked back to his car.

In the car parked opposite, Morton spoke into his transceiver, 'Alpha Four to Hydra. Cat's-paw on the move. We'll follow. Over.'

The voice that answered was easily identified. The little man was taking personal charge. He said, 'Hydra to Alpha Four. Keep distance. Let Cat's-paw pull his own chestnuts out of the fire. Kindly confirm.'

Morton sighed. He said, 'Alpha Four to Hydra. Message understood. Over and out.'

In Ida's listening room the duty operator entered the time in the log and rang Ida to report. At the finish he said, 'Jagger was calling Schramme from his own office. We picked up on both instruments.'

Ida thanked him, re-dialled and waited for an answer. When it came, Ida said, 'Jagger's turned over Schramme's office. He's on the way to see Schramme.'

The other voice said, 'How long do we have?'

'He'll be there inside half an hour, so get moving. And if you have to deal with Jagger, too, make it permanent.'

29. SCHRAMME—*Both or neither?*

IF GRATITUDE had been appropriate, Schramme had every reason to feel grateful to the country of his adoption. It had done well for him.

His Georgian house in Hampstead, high above the metropolitan sprawl, was one of an elegant terrace, but wide bay windows on each floor, triple-stacked like a showcase for gracious living, distinguished him from his neighbours like the only family in the street with colour television. The moon looked down through the leaves of a tall chestnut, dappling everything with movement like ripples on a lake of silver light.

He had taken Jagger's telephone call as calmly as if he'd been expecting it. In one way he had—the sense that, now things had started to happen, they would gather momentum. That was why he'd begun his withdrawing action. If the Americans did their part, he could be out of it before things got too hot.

He went back to his study, step-laddered with shelves, random-patterned with books, punctuated by precisely placed, carefully lighted works of art. He'd made money, but he'd spent it, too. That was one of his special privileges.

His pleasure pieces, as he called them, reflected no particular pattern of taste. Each item was unique. That was all that needed to be said about them. A ceramic plaque from Turku provided a burning backdrop for a T'ang horseman. A pre-Columbian turquoise death's-head separated an Egyptian funerary figure of the Twelfth Dynasty from a spindle-shanked, splay-armed Giacometti. It was possible he would have to leave them all when he went.

The telephone rang again. He went back. He wondered, as he had before, whether it would be Myra. He was both surprised and relieved that he hadn't heard from her since the break. It wasn't Myra. The voice was one he didn't know, but he knew the accent. That was another thing he'd been waiting for since yesterday.

'Schramme?'

'Yes.'

'Jagger just phoned you.'

'How do you know this?'

'Never mind. Did you know he called from your office?'

'My office?'

'Let's not waste time. Is there anything there you wouldn't want him to see?'

Schramme's wits began to function properly. The log jam had certainly broken. His office phone was tapped. Perhaps this one, too. He wondered for how long. They were thorough. Fortunately, so was he, though he should have anticipated such things.

He said, 'Anything I wouldn't wish him to see. It depends. Yes, if he's clever.'

'Let's assume he's clever. He's not paying social calls at this time of night.'

'What do you wish me to do?'

'Tell him the same story. The one you told us.'

'What?' Schramme's astonishment escaped his control.

'You heard me. Tell him everything. Everything except about the meeting at Victoria. Leave the rest to us.'

'What are you going to do?' He was too late. The dialling tone purred in his ear like a mechanical cat.

He went back to the study, completely at a loss. Instinctively he drew aside one of the drapes from the glass doors that opened on to his small garden. He peered out. The night was abrim with moonlight. With danger, too, but for whom? He let the curtain fall and sat down. He began to think, as if his life depended upon it. He had had plenty of practice.

When the doorbell rang he was as far as ever from an answer. He let Jagger in, looking past him at the sloping road that flowed with light like a still river. It was deserted except for parked cars.

Jagger followed him through to the study. Among the artistic fallout he saw things he would have liked to own himself, but it wasn't the time for cultural chitchat and anyway Schramme seemed a little preoccupied.

He sat down. The house heat was on but a small fire of birch logs rustled and shimmered in the hearth, hot embers coruscating like nascent rubies.

He said, 'It's late. I apologize.'

Schramme smiled, his tight, on-duty smile. He said, 'You were detained at the office. My office, I believe.'

Jagger's self-control took a silent mauling. He hadn't so much lost the initiative as had it pulled from under him. 'Why should you think a thing like that?'

Schramme said, 'Allow me one secret. I presume you have the rest?' He was still working furiously at his problem, like a man with a jigsaw puzzle. There must be a pattern but at the moment he only had the edges.

Jagger tackled his own problem. He said, ' "Curtsey while you're thinking what to say. It saves time." '

Schramme said, 'Forgive me. I do not understand.'

'A quotation. Lewis Carroll. *Through the Looking Glass*.'

Schramme saw the allusion at once. In a sense it cleared the air. He said, 'It is a book I have not read.'

Jagger said, 'You should. It's a revelation.'

Schramme made a small motion of irritation. 'Come. It is too late to play games. What do you wish to say to me?'

Some three miles away, Ida's car waited in the red glow of a stop light, the driver revving the engine with controlled impatience. The man beside him, hand in pocket, fingered his gun. Through his thin glove he could feel every indentation and protrusion. He shifted and reshifted the safety-catch —off, on, off, on. The lights turned to green.

Jagger was smiling at Schramme. 'What Management Search sells over the counter isn't quite the same as the stuff in the back room.'

'My company and my staff,' Schramme said, 'are not involved. Only I. You see? I am prepared to talk.'

'Are you? Why?'

'I am not a fool. I know when something is over. What I did, I had to do. I had no choice.'

Jagger said, 'I don't believe in free will either. Tell me

197

something. A pathetic, shabby collection of human weaknesses for everybody except Lusty. Why the exception? You knew about Lusty, too. That's why he's dead.'

'Oh yes,' Schramme said. 'I knew about Lusty. That is your answer. I knew about him before he passed through my hands. There is no point in recording what is already known, what is not the product of one's own research.'

'You mean someone else knew? Someone who sent Lusty to you. With instructions to fix him up in a nice little job with Pargeter Electromation.'

'Exactly.'

'Who?'

Schramme looked surprised. 'What do you think?'

'Someone whose home address is No. 2, Dzerzhinsky Street? Moscow?'

'You are better informed than I, but if I understand you correctly, yes.'

'And you had no choice. Tell me about it.'

'No one is immune to blackmail. If I provided the means for others to employ it, I was also its victim.'

Schramme was becoming edgy, though he concealed it from his visitor. In this room, things were moving slowly. He could only suspect how fast they were moving elsewhere. Following instructions that weren't accompanied by explanations made him nervous.

Jagger said, 'Don't stop.'

Schramme went on, though one part of his mind was still picking away ceaselessly at his puzzle. 'Schramme is not my real name. I am Polish by origin. I did not work for the Nazis as a slave labourer but as an interrogator.' He held up his hand to stop any interruption. 'No. I was not a traitor. I was responsible for translating during the preliminary interrogation of Polish prisoners—men from the Polish underground army. The Germans had my family in Cracow.' The lie, so many times rehearsed, came smoothly, naturally. 'My father, my mother, my brother and two sisters. I had no choice.'

He bent his head, silent for a while. 'During the last days of the war, when Germany collapsed, I escaped. By that time I had lost all contact with my family. I have never heard from them since.'

Another pause. A log slipped in the fire. A fiery drift of sparks floated up the chimney. Schramme glanced briefly. The warm light reflected coldly from his eyes, like sunlight on hoar frost.

'I took the papers of a dead man. A Pole whose father had been Flemish. Schramme. I went west, to Belgium. Finally I was able to come to this country, to start again. I concealed my past. It is one of which I am not proud.'

Ida's car, less than a mile away, had begun the steep climb up the hill towards Hampstead High Street.

'I should explain,' Schramme said, 'that when I first came to this country I already knew some English, also several European languages. I obtained a job as a translator. I met many talented refugees seeking work in Great Britain. This gave me the idea of opening an employment bureau. My experience of certain interrogation techniques led me to develop theories that resulted in my system of stress probing. Later I was fortunate enough to meet Sir Ben Pargeter. The rest you know.'

'Not all,' Jagger said. 'Go on.'

'When I became successful,' Schramme said, surreptitiously looking at his watch, 'I decided I would like to go to the United States. You will forgive me for saying it, but there they have greater appreciation of new thinking in the field of business efficiency. Others were developing techniques not unlike my own. I did not wish to miss an opportunity. I made inquiries at the embassy, but with my background I encountered many difficulties. I was told that I must wait. It was shortly afterwards that I myself experienced blackmail.'

He hunched his shoulders as if he were cold, squeezing his hands tightly together. 'A telephone call. An anonymous voice. A threat to tell both the British and American authorities that I had worked for the Nazis, that I had the papers of a dead man.'

'Unless.'

'Unless! All that was asked for was one small item of industrial information, secret but quite unimportant. The anonymous caller knew that the company concerned was recruiting through me, that it would not be difficult to get someone to talk.'

'So you agreed.'

'I agreed. What would you have done? Of course, you have never been a refugee.'

'After the first demand there was a second.'

'Naturally! There is no need to tell you the rest. When you came to see me, I knew that things were almost over.'

'How did you know I'd been in your office tonight?'

Schramme didn't answer. In a single instant of revelation he had solved the puzzle. He had been clever, but they had been more so. He was being used to lay a trail, a false trail. But for their plan to succeed there must be a final, irreversible climax. Irreversible for him. Perhaps he was already too late, but he saw what he must do. He loosened his tie, unbuttoned his shirt. A moment later a thin gold chain came over his head. He held it towards Jagger, a slim gold whistle swinging from it.

He said, 'Listen! We are both in danger. What I have told you is true except for one thing. The name of the control is Ida, but Ida is——'

The glass of the garden window shattered with a crash that tailed away in an atonal tinkle of falling glass, like the eerie music of a Japanese wind harp. One gloved hand dragged aside the curtain, another thrust a silenced pistol through the jagged gap.

Schramme's reaction was faster than Jagger's. He threw himself back and down as the first shot starred the plaster of the wall behind him. Jagger had turned instinctively toward the window. The assassin's face, just visible, was flattened and distorted by a black nylon stocking drawn over his head.

Jagger recovered and threw the first thing that came to hand, a small Brancusi head cast in solid, polished bronze.

It struck the edge of the window, scattering more glass. Schramme hurled himself at the door of the room, flinging it open. In the hall there was the sound of a brief scuffle, the solid thud of a falling body. A second intruder was in the house.

It was almost the last thing Jagger had time to register. As he reached for his own gun the man at the window fired again. Something smashed into Jagger's heart like a sledge-hammer. He ceased to see or hear anything even before he fell.

Schramme had been taken unawares, but his revelation had left him half prepared. Catching the second intruder by surprise, only just through the front door, he smashed him down, taking advantage of the man's forward momentum. By the time Schramme reached the street he was carrying out a long-prepared plan.

Ten minutes later he let himself into the rented lock-up garage. Using a shielded light he combed his hair sideways after rubbing in a paste that streaked it with iron grey, and slipped on plain-lensed glasses. A change of clothes completed a simple but effective transformation. The photograph in the passport he took from the glove compartment of the car matched his new appearance very adequately.

He pocketed currency and travellers' cheques, substituted the power leads of the pulse transmitter for those of the car radio, raised the garage door and drove out into the moonlight. He headed south and east towards central London, switching on the transmitter as he drove west along Charles Street from Berkeley Square. On the top floor of Management Search Limited, the magnesium fuse of the thermit-napalm bomb in the room behind the mirror flared invisibly but brightly, electronically fired. The thermit ignited. The black paint on the wooden chest beneath the bench began to melt and bubble only seconds before the wood itself burst into flame.

Schramme switched off the transmitter and turned towards Piccadilly, heading for the motorway and London Airport.

30. TINN—*Whose?*

TINN NEVER THOUGHT of himself as being happy or sad. He never really thought in terms of happiness or sadness at all. It didn't mean anything. Things went well, less well and, occasionally, badly. Usually they went well. Almost invariably so when he was left to himself. Undisturbed work was good. When it went well, as it had in the last few months, it was very good.

Though work was a concept that didn't mean much to him, either. What they called work was something he did all the time, and he did it no better because he was paid to do it. He didn't stop when he wasn't paid, either. Thinking was both a means and an end. You might not always think for the same purpose or about the same thing but basically you always thought in the same way.

The point was that somewhere at the back of existence, at the back both of the physical universe and of those things that up to now had never seemed quite to be physical, there was a oneness, entire and perfect, like a huge, complex and wholly beautiful pattern in which everything was linked with everything else and each was explainable in terms of all the rest.

Once, in his sleep, he had been on the brink of seeing the complete design, dizzyingly awe-inspiring, dazzlingly beautiful. Of course, when he woke up it had gone. Dreams of that kind were commonplace enough. But he knew that in his own case what he had almost dreamed really did exist. For a brief instant he had been permitted a glimpse of it. One day the dream would become reality. When it did, everything would be explainable.

In the meantime he followed his thoughts, and his thoughts were mostly mathematical because there was no other significant way of thinking. Nothing was meaningful unless it could be set free from emotion, from all the irrational exercises that substituted for thinking among most people. Nothing had meaning unless it could be proved or disproved, in terms that were beyond argument. If there were a great many things he

202

found difficult or impossible to understand it was simply because, as yet, no one had devised the means of expressing them in those immutable, indisputable terms.

As yet! That was the point. One day even the most intractable topics would be expressible in basic terms and there would be no more mysteries. The universe, with everything in it, was a mathematical concept. What couldn't eventually be explained in mathematical terms simply wouldn't exist.

Take music, for instance, if only because it interested him. Music was simply a product of air movement, of certain combinations of vibrations, tempos and silences. So why did he find Beethoven boring, Bach pleasant but predictable and Webern, say, reasonable, logical and exciting?

You could talk about an interplay between the living and the non-living, between physics and biology, between particle movement and gene chemistry, but that was just clouding the issue with words. Basically, music and everything else were simply different aspects of the one immutable unity, facets of a single structure that embodied everything from meson to Mozart, from matter to 'soul'.

But so far only isolated integrants had been discovered and studied. Until much more was known, a great many things would remain indefinable. Unfortunately for Tinn, they were the things, by and large, that most people seemed to like talking about most. One of them in particular cropped up constantly among scientists. It had cropped up now very personally. Was what he was currently doing 'right'?

Even though he'd already agreed to let someone else decide, he didn't see how the question could have any meaning, let alone an answer. If you were going to talk about 'right' and 'wrong', it could only be in mathematical terms, where what was right was provable and so was what was wrong. Mathematics dealt with facts. Facts *were*, always had been, long before there were men to discover and discuss them. One multiplied by itself was one and remained one, whether men existed or not. Facts were neither good nor bad. Only men could be good or bad, if the words meant anything at all, so why pick on scientists to discuss the social consequences of their work, any more than musicians or artists or poets?

He himself was concerned neither with right nor wrong in the meaningless moral sense; only with truth. At the present time he was in the final stages of proving the truth of a series of mathematical ideas so beautiful that their perfection made his mind swim. What could such abstract beauty have to do with social consequences, any more than the fact that one multiplied by itself was always one?

And in that case, why, against all reason was he——?

He stopped chasing his thoughts, realizing with the nearest he ever came to annoyance that thinking pointlessly had made him careless. The star had almost gone from the field of view of the telescope. He brought it back. The magnitude had fallen, according to his comparisons, by 2.4 since his first observations at the beginning of the week. That would mean a periodicity of—of 7.38. He called up the tables in his mind. Correct, within reasonably acceptable limits for non-instrumented observation.

He freed the clamp and started to swing the telescope towards the short-term variable in Pegasus. Instead he found himself staring, head back, mouth agape, at the three-quarter moon. He knew he must look foolish, his huge glasses clouding in his drifting breath, but he still enjoyed losing himself like this, projecting his mind across empty space to things at distances the mind couldn't really grasp. Out there lay the key to the tantalizingly glimpsed pattern. All he wanted, all he'd ever wanted, was to trace a little more of that pattern for posterity.

So why had he been persuaded to turn his attention away from the real task, even for a short time, and concern himself with the very thing he found most pointless? That again was a question he couldn't really answer.

It was nothing to do with sex. In any case, sex was another enigma. Why should people take a biological reaction that was almost as scientifically definable as magnetism or electron flow and talk about it as if——?

He couldn't even put it into words. Other people seemed to spend a lot of time trying to, but what they said had no real meaning. So-called love poetry was nothing more than a grouping of imprecise images in an attempt to portray the indefinable spin-off of physico-chemical reactions. Love was just a waste product of natural forces.

He faltered, unable to bring himself to any worthwhile conclusions. That was the way this sort of thing always ended. Molecules, atoms, particles were part of a mathematical, conceptual reality. The rest was a mess of woolly abstracts that broke all the rules by pretending to be greater than the sum of their parts—feelings, judgements, morals and so forth.

People.

Someone whistled, just once; low, clear, urgent. That was the signal and because he'd committed himself against his better judgement, he'd have to carry out his side of the bargain. How was it that you could be so confident of your intellectual superiority in certain fields and yet be persuaded to defer to someone whose actions were based on little more than strongly felt emotions? He sighed. It would have to be an incredibly complex pattern to embody everything.

He took the telescope and tripod into the shed, following effortlessly remembered instructions. He picked up the small case, closed the door quietly behind him and went through the moonlight to the gate at the foot of the garden. He walked down the lane.

He was surprised to note that his pulse rate had increased a little.

The car was waiting at the top of the hill. The nearside door opened as he came in sight. Neither of them spoke as he slid awkwardly in, Tinn because he could think of nothing to say. He never could, especially in circumstances like this. He knew he always looked stupid. He supposed he behaved stupidly. People with his kind of qualifications had often been idiots, in the literal sense. Perhaps he was one himself, according to standards he couldn't begin to comprehend.

He knew people made clumsily tactful attempts to humour him.

The handbrake of the car was released. It began to roll down the steep slope, its wheels making a gritty hiss like radio static. The engine started at the junction with the main road, the rapid acceleration thrusting him back hard into his seat.

Acceleration—the rate of change of velocity, measured as a change of velocity over a given unit of time. He watched the telephone poles fly by. In his mind figures began to whirl like the spindles of a computer.

31. IDA—'Not who! What!'

IT WAS THE TRIAL-SIZE hour of the new day but lights burned in the secret depths of New Strutton House like a candle stump in a turnip head.

The Master said, 'It's a pity you didn't concentrate on following Schramme.'

Morton said coldly, 'I followed orders, until it was obvious something had happened to Jagger.'

The Master said grudgingly, 'You were right to help Jagger, of course. One isn't entirely devoid of human feelings.' He sighed. 'As Machiavelli said, a wise prince relies only on what he can control, never on things beyond his power to control. I ignore a sound precept. When will the doctor finish with him?'

Jagger came through the door on cue. He looked pale, and he winced as he sat down. He gave the Master five seconds, put his head on one side, smiled crookedly and said, 'Great, thanks! How are you?'

Reproachfully, the Master said, 'I was just asking. You're a lucky man. What does the doctor say?'

Jagger grinned. 'That I should be in bed, but I had a feeling you'd be disappointed.'

With ill-concealed eagerness the Master said, 'Well, you must be the judge, but if you feel able to enlarge on what you told Morton——?'

Jagger patted the left side of his ribs gingerly. 'Heartache's a thing I never believed in. I was wrong, but it takes a bullet, not an arrow. Have you caught Schramme?'

Morton and the Master exchanged glances. The Master said, 'We're not entirely sure we want to catch him.'

Jagger said, 'What's this? Be Kind To A Spy Week? Or is your K.G.B. collection complete?'

The Master cleared his throat awkwardly. 'C.I.A., not K.G.B. There were good reasons for not telling you before. Morton!'

Morton, his eyes apologetic, gave Jagger a summary of the Bohm story and its sequence. Like a *Reader's Digest* condensed version, it left out all the nasty bits. Jagger found concentration difficult. The bullet had hit the butt of his shoulder-slung pistol and glanced off. It had been like being kicked over the heart by a mule. It had also left him with a ricochet wound below his left armpit that was superficial but painful.

When Morton finished, Jagger looked at them incredulously. He said, 'Perhaps I never came back through the looking glass! Lusty was spying for the Russians and it was Schramme who put him into Pargeter Electromation. Somebody's wires are crossed, and it isn't mine.'

The Master said, 'Certainly Schramme placed Lusty with Pargeter, but Schramme was working for the C.I.A. *Ergo*, Lusty also was working for the C.I.A. He and Bohm were a team.'

Jagger made a rude noise. 'Schramme didn't know a damn thing about Bohm! But he admitted openly that he and Lusty were controlled by the K.G.B.'

The Master looked aggravatingly superior. 'Of course he did! Neither we nor the Americans want an open confrontation. We're allies! It's mutually convenient for them to divert suspicion from themselves to the K.G.B. and for us to pretend to believe them.'

Morton said, 'We've had Schramme under observation for some time. Two nights ago he had a secret meeting with a C.I.A. man in a snack bar at Victoria Station.'

Jagger still couldn't swallow it. The holes seemed as big as the one he should have had in his heart. He said, 'You knew Lusty had worked on the same project as Tinn, down in Wiltshire?'

Morton said, 'We found out after he'd been killed. There was no particular reason why we should have known before and now you've seen Tinn you know why he wouldn't be likely to tell anyone. We weren't concerned with security clearances for Pargeter's own research staff. Tinn was working on his own.'

Jagger said, 'You won't deny the probability that Lusty had been spying long before he went to Pargeter? Schramme said as much.'

The Master stirred impatiently.

'You seem to believe everything Schramme told you. Of course Lusty had spied previously. That's how he guessed what Tinn was doing. That's why he and Bohm followed up.'

Jagger said, 'Look, Schramme knew I'd broken into his office. He didn't tell me how, but it's pretty obvious. I telephoned him, so either his office or home phone was permanently tapped. Possibly both. Schramme's friends must have told him to stall me until they arrived to take care of me. He did, by filling in on what he knew I'd already have guessed. He thought it wouldn't matter, once his friends arrived.'

He winced, shifting his left arm cautiously. The bullet graze was beginning to throb savagely. 'Of course, he had it wrong. They were going to take care of him too, he was no use to them any more. He realized it at the last minute and tried to get his own back by blowing his control.'

He plunged a hand into his pocket. 'Schramme said the name of his control was Ida.' He produced the golden whistle. 'He was going to tell me the rest when the two gents from

*Mokryye Dela** arrived, tarted up in black stockings like a couple of Soho whores, and he——'

He stopped. 'Now what?'

The other two were still staring at the whistle. The Master said, almost jovially, 'And you think Schramme was working for the K.G.B.!'

He opened a drawer and took out the twin of Jagger's whistle. 'We took this one from Bohm. Bohm was an American and we know beyond any shadow of doubt who employed him.'

It was a body blow almost as violent as the one Jagger had already taken. He looked at Schramme's whistle. Slowly he put it away. The evidence seemed conclusive, and yet— and yet——?

Increasingly conscious of the throbbing pain that was spreading to his armpit, he said, 'You'll raid Schramme's office?'

Morton said, 'Practically burnt to the ground. Some kind of incendiary gadget, according to the experts. They're still fighting the fire. There'll be nothing left.'

Jagger produced his one remaining card, the gamma sheet. 'That was in Schramme's secret hidey-hole. Unless I'm out of touch, it's from a K.G.B. one-time pad.' He gave it to Morton.

The Master ignored it. He said, 'If you'd found a dozen cases of vodka and the collected works of Karl Marx in Russian, one would still be unimpressed. The C.I.A. meant the trail to point towards Moscow, for our convenience as well as theirs.'

Jagger gave up. 'All right. Just tell me this. The Yanks are top of the league in technology. Why——'

'Would they be spying on British research work? They may be top of the league, as you put it, but no country has a monopoly. If they are to pay proper regard to their own

*The K.G.B.'s department for assassination and terror. *Mokryye Dela* means 'the department of wet affairs', 'wet' in this case signifying dirty or 'blood-wet'.

security they must keep the closest possible watch on the secret research work of other countries. We attempt to do the same in the United States, in our own small way. After all,' he added, 'allies we may be, but if we were compelled to decide between their survival and our own there is surely little doubt of our choice? Nor of theirs, in similar circumstances.'

Morton said, 'They can't expect to back all the winners themselves and they know we still have some of the world's best scientists. Why do you think they've been taking all this interest in Pargeter? In Tinn, rather?'

Jagger said, 'You're begging the question, but I was coming to that. Or hoping you would.' He felt for a cheroot before he could stop himself. It made him angry. 'I was your trained bloody ferret. All right, I've driven the rabbit from its hole. Don't you think it's time I knew what it's all about?'

The Master, the only one of them still looking fresh and brisk, said, 'Surely you've no doubt?'

Jagger said, 'Something to relegate the H-bomb to the age of gunpowder. Is it to be taken seriously?'

The Master's face lost some of its misleading benevolence. 'Seriously? Oh yes! Yes indeed! Morton will explain. He understands these things.'

Morton said, 'What do you know about lasers?'

'That they're about as militarily dangerous as radio. Useful, but as weapons, non-starters. Try again.'

'Quite right!' Morton smiled a little. 'And about X-rays?'

Jagger said, 'Tell me or don't. I'm not in the mood for Sunday supplement quizzes.'

Morton said, 'The X-ray laser's the most comprehensively deadly weapon imaginable. In theory.'

Jagger said, 'Theory never killed anyone.'

The Master said very deliberately, 'If Tinn solves certain problems this country will have a weapon system that could destroy a missile or satellite a quarter of a million miles out in space, slice a plane or aircraft carrier in half, turn tanks and men into burnt-out cinders. Neither the Americans nor the Russians have been able to solve those problems.'

Morton said, 'The principle of the laser is to reflect a beam back and forth until it's built up a lot of energy, then release it all at once. But X-rays don't reflect. They penetrate.'

Jagger said, 'So an X-ray laser's impossible by definition.'

Morton said, 'Stones are heavier than water, but you've played ducks and drakes? You bounce 'em across. Same with X-rays, in theory. It's the atomic bomb in reverse. Einstein defined a mathematical relationship between mass and energy which eventually produced nuclear energy. With the X-ray laser it's the other way round. The nature of the weapon is clearly understood. What's been lacking is the basic mathematical approach.'

Eventually Jagger said, 'And one man can solve it when everyone else has failed?'

The Master said simply, 'You've seen Tinn. He's unique. The full-scale research programme failed completely, just as it did in Russia and the States, but Tinn blurted out a hint that he was working towards a solution. The project head and the government's scientific adviser were convinced, the Minister for Scientific Development approved a decision to terminate the large-scale work and put the project underground with Tinn as a one-man research team. A kind of human computer.'

He sneered condescendingly. 'Of course, the Minister saw an opportunity for personal glory. He fixed things with his pal Pargeter. The rest you know or may guess. Lusty and Bohm almost succeeded in photographing one of Tinn's rare scribblings, but luck was on our side. The leak was stopped.'

He looked at the golden whistle on his desk and added regretfully, 'Our counter-measures have been partially successful. Schramme has been smoked out. Unfortunately, without knowing the identity and whereabouts of Ida, the job is only half done.'

He toyed abstractedly with the whistle. 'We may guess

211

what this operates. An automatic communication system based on the infinity transmitter. We have the key. We have the name of Ida. But there we come to a stop. We lack the lady's telephone number. In the meantime, now that Schramme has vanished, we are placing Tinn under protective surveillance.'

Something else had just occurred to Jagger. He said, 'I was the patsy, wasn't I? Ready to foot the bill if someone wanted payment for Bohm.'

The Master said smoothly, 'Oh, come, not a mere pawn, dear boy. Let us say a stalking-horse. No real danger.'

Jagger said, 'Let us say balls!'

One of the Master's phones rang. He motioned to Morton to take it and said, 'You are too harsh in your judgements. You always were. Morton will arrange for a car to take you home.'

Jagger stood up. 'I'll take my own. From now on I prefer to keep my fate in my own hands.'

Morton interrupted, still holding the telephone. He looked shaken. 'It's Bailey, ringing from Leatherhead. Tinn's vanished.'

Jagger watched the ant-hill boil into frantic life. After a while he thought of something. It would have been worth passing on if he'd felt less bitter, if he'd been convinced by everything he'd heard in the last half hour. He felt neither, so he decided to follow it up on his own. Nobody noticed him leave.

Lights were still on when he pulled up outside the house in Cheyne Square. It wasn't all that long since his last visit, but that had been someone else in another life. Myra seemed half surprised, half relieved to see him. He followed her into the well-bred artificiality of the drawing room before he realized she was more than a little drunk.

She stood close against him, resting one hand on his arm, and said, 'I didn't expect to see *you*! Still, now you're here, have a drinky.'

He said, 'No thanks. I've had my fun for tonight.' He freed his arm.

She staggered a little, and forced a smile. In a light, over-careful voice she said, 'Well, I'm going to, even if you won't. What did you come for, anyway?'

He said, 'Where's Patti?'

She was pouring gin. 'Out. Ages ago. If you want to know, I thought she'd gone with you.'

'Why?'

She shrugged. 'I told you before. She's fallen for you.'

'Why did you think she'd gone with me? What time did she leave?'

She wandered away, her glass to her lips. She spoke into it, her voice ringing hollowly. 'She took a case. Packed a case, to go away. When? Eight? Nine, ten. I don't remember. Didn't see her leave. Just heard.'

She still had her back to him. 'How do I know she'd packed a bag? Looked round her room, ducky. Mother-daughter relationship!'

Jagger remembered Patti telling him she listened at keyholes, her father complaining that he didn't understand his own child.

His side hurt, his chest hurt, he wanted to sit down, lie down, fall down. He could hardly think two consecutive thoughts. Related facts lay scattered about his mind like beads from a snapped necklace. He was too tired to pick them up but a wild suspicion was becoming tamer every minute. He knew it would soon be eating out of his hand.

He said wearily, 'Listen. I think Patti may have done something rather silly. Where's the phone?'

She pointed. He went to pick it up. Neatly printed on a writing pad at its side was a message. It said: RING IDA BEFORE 9.30 THUR.

She'd followed him. He picked up the pad. 'Who wrote this?'

'Ben. My husband. Why?'

'What does it mean?'

She frowned. 'What it says, I expect.'

'Let's start again. Who's Ida?'

'Ida? Oh! No, not who! What! It's short for International Data Analysts. A company.'

'Any connection with Data Corporation of America?' He knew the answer before he asked the question.

'Of course. British subsid—subsidiary. Man called Simmons.'

He saw directories under a table. He bent down. She said, 'Nobody there at this time of the night, ducky, but if you want the number, it's in here.' She was holding out an expensive-looking leather gadget.

He pressed a key marked *I*. It flew open at *K*. He turned back.

He began to dial the number, fumbling in his pocket. He waited for the click of the relays, then blew one brief note on the whistle. Myra was saying, thick-voiced, 'Is that his? Ralph's? He had one just like it.'

In his ear a female voice, expressionless as a computer with a larynx, intoned, 'Ida to all contacts. Break and wait. Ida to all contacts. Break and wait. Ida to . . .'

He put the phone down, dialled another number. Myra sat down, still watching. For some reason he couldn't be bothered to understand, tears swelled beneath her lashes like slowly melting ice.

A woman's voice came on the line. She said, 'This is the supervisor. What number are you calling, please?'

He said, 'I'm calling you, sweetheart, but I don't know the magic words. Just pass a message. Tell them to ring this number and ask for Ida.'

The voice said, 'You wish to have it tested, sir?' but she repeated the number carefully enough. She said, 'May I have your name and number, please? We may wish to call you back.'

He said, 'Don't bother. They'll know my name. Oh, and if Morton wants to find his wandering boy he might do worse than trace the movements of Miss Patti Pargeter.'

He put down the phone. He looked at Myra. 'Don't worry. Patti won't have gone far. Unless I'm mistaken, she's picked up some rather awkward baggage.' Privately, he was half afraid he was going to find it on his own doorstep.

32. PATTI—*Herself*

THE DC9 FLOATED GENTLY down a pathway of darkness. The no-smoking-and-seatbelts warning came on. There was a thin scatter of lights to port, as remote and unreal as the first glimpse of another planet. The stewardesses had disappeared, the cabin lights were dim, the other seats might have been unoccupied.

Patti looked at Tinn. He was asleep, his mouth open, his glasses perched almost at the tip of his button nose. The engines were so quiet she could hear the faint whisper of his breathing.

The plane made a slow, shallow turn and shuddered as the landing gear thumped down. The sound of Tinn's breathing cut out for a few seconds, then began again, sparse, rhythmic. His glasses slipped a little further.

She felt she wasn't there at all, except in mind. Her body was far, far away. She wouldn't even wake up and find it was all unreal. She would go on just like this, floating beyond space, out of time, forever.

But she wouldn't! They were landing. There was no quicker way of dispelling a trance than arriving at an airport an hour before dawn, nothing less transcendental than going through customs and immigration control.

As if some nerve-paralyzing injection had suddenly worn off, she felt the cold, squeezing fingers of fright. The flame had burned out, the fall begun. There seemed little below but jagged peaks of impossibility.

Not long ago she'd had nothing but this restless churning certainty that somewhere there must be *something* worth doing, and she had to find it and do it—quick! quick! quick! —before it was too late.

But nobody could tell her what it was. The only people she'd ever seemed to meet were the self-seekers, who'd see the world in smoking ruins before they'd give a second thought to anyone or anything but themselves. Even among her own generation, who went around saying that life stank and the one way to bear it was to do your own thing, she'd found little but the old selfishness with new names.

And then, when it was almost too late, her life had taken a giant step forward. First she'd met Jagger. Not much later, she'd found her thing. It had been like discovering the ocean after a childhood of splashing in puddles. She'd nearly drowned first time in! So far as Jagger was concerned she knew now where she'd gone wrong. You didn't catch someone like that quite so simply. She'd picked herself up, squeezed herself dry and she was all set to try again.

But first she had to do her thing. It was as inevitable, as compulsive as if the entire purpose of the universe had been to bring her and it together. The fact that virtually everyone she could think of would tell her she was crazy was the best possible reason for doing it. Nothing really worthwhile ever happened unless you went out of your way to make it. If this one didn't work out, well, at least she'd have tried.

So that was why she was here, with a sort of human time bomb snoring softly at her side. It had been as easy as stealing a baby from a pram, because he was so brilliantly clever about so very little. He'd given in with surprising ease once she'd dug out the truth, and it hadn't taken her long to do that. After that, she'd simply wound him up like a toy, pointed him in the right direction and led him like a lamb from the slaughter.

Except! Except that the way things had looked then and the way they looked now were altogether different. Then, the problems had been somewhere over the horizon, hadn't even cast a shadow before them. Now, literally, they were coming nearer by the minute.

216

The aircraft settled steadily, evenly. The planet seen from space had vanished. In its place lights fled past the windows, glaring, vanishing, glaring, vanishing. Beyond them was a bleak familiar world with some bleak and unfamiliar problems.

The wheels touched lightly, shrieked, lifted, touched again. The engines began to howl in reverse thrust. Tinn grunted, stirred, awakened. He took a little time to orientate himself. His face turned towards Patti. He smiled tentatively, his eyes innocent, unconcerned. She smiled back.

She pulled herself together. Nothing seemed easy any more, but the first thing was a hotel. A little sleep. She couldn't hope to achieve very much today. She didn't even know what time the Secretary-General would be arriving, or where he and Kia would be staying. Into her mind came a dark-skinned, merry-eyed face built around a blend of mischief and timeless wisdom. It cheered her up. Once she and Kia met, friendship would do the rest. She'd beat them all yet!

The night was slowly bleeding white, nailed to the sky by a three-quarter moon, but the sun was deep down below the mountains, crossing the Iron Curtain. The early papers were on the news-stand. She bought a copy of *La Suisse*. The main front page headline said *LES YEUX ET LES ESPOIRS DU MONDE SONT AUJOURD'HUI SUR GENEVE.* A smaller one half-way down the page drew her attention. She read: *La fille du Sécrétaire-Générale reste à New York. Elle souffre de la grippe.* The day died before it was born.

Tinn said, 'W-w-what happens now, Miss P-p-pargeter?'

She said, 'I'm not sure, Jack. Something's gone a bit wrong.' She fought back a choking sense of panic and futility.

Before he could ask questions she said, 'Come on. Let's get in the coach.' She'd think better after a few hours in bed.

Behind her, one of the first-class passengers from London was staring, astonished. From a safe distance he watched them climb into the coach. He looked quickly for his car.

The driver must have identified him almost at once. He brought the car into the kerb, wound down the window and spoke the first half of the *parol*. Schramme replied with the second and slid in. He said, 'Pull across and wait. I want to follow that coach into Geneva.'

33. MORTON—*We*

HE LAY ON HIS BACK in a huge press. Faces he could barely see floated over his head like a cluster of pale balloons.

Someone said again, 'Where is she?'

He said, knowing, 'I don't know. I don't know.'

Another turn of the screw. The pressure on his chest increased. Something would snap—his rib cage, his sternum. When you pressed down sharply on the breast-bone of a bird it died instantly.

The voice that sounded—why hadn't he recognized it before?—like Schramme's, said again, 'Where is she?' They put a red-hot poker to his side. Schramme said, 'It is my function to lay bare the true man. You are your own judge and jury and a stern one. Where is she?' The vice tightened until he knew his heart must burst. A bell began ringing, high-pitched, spiteful.

The bell rang maddeningly. He was awake. Dawn light seeped round the edges of the curtained windows. He fumbled into a dressing gown that hid its arms from him like a live thing, and went downstairs.

It was Morton. He had a car outside. He said, 'We tried your phone but it's out of order.' His face was dark with overnight stubble but his eyes were still bright. He followed Jagger upstairs and stood about the small kitchen, watching him make coffee.

Jagger said, 'My days only come in the handy twenty-four hour pack. I hadn't even begun to knit up the ravelled sleave of care.'

Morton said, 'Don't give up now. You're just coming to the glory bit.'

Jagger said, 'As a friend of mine said very recently, "Glory! *Je m'en merde!*" '

Morton sipped and scalded his mouth. He said, 'You don't really mean that. Yes, you really do! Never mind. You're a hero whether you like it or not. How did Ida come to give you her telephone number?'

Jagger said, 'My fatal charm,' and told him.

Morton said, 'Anyway, we paid the lady a visit.'

Jagger was still feeling as if he'd been trampled and left for dead, but the hot coffee was like a blood transfusion. 'I thought you didn't want to come face to face?'

Morton grinned. 'We took a leaf from their spy book. They gave us a fire. We gave them a burglary. By the time the police were told officially, the place had been pretty thoroughly turned over.'

He shook his head in mock sorrow. 'What a mess! Filing cabinets broken into, safe opened, strong boxes taken away. Oh, and they also played havoc with a lot of electronic equipment.' He poured himself more coffee, exuding satisfaction.

'Did you—they—find anything?' Jagger asked.

'Just a stack of technical stuff. The kind of thing Data Corporation specializes in. I can't imagine why the thieves thought it was important.' Morton stopped being jokey. 'We haven't really had time to check properly yet, but a lot of the data came from places that aren't on their client list.'

He loaded his cup with sugar. 'The cops had to get Simmons out of bed. He's still there. They want him to make a list of what's missing. I have a feeling that he's nearing the end of a promising career. Still, that isn't the only reason I got you up.'

Jagger didn't say anything. Morton said softly, 'Is this the Jagger I heard so much about?'

He said, 'I don't know what you heard.'

Morton said, 'We haven't exactly found Tinn, but we know where he is. And who he's with. Or are you a stickler for whoms?'

219

Jagger said, 'You know where he is, so you'll soon have him back. What more do you want?'

'Tinn is with the Pargeter girl. You knew that much. Somebody with a suspicious mind might think you knew more.'

Jagger said, 'And we both know someone with a suspicious mind. All right. Where are they?' He knew the answer. He'd half-guessed it on the way from Cheyne Square, fallen asleep trying to disbelieve it and revealed it under duress as the doorbell dragged him from his dreams.

Morton looked at his watch. 'Tinn and the girl took a flight to Geneva. They arrived about an hour ago, just too late for us to intercept them. We thought you might know what they'd do next.'

Jagger slipped off his stool and went back to the living room. He drew the curtains. The sky showed the bright pink symptoms of sunburn. An early bus, lights still on, trundled along the far side of the Common.

He'd known. With anyone else but Patti it would have been unthinkable, but he'd known. This time she hadn't waited for someone to tell her she didn't understand. You don't wait for things to happen; you make them!

Morton was standing almost where Patti had stood in those final, fatal seconds two nights ago. He liked the man well enough but at this moment he felt he'd rather strangle him with his bare hands than betray an enterprise so absurd, so magnificent, so doomed. He said, 'What will they do next? How the hell would I know?'

Morton nodded. There were dark smudges under his eyes. His unshaven cheeks were grey and hollow with fatigue. He said, 'You weren't my ferret. You were his. I believe in flushing out my own ratholes. Schramme worked for Ida. Ida's European headquarters are in Geneva.'

Jagger had turned back to the window. On the grassy common the dew shone like wet silk. 'So Schramme was a C.I.A. man all the time. You don't need me, someone who refuses to recognize the obvious.'

Morton said, 'Schramme worked for the Yanks. But what if he was already working for someone else?'

This time he struck a spark. Jagger said, 'What makes you say that?'

'There was plenty of evidence of Schramme's work in Ida's offices, but it was all technical data. No blackmail information, nor any indication at all that Ida used it. But Schramme was collecting it for somebody. And in Lusty's case, at least, we know it was used.'

Jagger took a chair. 'It's just possible you feel worse than I do, but I doubt it. You tell me.'

'What if everybody's right? The Master, you, Schramme? Schramme gave you the whistle and started to tell you something about Ida, but he hadn't time to finish. Supposing he was switching his story? That would mean he'd been going to tell you he'd really been working for the Americans. Why would he do that? And if it was true, how could he be sure?'

Jagger buried his face in his hands. After a while, he said, 'If he was really a Russian agent, already working for Moscow when the Americans put the bite on him.' Now he'd said it, he felt it had been somewhere in his mind all the time.

'Right! So what if he'd come over as an "illegal"*, with a long-term programme? First, to establish himself as a British citizen, with a business that was not only reputable but invaluable to Moscow? The Russians are a technology-hungry people. And that isn't all. It could be that Schramme genuinely wanted to emigrate to the States, had been ordered to do so as soon as his cover was deep enough. He'd have been even more useful to Moscow there. The pickings are richer.'

Jagger was listening carefully enough now. 'The Russians and the Americans had the same idea? The interview technique?'

'Why not? It wouldn't be the first time. Every espionage service is on the look-out for people like Schramme, people

*Illegals are Russian deep-cover agents working in a foreign country. After lengthy training they virtually become citizens of the country to which they are assigned, and work independently of other Russian espionage groups.

who have access to valuable information as part of a normal, respectable job. The Russians dreamed up Schramme's technique, blackmail included. The Yanks obviously penetrated his cover far enough to put the black on *him*, then decided to use him almost exactly in the same way as the Russians, but minus blackmail candidates. How's that for irony. Moscow must have laughed!'

'If Schramme really was working for Moscow, why did he go out of his way to tell me? He could have caused a lot more trouble if he'd said he was a C.I.A. man.'

Morton said, 'You're tired and you've taken a beating. Schramme had to tell you the story he thought you were most likely to swallow. So long as he believed you were to be knocked off, it didn't matter. When he realized the Americans would gain most by killing you both, he tried to change his line so as to do as much damage as possible to Anglo-American relations as well as wrecking the C.I.A.'s technical intelligence operations in the U.K. He knew we'd interpret all the Russian overtones as a clumsy attempt by the Yanks to fool us.'

Morton snapped his fingers, thinking of something else.

'And I can guess why he arranged that rendezvous with the C.I.A. at Victoria. When you started poking around he thought the game was up. He didn't mind being blown with us so long as he could preserve his cover with the Yanks and maybe still get himself to the States, as a K.G.B. double agent. Want to bet? He told them the Russian story, betting that because they thought they'd been controlling him they'd never realize he'd been playing double, that he was really Moscow's man.

'Mind you, the Master won't have it. So far as he's concerned, all the Russian trimmings are Yankee red herrings. Pardon the pun!'

Jagger said, 'He could still be right. There's no proof.'

Morton shook his head. 'There's no proof, but I know I'm right. Still, what we have to worry about now is why Tinn and the girl have gone to Geneva.'

Jagger had already made up his mind. She hadn't a hope,

but he'd destroyed her illusions once. He wasn't going to do it a second time. He said, 'How would I know? I've done my stint. From now on it's all yours.'

Morton said, 'Pity! I had an idea that you wouldn't want to see her harmed.'

'I wouldn't.'

Morton looked at his watch again. 'I wouldn't under-estimate the C.I.A. If they could get their hands on Tinn before us they wouldn't be likely to let anything stand in the way. Especially not a girl.'

He let the point sink in. 'There isn't another commercial flight to Geneva until eleven. I've a service plane standing by. We've just time to clean up a little. Our embassy at Berne's working on the Swiss but they're at full stretch because of the conference. Anyway, we would much sooner find Tinn ourselves.'

Slowly, reluctantly, Jagger said, 'It'll take me ten minutes.'

Morton said, 'After you with the razor. By the way, I think I might be able to fix your phone. You've been using some-thing of ours that you don't really need any more.' He began unscrewing the bottom of the telephone. He called out above the sound of running water. 'We bugged you a couple of weeks ago, when the little man was still suspicious. I tried to get you a couple of times before I drove out here but the line was engaged. We couldn't pick anything up on the monitor, so our bug's obviously gone on the blink. We shall have to——'

His voice tailed away for a moment. He said, 'One of the damned screws is stuck. I'll have to send somebody round afterwards.'

A moment later he came into the bathroom. Against the background of running water he said softly but very clearly, 'There's nothing wrong with the screws. Somebody's swapped bugs. We aren't the only ones who know Tinn and the girl are in Geneva. Hurry up with that razor.'

34. D.C.I.—*If not us, not them!*

As he closed the door behind him the White House security adviser said, 'It can't be world war three. I'd have read it in the papers.'

Head of Plans said, 'Boy, you certainly took some finding!'

White House said, 'If you fellers can't find somebody, who the heck can?'

The Director said, 'That's a very loaded question. That question is so loaded it's hard to believe it's just coincidence.' He didn't appear to be joking.

White House took off his glasses as he sat down. He began to polish them, blinking myopically. 'Somebody missing?'

The Director took a long, deep breath. 'Tinn.'

White House dropped his glasses, made a grab at them and succeeded in knocking them a yard across the carpet. Head of Plans retrieved them. White House held them up to the light, squinting to see whether any damage had been done. He put them back on. He said, 'Tinn, huh? Them or us?'

Grimly, the Director said, 'Not us.'

White House said, 'Tell,' his voice angry.

The Director looked at Head of Plans. He said, 'Henry, tell.'

Head of Plans said, 'Not much to tell and none of it good. Tinn disappeared from his lodgings. They missed him at one a.m., British time—around seven p.m. here—but he could have been gone anything up to two hours earlier. We heard as soon as they did. Wire tap.'

White House said acidly, 'Disappeared? That's kind of a vague word.'

The Director said, 'Maybe, but they don't know where he is.'

White House narrowed his eyes. 'Mart, did you bring me out here just to tell me that? What about your boy on the spot? Does he know anything?'

The Director cleared his throat. 'He doesn't have too much to say at this present moment. He's blown. The whole goddamed technical intelligence operation's blown.'

White House sat up straight. He said, 'Oh *no*!' with as

many shades of feeling as if he'd recited the whole of 'To be or not to be.'

Head of Plans said, 'You can't win 'em all. They didn't just lay Ida. They took her more ways than there are in the *Kama Sutra*. Simmons is still picking up the bits. Of course, they won't press anything, officially or otherwise. Everything in the very best tradition of British tact, but Data Corporation doesn't have an English subsidiary any more.'

White House pinched his nose hard for several seconds. He took pity on it, let it go and said, 'It's obvious, isn't it? They say they don't know where their boy is but that's for our benefit. They clean up the whole business at one go. Out with Ida, in with Tinn, and that to Uncle Sam.'

The Director said, 'I'd love to settle for it, but there's more. You know about this guy Schramme?'

'Only what you've told me,' White House said.

'Schramme's vanished too. Round about the same time.' The Director gave him a summary.

White House abandoned any pretence of calm. His eyes burned coldly and the blood showed in his cheeks. 'There has to be some connection! Schramme first, then Tinn and——' He stopped. He said, 'Hey!'

Head of Plans said, 'We saw it. Schramme's a Russian double agent. It's the only thing that figures. He worked for us, but his heart belonged to daddy.'

'The K.B.G.!' White House snapped. 'Mart, I don't have to tell you the President's not going to be too pleased about this.'

The Director looked angry in turn. 'You're damned right you don't. *I* don't like it! I'd hoped you'd be the first to realize that.'

White House held up a hand. 'Okay. Cool it. I'm sorry. Where do we go from here? And incidentally, let's try to use our own brains instead of relying any more on computers. That COMSTAR's run out of credit at my bank.'

The Director's intercom brayed. He pressed a key. Charlie

Osgood's voice said, 'Sorry to bother you, but I have to see Henry fast and they tell me he's with you.'

The Director said, 'Is it important? We're kind of tied up right this minute.'

Osgood said, 'I think this might loosen a few knots.'

The Director said, 'Come on up.'

White House said, 'Well, you have to hand it to those boys in the Kremlin. They go back on their secret promises, persuade us it's all our fault, get us going the wrong way by kidding us they'll kiss and make friends if we do something to block Tinn, and all the time they're planning to hijack him themselves. Mart, I hate to say it, but this is the biggest foul-up for *La Compania** since the Bay of Pigs.'

When Osgood came in he looked unprofessionally excited. He said, 'We just had a message from Simmons's deputy. They planted a bug on one of the British S.I.S. men last night and it's paid off in a big way. Funny thing was, the phone had already been bugged. Not an infinity transmitter, like ours, but they had to switch——'

Head of Plans reached out a long arm and pulled Osgood into a chair. He said, 'First things first, Charlie.'

White House said, 'Infinity transmitter?'

Head of Plans explained. 'A little gadget you wire into a telephone receiver. One of the neatest and simplest bugs. It's triggered by a pre-set signal, a fixed note from a whistle or a tuning fork. All you do to operate it is to dial the number and trigger the bug. It cuts out the phone circuit, gives the engaged signal to anyone else who happens to call and turns the receiver into a microphone. You can listen to anything in the room and you can do it from the other side of the world if it suits you. That's how it gets its name.' He nodded at Osgood. 'Go ahead, Charlie.'

Osgood said, 'Tinn wasn't picked up by Schramme. He's in Geneva, with Pargeter's daughter.'

He got his sensation. Everyone spoke at once.

*A slang name for the C.I.A., especially in Latin America.

The Director said, 'With Pargeter's daughter? But——'

Head of Plans said, 'Geneva? Judas Priest!'

White House said, 'Isn't that where Dobereiner——?'

Head of Plans said, 'It sure is! It sure is, by God! Charlie! Operations room!' He left like an ill-trained long-distance runner, all knees and elbows. Osgood followed.

White House said seriously, 'Mart, where's your lucky rabbit's foot?'

The Director said, 'Nobody's making me uncross my fingers to look for it.' He thought for a moment. 'You didn't see Dobereiner's last report? This Pargeter girl. He met her. He said she's an oddball. As pretty as all-get-out but an oddball. Idealistic, intense. The kind that pickets the Pentagon. Dobereiner had the impression she was up to something.'

'Do you mean,' White House said quietly, 'a kook? Or something more?'

The Director didn't answer. Head of Plans came back, breathing hard through his nose, his pipe streaming a blue, evanescent whirl of smoke. 'If this outfit,' he said, 'is only a half of what we think it is, we might track those two down before the British. There's just one more thing I have to know.'

He stood over them, his hands on his hips, an ectomorphic caricature of Dürer's golden mean. 'Tinn's apparently up for grabs. Do we play like my great-aunt Mary-Lou, who can't bear to lose her match-sticks? Or do we go for broke?'

The Director and White House exchanged looks. The Director said, 'So long as we keep our noses clean with the Swiss, we go for broke. If we can't have him, let's make sure no one else does.'

Head of Plans said, 'I bet the poor little bastard never thought higher mathematics could be dangerous.'

White House said, 'Like it's that kind of world, man.'

35. ONE AND ALL

PATTI AWOKE with a physical start. The room was in near darkness, shuttered against the daylight. She switched on the bedside lamp and looked at her watch. Less than an hour to noon. She slipped out of bed, opened the window, pushed back the shutters, The street outside wore its window boxes of late summer flowers like medal ribbons. The day was bright.

She dressed quickly. Her plan was in tatters. It might not have gone far anyway, but with Kia still in New York there wasn't a chance. She'd been beaten by a bloody little 'flu virus.

It left her in a mess in more ways than one. Her sense of urgency and her usual high octane enthusiasm had made her cut corners and she'd made one-way flight bookings. On top of that she hadn't been able to rake much currency together at such short notice. What she had, apart from a little sterling, she'd 'borrowed' from her father's business reserve.

She spilled out the contents of her bag, prodding disconsolately at a cosmopolitan mixture of coins and notes. Enough to pay for the hotel. Not enough for two return flights. She'd asked Tinn already. Typically, he'd practically no money at all.

She sat on the bed, gnawing her thumb. The first thing was to decide what to do. It occurred to her that Tinn's disappearance might have caused a bit of a stir. You didn't think about that kind of thing when you started because if you did, you'd never start. All the same they must have realized by now that Tinn had vanished. They'd be trying to find out who'd done what and why. It cheered her up, briefly. Then it made her realize that what had begun as a snowball could finish up as an avalanche.

What she desperately needed was someone to help her sort everything out. Someone, in fact, like——

She was astonished at the turbulent cross-currents of emotion. All right, he was the one person who'd be able to find a way out of the mess. But he was also the one person

228

she couldn't ask, because she'd asked him for something before, and he'd turned her down.

Hunched on the edge of the bed, she stared hopelessly out of the window at a Dayglo splash of scarlet geraniums across the street, checking a long list of reasons why she couldn't telephone Jagger.

Then she decided to ask him anyway.

She went out into the corridor. It was deserted but an unseen vacuum cleaner filled it with noise like a wind in a forest. She knocked on the door of the next room. There was no reply. She knocked a little louder, tried the handle and found the door opening.

Tinn was still asleep, face buried deep in the pillow, legs drawn up like a child. From the bedside table his glasses watched her emptily.

So long as he stayed where he was, she had one worry less. She went back to her own room, found one of the hotel's business cards and printed: *Please stay here until I get back. Shan't be long.* She propped the card against his glasses, hung the 'don't disturb' sign on his door and went downstairs. Hotel telephones went through hotel switchboards. She wanted something more private and the central post-office was less than five minutes away.

The man in the Citroën parked across the road nudged his companion. 'Here's the girl now.' The other lowered his paper and peered over the top. He'd learned a lot since arriving in Geneva and making his report to the Centre.

He folded the paper neatly and opened the door. '*Podozhdité zdes,*' he said. 'Wait here. If the man comes out before you hear from me, follow him. If he doesn't join the girl and me, phone in at the first chance. *Ya pommáyu?*'

The driver said, '*Khorishó, tovarich.* I understand.'

Schramme shut the door and strolled slowly after Patti.

The car provided by the Berne embassy swished them smoothly down the Rue de la Servette. Morton said, 'All right. I know I'm harping on it, but it takes some swallowing.'

Jagger said, 'You don't know her. I do.'

Morton said, 'I'm sorry. It's obviously my loss, but you must admit!'

Jagger said, 'Morton, my friend, you've forgotten what it's like to be young. When you're young, you care. If you care enough, you do something. Or you try.' He winced as the car jounced his arm against his sore side.

'Are you trying to tell me,' Morton asked maliciously, 'that you too once cared?' Getting no reply, he said, 'Anyway, the other girl stayed in New York with the 'flu, so if you're right, the thing's stillborn. Not that anybody in their right mind would have had such a crazy idea in the first place.'

'Since when,' Jagger said, 'did you have to be crazy to have ideals? Arteries aren't the only things that harden as you grow older.'

'Were you ever that idealistic?' Morton asked.

Jagger said, 'No, but I have the grace to feel ashamed.'

Morton said, 'Well, we're walking on eggs from now on. This place is full of conference delegates. Everybody has his secret service uncle in town, the Swiss police and security people are at full stretch, and we have to find two people among a quarter of a million and get 'em back home without saying why. The embassy's doing its nut!'

The car skirted the Cornavin station, turned into the Rue de Lausanne and began to thread through buff-coloured sidestreets lined with elegantly balconied apartment buildings. It glided to a halt outside a hotel like a stone and glass bookcase. Directly ahead of them, plane trees flanked a misty vista across the open lake towards a lush promontory. Beyond lay the cloud-banked ghosts of mountains.

The lobby was thronged with a Heinz variety of nationalities. Morton said, 'In the bar. You might guess, with an embassy type!' He led the way through a series of interconnecting rooms like antique dealers' showrooms. Unreal people posed against unreal backgrounds of overstuffed furniture, bronze heroic statuary and flowers arranged like

230

butterflies on pins. Even the air, throbbing with electronic music like a mortician's parlour, smelled artificial.

The bar was Regency stripes and plush-upholstered hush. A man in suede boots put down his glass and fluttered ballet dancer's fingers at them. He wore a suit that spoke of Burlington Gardens in mildly eccentric accents, a pale mauve button-down shirt and a Guards tie that held everything together like a drill sergeant with a bunch of gentlemen cadets.

Morton said, 'This is Creevy. He's been kind enough to nip over from Berne.'

Creevy draped his fingers briefly over Jagger's without giving him the privilege of holding them. He said, 'A drag for one and all, but needs must, *mmmmm*?' He discovered a brand-new vowel in 'drag'. He waved at a stocky, dark-haired man shaped like a spinning top and said, 'Let me introduce you. Herr Wipfli. Swiss security police. He's a trifle fraught but he's doing what he can.'

Wipfli bowed slightly from an indetectable waist. In the voice used by Nazi generals in American films made in England he said, 'We shall do our best, my dear sirs, but you will appreciate the problems. We are stretched to the limit of our abilities. One mistake of judgement at present and we have an international incident. One international incident and the conference ends before it begins. You understand clearly?'

He smiled apologetically but the warning wrapped up in the round, pink package of his face showed quite clearly through the pale grey holes of his eyes.

Creevy said, 'We all understand perfectly, Herr Wipfli. The last thing Her Majesty's Government wishes is any incident of any kind.'

Herr Wipfli bent once more from his hidden middle. 'Thank you. Switzerland is a neutral country and naturally cannot permit ideologic conflict on its soil.' He hid his chilly stare among a sudden sunburst of smile wrinkles and said, 'We do what we can. But this is unmannerly. You will permit me to buy you a drink?'

The telephone on the bar tinkled discreetly. The barman answered and looked up. As if they were all at the far side of the room he shouted, 'Monsieur Wipfli?'

Wipfli spun his top-shape on the tips of his toes. '*Me voici!*' He took the telephone, repeated his name, listened, said, '*Ils viennent d'arriver. Je les mettrai au courant. Merci.*'

He replaced the phone. With the merest trace of complacency he said, 'So! This is not so bad. We check the hotels and your friends are found.' He took out a notebook, scribbled, tore out a sheet and handed it to Morton. 'Hotel du Mont. By car, five minutes.'

With unexpected quickness Creevy said, 'Get you a cab.' He floated out like a willowy Mercury.

Wipfli produced a card. 'I shall hope for many reasons that you are back in London tonight, but if not, I am again at your disposal.'

Creevy reappeared and waved. As they passed him he said, 'For God's sake be careful. The Swiss won't stand any funny business. I'll wait here until I hear from you.'

For Tinn, wakefulness and sleep were two extremes of the same state. He drifted back to consciousness cell by placid cell. His eyes opened, but without his glasses the green walls and gleaming mirrors of his surroundings remained vague, dreamlike, somehow sub-aquatic. He fumbled for his glasses in the shuttered shade. Patti's message slid from the table and wafted sideways under the bed. He sat up, thumbing his glasses into place. He remembered where he was. He got up.

Washing and shaving methodically, his mind sifted through the events of the past twenty-four hours, making unpredictable leaps as he discarded whatever seemed unimportant.

He was in Geneva, with Patricia Pargeter. Taken as an unrelated fact, that was good. He trusted her, otherwise he wouldn't be here. But today there were problems to be faced. Miss Pargeter's plan might not work, because her friend had caught influenza. What would happen next he didn't really know.

There were a good many things he didn't really know, but Pa—but Miss Pargeter would sort everything out. He supposed she was what you would call worldly in the nicest kind of way. She seemed to understand all the things he'd never really given much thought to.

She even understood the fascinating piece of reasoning he'd begun down in Wiltshire. Bit by bit, a series of complex and beautiful concepts had emerged. With their guidance you could persuade certain kinds of high-energy wave motions that they weren't themselves, that they were other kinds of radiation with quite different properties.

With the proper apparatus they could be made to 'think' —though the word was absurd!—that they were penetrating solid surfaces when in fact they were being reflected, and without losing any energy. He'd tried to explain it to Miss Pargeter. She'd been so insistent. He'd had to tell her.

Of course she'd thought of something more fanciful. She said it was like a man being hypnotized into doing things that were stupid and quite unlike his normal behaviour. Then you woke him up and told him what he'd done and he flew into a blinding rage and smashed everything for miles around. She'd said something about hypnosis being dangerous in the wrong hands.

But was it really your fault if—well, if you found a pebble on the beach, a beautiful pebble, and somebody else took it and put it in a—in a sling and used it to kill Goliath——? He jerked in surprise and cut his face with the razor. Now he was being poetic and fanciful. That was what happened when you spent time with people like Pa—like Miss Pargeter.

Well, maybe it wouldn't be your fault, but it wasn't a very satisfactory way of employing aesthetically pleasing ideas, either. After all, mathematics was every bit as aesthetically pleasing as poetry and things like that. So he agreed with her —such ideas shouldn't be allowed to benefit people like Arnold Parsons, who was kind enough but very crude, or Sir Ben Pargeter, who made him feel awkward and foolish. And certainly not the director of the advanced weapons research

233

establishment, who'd forgotten what it was like to be a scientist in the excitement of finding out what it was like to be a politician.

He'd admitted—or had she suggested?—that it might be a good idea to talk about his work to someone who'd appreciate its elegance, and Patti—he meant Miss Pargeter—had said that all he had to do was explain it to someone high up in the United Nations Organization and leave it to them to find the right person.

Now it was all over before it had started. Or was it? He wouldn't put it past her to think of something. He dried his face, dabbing awkwardly at his cut cheek. It was nearly midday. He dressed and peered out into the corridor. Nobody about. He tapped timidly at her door. No reply. He tried again, a little louder. A middle-aged woman came round the corner at the end of the corridor, carrying a vacuum cleaner. She said something in French.

He fled before her, mumbling stupidly. In the foyer the receptionist spoke to him in English. He supposed they could tell. He asked if he could ring Miss Pargeter's room. She said, 'Oh, but the young lady is out, half an hour ago.' He felt foolish again, muttered that he'd look for her but if he missed her he wouldn't be long. She smiled, but he was sure she was secretly laughing at him. People did. He couldn't blame them. He blundered out into the street.

He was only a short distance from a main shopping thoroughfare. He crossed it as soon as there was a gap in the traffic. A policeman blew his whistle loudly, angrily, pointing at him and then at the traffic lights. He pushed his glasses hard against the top of his nose and walked quickly up the nearest side turning. He felt everyone was looking.

He came out on a river bank with a bridge and an island with an old, tall building on it. A lot of clear, very cold-looking water was flowing under the bridge. There were other bridges in either direction and he could see swans in the distance. A man following behind him looked as if he might be going to catch up and speak. Tinn crossed the bridge at a shambling trot. He turned up a long straight street that led towards trees and big blocks of flats.

It was lined with a jumble of offices, garages and workshops. Inside a radio and television wholesalers' a hugely amplified voice shouted in French, officious, threatening. He crossed the road to avoid it and was almost run over by a cream and orange trolley-bus.

He walked up the shady side of the street towards the distant trees. The man he'd seen on the bridge was still following some twenty yards behind. It could have been coincidence, but he remembered a trip to Paris when a man had stopped him and shown him some very embarrassing photographs. He didn't want it to happen again. He quickened his pace, pursued by the huge angry voice from the radio shop. He was approaching a large drab building like a nineteenth-century railway office. It had a little balcony that hung over the street, and sprouted a stubby flagpole. It would only have served to review a very unimportant parade but it seemed to go with the dictatorial voice and made him feel uncomfortable. As he passed it, something caught his eye in the doorway.

He thumbed up his glasses, went a little closer and peered at a mosaic of company names on metal plates. One of them said: DATA CORPORATION OF AMERICA.

He remembered. Mr Dobereiner, who'd seemed to get on so well with Miss Pargeter. And Mr Simmons, who'd been very polite to Tinn himself. Of course! Mr Dobereiner lived in Geneva. If Miss Pargeter had been with him now they could perhaps have called in to say hello, but Tinn couldn't think of doing it by himself.

As he turned away he saw that the man who might have been following him had almost caught up. He was definitely going to speak. Tinn plunged hastily into the dark entrance hall. The Data Corporation plate had said the first floor. He went up and saw the name on a frosted glass door. He'd no intention of going in but he had to lose that man.

He looked down the stairs and saw the man silhouetted

against the light from the street. There wasn't much option. Tinn knocked nervously at the glass door, opened it and went in.

36. OURS

Moscow's INSTRUCTIONS on Tinn were classically simple. Alive if possible. If not, not. Schramme might have been blown with the British and the Americans, but he was the only one who was familiar with Tinn and the Pargeter girl and he knew just how much was at stake.

He followed Patti to the foot of the post-office steps, saw her hesitate and turn away. She went on towards the Quai du Mont-Blanc, crossed the road and walked slowly along the water's edge with the gulls wheeling and the yellow buoys bobbing like outsize grapefruit. He crossed too, waiting. There was still no clue why she and Tinn had come to Geneva. He could recognize her uncertainty without understanding its meaning.

She recrossed the road to a café, took a seat and ordered coffee. He stayed where he was, keeping watch behind his newspaper as he leaned against a stone urn of mauve and white petunias. After two or three perfunctory sips she seemed to reach a decision. She paid her bill and turned back into the town. He had to hurry not to lose her.

This time she went into the post-office without hesitation. He caught the inner door before it stopped swinging. She headed for a telephone booth. Before she could shut herself in he joined her, closing the door behind them. She turned, startled and indignant, then alarmed when she saw him. He said, 'Good morning, Patti.'

Before she could speak he added, 'It is regrettably melodramatic but I am holding a loaded, silenced pistol in my pocket. You must believe me when I say that I should not hesitate to use it.'

236

She found herself breathing fast, her heart thumping uncomfortably. She said, 'What do you want?'

He said, 'You were going to make a phone call? Let me make it for you. Then arrange for Tinn to meet us.'

He took the receiver from its rest, laid it down, dialled, picked it up and listened, then said, '*Un moment, s'il vous plaît.*' He handed her the phone. As she reluctantly put it to her ear, he stood even closer, bending his head so that he could hear what was said from the other end. She found his nearness repellent.

Speaking her good French, she asked for Tinn. The girl said instantly that he had gone out.

Schramme whispered, 'Where?'

Patti repeated the question. The girl said, 'He was going to look for you. He left ten minutes ago. He said he wouldn't be long.'

She looked round at Schramme, biting her lip. He nodded. She said, 'Thank you,' and replaced the phone. Schramme dialled another number. The hidden gun pressed uncomfortably against her side. After a moment Schramme began to speak a language Patti couldn't understand, though she thought it might be Russian.

He was asking a series of questions. She sensed a note of urgency in his voice. He finished the call and steered her out of the booth. He took her arm. He said, 'If you wish no harm to come to your friend or yourself you will do nothing foolish.' They stepped out into the sunlight.

He said, 'Why did you come to Geneva? What number were you going to call just now?'

She said, 'I don't see why I should tell you,' angry to find her voice a little breathless.

'I will give you a reason! It may save your Mr Tinn's life.'

She repaid his half-truth with one of her own. 'I brought him here to get him away from them.'

'Them?'

'My father. Other people. They're driving him too hard. He's on the edge of a breakdown.'

'Not to arrange a secret meeting with the Americans?'

'Americans? Here? Of course not! He doesn't know anyone in Geneva.'

He squeezed her arm painfully. 'No? Then why has he gone to pay a call on Data Corporation of America?'

She stared, astonished. 'Jack? He hasn't. Who says he has?'

They came out again on to the Quai du Mont-Blanc. He led her to a seat. The flat-topped shadowy bulk of Mont Salève faced them like a piece cut out of the sky. He said, 'You're being foolish after all. He has been followed by one of my colleagues, who reports that he is with Data Corporation. Do you expect me to believe you know nothing of this?'

'You can believe what you like. I know Data Corporation, yes. I met two people yesterday who belonged to it. So did Jack. It was the first he'd ever had to do with them.'

'What two people?'

'A man called Dobereiner, who comes from——' She stopped.

He prompted her. 'Yes?'

'From Geneva. The other's called Simmons. He's in charge of the London subsidiary. International Data Analysts.'

'International Data Analysts?' He was staring at her oddly. His face changed in a way she didn't understand. He said, 'Ida!'

'If you like. That's what Daddy calls them.'

He was pulling her up. He seemed excited. 'Come!' He waved for a taxi, bundled her in and gave the name of her hotel. In a low voice he said, 'How stupid you must think me. But I think it is you who are stupid, to allow them to involve you in this business. Now the conference is over before it begins.'

They sat in silence, Patti because she couldn't understand anything at all, Schramme because he was deep in thought, though the gun still pressed uncomfortably against her. They reached the Rue de Chantepoulet and slowed for the turn that would bring them to the hotel. Suddenly Schramme

238

said quickly to the driver, 'I have changed my mind. Go on. Rue du Stand.'

She knew at once why he'd changed his mind. She'd seen it too, though it was still difficult to believe. On the pavement, turning to enter the foyer of the Hotel du Mont, had been two men. One she'd never seen before. The other was Jagger.

Tinn shifted awkwardly on his uncomfortable chair. The girl at the desk stopped typing and said in her American-accented English, 'I'm sorry, Mr Tinn. Mr Dobereiner should have been here by now. Are you sure no one else can help?'

She knew that Dobereiner only dealt with certain clients. M. Gainsbourg handled the company's day-to-day business.

Tinn said, 'N-n-no, thanks. It's Mr D-d-dobereiner I came to see.' He looked at his watch. At first he'd only been concerned to get away from that street tout. Then he'd remembered they were short of money. If Miss Pargeter had thought of Dobereiner, Tinn was sure she would have asked him to help. The least Tinn could do in the circumstances was to tell Dobereiner they were here and in difficulties. He wouldn't have dared, normally, but for Pa—for Miss Pargeter it was different.

Still, he'd waited half an hour. Perhaps he'd better go back and tell her first. He stood up, shuffling. The girl looked round. He was sure he amused her. It was something he should have been used to by now, but he never was.

He said, 'I don't think I c-c-can wait any longer. P-p-perhaps if I left m-m-my name and address?'

She took it down and he left thankfully. If he'd actually seen Dobereiner he'd only have made a fool of himself. It was much better if Pa—if Miss Pargeter spoke to him. He stepped out into the street and turned back towards the hotel.

Five minutes earlier Schramme, in the same street, had stopped his taxi to pick up the man who'd been following

239

Tinn. Schramme was saying now, 'It would not have been safe to wait. You might have drawn attention to yourself. He has friends in that place, and more friends at the hotel. We'll take the girl with us. I need time to think.'

Patti, sandwiched between them, could understand nothing, though she was sure now that they were both speaking Russian.

Schramme said, 'On second thoughts, leave the girl with me. They know me but not you. Go back to the hotel. Keep your eyes open, be careful and find out what you can, then come back to Rue Forget. I'll be waiting.'

He leaned forward to give the taxi driver fresh instructions.

In Data Corporation's outer office the phone was ringing. The girl stopped typing to answer it. She said, 'Oh, Mr Dobereiner! What a pity! There was a gentleman here to see you and he's only just this minute gone. Yes, he did. And his address. His name's Tinn. There's no need to shout, Mr Dobereiner! That's what I said. Tinn.'

In the lobby of the Hotel du Mont, Morton said, 'I don't like it. How long do you think we should wait? I promised Creevy I'd ring.'

Jagger said, 'You're the boss. You make the decisions.'

Morton said, 'I wouldn't worry about the girl. But when Tinn goes out by himself——'

Jagger said, 'Who cares about Tinn?'

Morton shot him a sidelong glance. 'Don't misunderstand me. I want to find them both and get them back safe and sound. But Tinn's the one who matters. At least, that's the way the people who call the tune will see things.'

Jagger said edgily, 'They may call your tune, but I'm nobody's piper. Not any more.'

Morton wasn't listening. He was staring at the door. It swung open and Tinn walked in. He didn't see them. He went towards the reception counter. Behind him, the door was opening again. A broad-shouldered man with a broken-veined, toughly handsome face and a crewcut the colour of pewter pushed through fast, his eyes bright and hungry. He called out, 'Hey! Jack Tinn! How've you been?'

Jagger stood up. For the first time in days he felt pleasure. He said, 'Well, Mr Dobereiner! How have *you* been?'

37. THEIRS

THEY WERE WAITING for Wipfli. Morton began to laugh again. 'Ever rescued a mouse from a cat? That's just how Dobereiner looked. And there wasn't a thing he could do.'

Jagger said, 'Or say. Not even about Patti.'

'He doesn't know anything about her. I'll stake my life on it.'

'It isn't your life I'm worried about.'

'I'm sorry.' Morton looked it, too. 'I just don't think she's in danger. If Dobereiner had her he'd have made sure we got the message.'

He turned to Tinn. 'You spoke to no one except the typist?'

Tinn shook his head. 'No one.'

'You never mentioned Miss Pargeter?'

Tinn shook his head again. Morton turned back to Jagger. 'You said yourself she doesn't give up in a hurry. So she's somewhere around the Palais des Nations and Wipfli's people will find her. If they don't she'll be back here before the afternoon's over. Relax!'

Jagger suddenly realized that Morton, for all his assurance, was worried too. Then he saw that what concerned Morton wasn't so much the girl's safety as whether she'd talk out of turn. It didn't improve his own state of mind.

They were all in Tinn's room. Morton sat on the bed, Tinn and Jagger in two uncomfortable basket chairs. The remnants of a cold lunch sat messily on a tray. Tinn said apologetically, 'I wouldn't have called on Mr D-d-dobereiner if the man hadn't been following me.'

Jagger and Morton looked up as one man. The telephone

rang. Morton dithered uncharacteristically before answering. He listened and said, 'Wipfli's on the way up.' He turned on Tinn and said more fiercely than he'd intended, 'What man?'

Tinn blinked. 'I don't know. I think he m-m-might have wanted to s-s-sell me something.'

There was a knock. A voice said, 'It is I. Wipfli.'

Morton let him in, unable to pursue Tinn's remark any further. Wipfli looked curiously at Tinn. 'This is the man?'

Morton introduced them. Tinn mumbled, shoving at his glasses. Wipfli said, 'And the young lady? You have heard nothing?'

Morton said, 'Nothing.'

Wipfli said, 'We have circulated the description. We look. We can do no more.' He was watching Morton and Jagger with an odd intentness.

'She's somewhere around that opening ceremony,' Morton said. 'You can bet on it.'

Wipfli said, 'I do not bet, which is just as well. The opening ceremony is postponed. Perhaps for good. The Russian delegation once more accuses the Americans of bad faith and threatens to return to Moscow.' He studied the effect of his news and added, 'My government wishes you to leave Switzerland as soon as the girl is found. Mr Creevy has been informed. You will be one problem less.' He held open the door of the room. 'There is a car outside. Mr Creevy expects you.'

Morton and Jagger exchanged glances. Jagger mentally deserted his post. He said, 'I'm waiting here. She may come back.'

Wipfli hesitated, then nodded. 'Very well. This will release one of my men.'

At a sign from Morton, Tinn started downstairs with Wipfli. Following a few steps behind with Jagger, Morton said in a low voice, 'Something's up. You could see it in Wipfli's eyes. And another thing! It's a hundred to one that whoever followed Tinn wasn't trying to sell him anything. I'll pump him as soon as I can.'

Jagger nodded. 'He wasn't a C.I.A. man, either, or Dobereiner wouldn't have made such a balls-up.'

'Which leaves a very unpleasant possibility,' Morton said, 'remembering friend Schramme. K.G.B.! The chap who followed Tinn would report back that Tinn had a clandestine rendezvous with the Yanks. The Russians wouldn't like that. The sooner I get Tinn out of this town, the happier I'll feel.'

Jagger said pointedly, 'Just Tinn?'

'We may have to skip without waiting for the girl. The Swiss want us out, even if they're not sure why. She'll turn up. You'll see.'

They reached the lobby. It was almost deserted. In the far corner a fat man slept off his lunch, head back, mouth open, one hand hanging limply over the arm of his chair. A little nearer, the man who'd followed Tinn screened himself behind a fully-spread newspaper. Tinn, fidgeting nervously as he watched the other, never once looked towards him.

Wipfli was murmuring instructions to a man with dark glasses and acne. Morton joined Tinn, then called back to Jagger, 'If Creevy agrees, we'll wait another three hours after we're back in the hotel. If she hasn't shown by then, we're on our way to the airport. So far as you're concerned——'

Jagger said flatly, 'I'm staying until she shows.'

Morton didn't argue. They all got into Wipfli's car. Jagger watched it slide away. He spoke to the receptionist in case Pattl should telephone Tinn, then sat down. He felt the weariness of aeons. He closed his eyes. After a while the man behind the newspaper lowered it, looked at the clock, yawned widely and stretched for the benefit of the receptionist. He stood up, stared briefly at Jagger and went out. He'd learned what he could. It was time to report to Schramme.

Leaning forward, hugging himself as if he had stomach-ache, the Director listened grimly. At the finish he said softly, 'Jesus Christ!' It was more a prayer than a blasphemy.

Head of Plans said, 'Dob did the natural thing. All he knew was that Tinn had paid a personal call and gone back to his

243

hotel. Dob followed. The British S.I.S. people had only just arrived.'

'They saw him,' the Director said stonily. 'We've had three strikes and we're out. What the hell is going on, Henry?'

Head of Plans pulled a face. 'Don't ask me! But whatever it was, it's over. They'll have Tinn back to London before you can say "Shortchange".'

The Director nodded sombrely. 'So they won and we lost. But are our dark brothers in Moscow going to believe we lost, or will they think we threw it?'

A telephone rang. He picked it up and listened in silence. His face became as shut and guarded as Fort Knox. He said, 'Thank you,' and replaced the phone. 'The Russians have done a Krushchev over there in Geneva. The conference is stalled, *sine die*. There's our answer.'

Henry fumbled for his pipe. 'Well, there isn't another thing we can do about it.'

The Director picked up another phone. 'There is. We struck out, but if the President agrees we're going to send dark brother in to bat.'

Henry stretched out a long arm and cut the phone off. 'Wait, Mart,' he said. 'You mean, tell Moscow everything we know and ask them to help?'

The Director stared impassively at him. 'Do you have a better idea?'

'What if they snatch Tinn? That would give them Short-change.'

'That's a chance we have to take. STARCOM says it's not too big.'

Henry's eyebrows climbed comically. 'STARCOM!'

'I played a hunch this morning, Henry. I asked STARCOM what we should do if everything else failed. STARCOM said we should sign up the Russians on our team as guest players. Strictly for one appearance. The probability of success was nearly thirty per cent above the nearest alternative course.'

Head of Plans stared for the better part of a minute. Eventually he said, 'Trust them! You mean trust the Kremlin!'

The Director said, 'It has to happen sooner or later. There might not be a later.'

Henry took his hand away from the phone. When the operator answered, the Director said, 'Get me the President, fast.' To Head of Plans he said, 'Have them ready the hot line, Henry.'

Jagger awoke instantly when the receptionist touched his shoulder. The sun had gone from the street outside. In the far corner the fat man snored lightly. The clock behind the reception desk said twenty to four.

The receptionist said, 'A telephone call, sir. Miss Pargeter.' She pronounced the name to rhyme with care.

He said, 'Patti? It's me. Jagger. Tinn's not here. Where are you? Are you all right?'

She laughed, over-excited, shaky. 'You sound worried. Yes, I'm all right. I've been for a little ride with Ralph Schramme and some friends of his, but they've gone and I'm all right. Is Jack safe?'

'He's safe. Where are you?'

'A little place called Ste. Anne de Marchairuz. In the mountains near the French border. They took me to some house in the middle of nowhere and pinched my shoes so I couldn't escape, but I don't think they knew what to do with me so they finally pushed me out of the car a couple of kilometres from here. I think they've crossed the border into France. Listen, did you know Ralph was Russian? At least, I think so. Am I making sense? It doesn't matter. Come and fetch me and I'll tell you everything. Will you? Or am I in disgrace?'

He still couldn't believe it. 'You're sure they've really gone? Look, give me your telephone number. I'll ring back as soon as I've fixed things. Don't——'

'Yes?'

'Don't do anything else silly.'

'I won't. I promise. You sound as if you minded. Or perhaps I don't understand again.'

He said, 'You understand well enough.'

Head of Plans and the Director, joined by Head of Support, had moved to the operations room. A small group of department and section heads stood around to help in handling the situation developing half a world away.

'Well, it's a bit thin,' Head of Plans said finally. 'A bit thin and makeshift, like most improvisations, but holding the girl bought us some time. No reason why it shouldn't work, provided our temporary friends do their part.'

The Director said, 'Let's concentrate on doing ours.'

Head of Support said, 'No sweat! The gasoline tanker's on its way to the airport right now, but——' He stopped, grinned uncertainly and said, 'It's just hard to take, that's all. All this'—waving a hand to embrace the operations room—'and we end up putting it to work for them.'

'Not them,' the Director corrected. 'For the moment they're "us" and the British are "them".'

Head of Support wagged his head incredulously. 'Well, if war games are a simulation of war, what we're playing has to be a peace game. It sure is a goddamed screwy world.'

A teleprinter began to rattle, jerking out a hundred words a minute. They bent over it. The Director said, 'Here we go! That means Dobereiner's back from his meeting with the other——' He stopped, then said carefully, 'With our unofficial, strictly foul-weather friends.' He glanced at a clock. 'Our friends, if everything goes right, for no more than the next couple of hours.'

Head of Plans took out his pipe, looked at it and put it away again. 'Well,' he said, 'they call mine the Department of Dirty Tricks and this time they're sure as hell right, especially with the girl involved. It's a goddamed nasty way to die.'

The Director turned away. 'Speaking personally,' he said unemotionally, 'I don't know of a nice one.'

When Wipfli arrived they were all in a private suite at the President. He looked at Patti with something more than

246

appreciation, though that was there too. He said, 'It is a pity I agree to ask no questions.'

Creevy said smoothly, 'All for the best, Herr Wipfli. No infringements of sovereignty or neutrality, believe me.'

Disbelievingly, Wipfli said, 'But of course! And now you will be leaving at once?'

Patti suddenly remembered something. 'Oh, my bag! My things! They're at the other hotel.'

'They're here,' Morton said. 'In the bedroom.' He nodded at a door.

'In that case,' she said, 'you won't mind if I change.' She went next door before anyone could speak.

Creevy said, 'Women! Time you were off when she comes back. You're already two hours later than we'd planned because of her. London isn't too pleased.'

Jagger said, 'Did you expect them to drop her back at the hotel? Those mountain roads are no joke, especially when it's getting dark. You're lucky we didn't take longer.'

'No doubt!' Creevy said disinterestedly. 'I'll consider myself still more fortunate when you're out of Swiss airspace.'

When Patti emerged they went through the back reaches of the hotel to the underground garage. Two cars waited. The first held two of Wipfli's men. Morton got in front of the second, with the embassy driver. Patti sat in the back between Jagger and Tinn.

Wipfli said dryly, 'A totally unnecessary precaution, we all agree, but you will also have a motorcycle escort as far as the airport.' He distributed his one-stroke handshake and his half-bow among them, said *'Glückliche Reise!'* and closed the door on Morton. The cars pulled away up the slope. Two waiting police motorcyclists kicked a thunderous response from their machines as they turned into the street.

Morton took a deep breath and said, 'Phew!'

'Who but you,' Jagger said, 'with your unrivalled eloquence, could phrase things more appropriately?'

Tinn asked, 'Are we g-g-going home now?'

'We are, old chap,' Morton said. 'We most certainly are.'

Patti said gloomily, 'All right. Who's going to be the first?'

Morton looked round. 'The first?'

'To start the row. After all, you have the advantage of being at the head of the queue.'

Morton said gently, 'My dear Miss Pargeter, I forgive you because you knew not what you did. Others, I'm afraid, will be less charitable.'

'Oh, but I did know!' Patti said. 'I knew exactly.'

'In that case, my girl,' Morton said, 'don't push your luck.'

After a while she said, 'What about Ralph Schramme, though?'

'Take my advice,' Morton told her. 'Forget him. Just consider yourself fortunate you didn't know enough to be important. You're lucky to come through whole. Damn it, they even gave you your shoes back.'

Jagger said, 'And you're lucky it was only your shoes. If it had been a man they'd have taken his clothes.'

'If you think,' Patti said indignantly, 'that taking my clothes would have stopped me trying to escape!'

'No!' he said with some feeling. 'I don't! Not you!'

Unexpectedly, he began to laugh. He reached forward to tap Morton on the shoulder. 'Has it occurred to you that we're the only ones who know Schramme's a K.G.B. man? The Master wouldn't believe me, so unless you can enlighten him he'll spend the rest of his days thinking it was all due to the C.I.A.'s double-dealing.'

Morton began to laugh too, with Patti unable to see the joke.

After that they sat in silence. Tinn had retired into the impenetrable depths of his thoughts. Morton exchanged a few words with the driver and lit a cigarette. Jagger, taking a little restrained pleasure in Patti's closeness and despising himself for it, reminded himself that there was still the generation gap. He also noted that the way Morton smoked his cigarette betrayed his underlying nervousness.

They swept through the tree-lined residential avenues of Petit-Saconnex, turning on to the Route de Cointrin. Ahead of them the glow of the airport brightened against the blackness that the slowly swelling mountains bit from the night sky. When the second car drew up before the brilliantly lit entrance to the passenger terminal, Morton released a barely audible sigh. 'By God!' he said with an artificial lightness, 'We made it! It'll take a physiotherapist to uncross my fingers.'

Jagger slid out and held open the door for Patti to follow. As soon as she was clear he closed the door, the motorcycle police revved their engines and the little procession moved off.

Patti stared after it. She said, 'Hey!' turning to Jagger.

He smiled. 'They'll take the high road and we'll take the low road and they'll be in London afore us. We came out in a service plane. That's how Morton and Tinn are going back. You and I have to wait for the scheduled flight, which means we've time for a drink.'

She was still glaring indignantly after the diminishing tail-lights. 'Why couldn't we go with them?'

'We fixed it up while you were changing. Morton couldn't wait to get Tinn away from you. He has this strange idea you're not to be trusted.' He took her arm. 'I'm afraid they'll clobber you with the Official Secrets Act when we get back. If I were you I wouldn't be in too much of a hurry to arrive.'

She drooped her shoulders. The fight seemed to have gone out of her at last. 'I've well and truly messed it up, haven't I? The big thing, and I boobed.' She turned towards the big glass doors. Indifferently she said, 'They've still got my case in that bloody car,' and in the same moment the sky about them flared in a false dawn, briefly dimming the geometrical constellations of overhead lighting. A fierce bark of sound slapped viciously at their ear-drums. The ground shook. Glass clashed and tinkled.

Jagger grabbed Patti, pulling her under a sheltering canopy. Flaming fragments were soaring above rooftops like ragged orange stars from a giant Roman candle. A steadily brightening glare from somewhere along the airport peri-

meter shimmered in convection ripples of heat. A soft furnace
roar of sound provided sinister counterpoint to the growing
clamour of shouts.

'It's a crash!' Patti said dazedly. 'There's been a plane
crash!' The strident ululation of sirens seemed to confirm her
belief but Jagger, staring at the burning skyline that marked
the direction taken by Morton and Tinn, knew that Morton
had uncrossed his fingers too soon after all.

In the restaurant of the Hotel President, Jagger finished a
meagre breakfast, his toast untouched. It reminded him
disquietingly of something he was trying to forget. His
wounds ached, he was in a stupor of weariness and what he
had seen at the morgue would haunt him for ever.

Patti hadn't come down yet. Creevy, back from Basle for
the second time, had already begun telephoning. Jagger
looked up to find Wipfli occupying the chair at the other side
of the table.

Wipfli helped himself to a cup of black coffee, lit a cigarette
and sat back, his eyelids drooping deceptively. He poured
smoke through his nostrils in a seemingly endless stream,
sipped a little coffee and said, 'The charge against the young
lady would be conspiracy to murder. The chief charge.
There would be others.'

Jagger said nothing, giving himself the last of the coffee.

Wipfli felt in his pocket, found a thick manila envelope
and emptied its contents carefully on to a plate. He pushed
the plate across, sipped coffee and appeared to study the tip
of his cigarette.

Jagger looked at the plate. Fragments of blackened, half-
fused metal surrounded a charred and almost unrecognizable
object that was still somehow familiar. He finally identified
it. A Cuban heel from a woman's shoe. It had been hollowed
out. The cavity held more fragments of twisted metal.

Wipfli waited for the sudden comprehension in Jagger's
eyes. 'One of the shoes of your pretty Miss Pargeter, who is
missing all of yesterday afternoon. Parked by the R.A.F.

plane, as you know, was a tanker of high octane fuel. No one, it now seems, knows exactly where this tanker is come from, but it appears that it is fitted with a clever fuse operated by radio.'

He pointed at the shoe heel. 'It is not difficult, I think, to see what happens.'

Jagger prodded fragments. 'A miniaturized transmitter in the shoe heel. They drive alongside the plane. The transmitter triggers the fuse. The tanker turns into a particularly nasty bomb.' He remembered the fire at Charles Street. It could have been caused the same way, by the same man.

'Exactly so,' Wipfli said.

Jagger drank coffee thoughtfully. 'She changed her shoes just before we left. Her case was left in Morton's car by mistake. And she thought we were all flying in the same plane. So, apparently, did someone else.' He knew now why they'd abandoned her in the mountains. They'd needed the time to set things up. And the episode of the shoes was self-explanatory.

Almost irrelevantly Wipfli said, 'You have heard the news this morning?'

Jagger shook his head. 'I suppose it made the headlines?'

'Not that. There is much bigger news. Bigger and more surprising. The Russians change their minds. The conference will open today.' He sat looking at Jagger while Jagger looked back.

Wipfli tipped the scraps on the plate back into the envelope and stood up. 'Of course,' he said, 'there could be no possible connection, you agree?' He put the envelope in his pocket.

Jagger started to get up. Wipfli pushed him back, bending over him. 'The tanker, one understands, may be American property. Stolen, of course! Our experts believe the transmitter contains Russian components. Black and white together make grey, which is a neutral colour. My government accepts the whole affair to be an unfortunate refuelling accident.'

He crushed his cigarette in an ashtray, shook hands with

his customary forward jerk and walked away. Over his shoulder he said, 'There is a flight to London in two and one half hours. Your Mr Creevy arranges reservations for you and the young lady.'

Jagger watched as Patti met Wipfli at the entrance to the restaurant. Wipfli didn't stop, aiming his half-bow at her as he passed. She turned to stare after him before coming on rather faster towards the table. She'd won after all, in a way, but for how long? And with whose help? Jagger knew where the Master would place the blame. The hell with him! Let him!

GIGO—... *is the end*

... we ended up working with the K.G.B. in Geneva.

The small man had withdrawn again, politely but unmistakably. The Central American ambassador, still prodding, said, 'If one is to choose between the appearance of infallibility in a man and the certainty of infallibility in a machine, surely the machine is preferable?'

Henry said, 'What makes you think computers are infallible, Mr Ambassador?'

'Oh, but surely? A computer deals only in facts, while a man is influenced by his emotions, his prejudices, by a hundred and one things that affect his judgement.'

Henry said, 'You're overlooking something. Something that computer men never overlook. In fact they summarize it in a little mnemonic. GIGO!'

The South East Asian ambassador frowned. He said, 'GIGO?'

Henry nodded. 'A synthetic word. The letters stand for "garbage in; garbage out". In other words, what you get out of a computer depends entirely on what you put into it. If what goes in is junk, what comes out is junk. And as every last thing that goes in is provided by fallible, emotional, prejudiced men——'

The Asian ambassador shook his head smilingly. 'How remarkable is your language! It has even given birth to its successor. GIGO! NATO! SEATO! UNO!'

'SNAFU!' the White House aide added, but he said it so softly that no one heard.

The Asian ambassador turned to the small Englishman, finding it pleasant to talk to someone shorter than himself. 'Your alliance with the United States has an immeasurable advantage over all others, Mr Robinson. You speak the same language.'

253

'A vicious lie,' the Master said impassively, 'fostered by our enemies to set us against each other,' and was the only one not to laugh.

He does know, by God! Henry thought. The others were turning away from him as a well-known voice approached. From the side of his mouth Henry said to White House, 'He knows.'

White House muttered, 'He can't *know*. And if he suspects he can't say so.'

Glancing quickly at the Master's face, Henry mumbled, 'You'd better be right. If you're wrong he has a great opportunity coming up.'

White House, a smile glued unbecomingly to his face as he prepared to exchange greetings with his own master, said quickly, 'No chance! He's his own computer. He'll have it all weighed up.' His voice assuming a grating joviality he added, 'Good evening Mr President. You remember Mr—ah—Robinson?'

The President stretched out his hand. 'Mr Robinson! Good to have such an old friend with us.'

Henry held his breath during the fractional pause. Then the Master took the proffered hand. 'How do you do, Mr President? It's pleasant to be among old friends.'

Garbage in, Henry reflected wryly, garbage out!